ALSO BY JOHN DAVID ANDERSON

Ms. Bixby's Last Day

The Dungeoneers

Minion

Sidekicked

Walden Pond Press is an imprint of HarperCollins Publishers.
Walden Pond Press and the skipping stone logo
are trademarks and registered trademarks of Walden Media, LLC.

Posted

www.harpercollinschildrens.com

ISBN 978-0-06-233820-4

Typography by Carla Weise
17 18 19 20 21   CG/LSCH   10 9 8 7 6 5 4 3 2 1
❖
First Edition

For those who have something to say.

Half the world is composed of people who have something to say and can't, and the other half who have nothing to say and keep on saying it.

—Robert Frost

POSTED

To Olivia
Stay #awesome and
enjoy the book!

John D _[signature]_

I PUSH MY WAY THROUGH THE BUZZING MOB AND FREEZE, HEART-struck, dizzy. It takes me a minute to really get what I'm looking at.

Notes. At least a hundred of them. Pressed all over the freshly painted locker.

Some clump together, overlapping like roof shingles. Others orbit like satellites, reaching up toward the wall. They vary in color—pale blue, fluorescent pink, lime green—but most of them are yellow, like dandelions before they fluff white and wither away.

I stand motionless and read a few of them, softly enough so only I can hear. They are just words and they are not just words. I think about everything that's happened. About Bench and Deedee and Rose. And Wolf. About all the terrible things that were said. About the things that should have been said and weren't.

There was a war. This was where it ended.

I can't tell you exactly when it changed, when it spiraled out of control like a kite twisting in the wind. When it stopped being something funny and clever and became something else. Maybe there was no single moment. Maybe underneath all the squares plastered on the walls and the notebooks and the windows there was the same message over and over—we just ignored it because it was easier to stomach. And now I'm standing here, dumbstruck, wondering if this changes everything.

I know what you are going to say: sticks, stones, and broken bones, but words can kick you in the gut. They wriggle underneath your skin and start to itch. They set their hooks into you and pull. Words accumulate like a cancer, and then they eat away at you until there is nothing left. And once they are let loose there really is no taking them back.

Truth is, I can't tell you exactly when it changed. I can tell you how it started, though. And I can tell you how it ended. I will do my best to line up the dots in between.

I'll leave it to you to draw the line.

THE CATALYST

IT STARTED WITH RUBY SANDELS.

That's her name, swear to God. Ruby freaking Sandels. Yes, sandals aren't slippers, which would have been worse, and it's not even spelled the same, but it still counts as a form of child abuse, IMO. Might as well just fix her black hair into a permanent ponytail, buy her a shaggy terrier to stuff in a wicker basket, and teach her to sing about rainbows. I'm sure her parents thought they were being cute with that name, but a thing like that could mess a kid up for life.

It didn't, though. Mess her up for life, that is. But only because Ruby looked nothing like a lost farm girl from Kansas. With her dark brown skin and tight jeans, Ruby was no Dorothy, and she was hard-nosed enough to stare down anyone who even *thought* about teasing her, which was always somebody. This was middle school. Everyone got teased by somebody sometime about something. At the very least Ruby would give back double what she got. You had to admire that.

Don't get the wrong idea. Ruby and I weren't friends. I will just say that up front. In fact, you can just assume that anyone I talk about isn't a friend of mine unless explicitly stated otherwise. Ruby was just a girl who sat in front of me in math class and ignored me out of habit. She had a backpack covered in faux sapphires. You didn't have to look close to tell the dark blue stones weren't real. This is Branton, not Beverly Hills. Anything flashy around here is fake.

That's Branton, Michigan, by the way. Don't try to find it on a map—you'd need a microscope. It's one of a dozen dinky towns north of Lansing, one of the few that doesn't sound like it was named by a French explorer. Branton, Michigan. Population: Not a Lot and Yet Still Too Many I Don't Particularly Care For. We have a shopping mall with a JCPenney and an Asian fusion place that everyone says they are dying to try even though it's been there for three years now. Most of our other restaurants are attached to gas stations, the kind that serve rubbery purple hot dogs and sodas in buckets. There's a statue of Francis B. Stockbridge in the center of town. He's a Michigan state senator from prehistoric times with a beard that belongs on Rapunzel's

4

twin brother. He wasn't *born* in Branton, of course—nobody important was ever born in Branton—but we needed a statue for the front of the courthouse and the name *Stockbridge* looks good on a copper plate.

It's all for show. Branton's the kind of place that tries to pretend it's better than it really is. It's really the kind of place with more bars than bookstores and more churches than either, not that that's necessarily a bad thing. It's a place where teenagers still sometimes take baseball bats to mailboxes and wearing the wrong brand of shoes gets you at least a dirty look.

It snows a lot in Branton. Like avalanches dumped from the sky. Like heaps to hills to mountains, the plows carving their paths through our neighborhood, creating alpine ranges nearly tall enough to ski down. Some of the snow mounds are so big you can build houses inside them, complete with entryways and coat closets. *Restrooms are down the hall on your right. Just look for the steaming yellow hole.* There's nothing like that first Branton snow, though. Soft as cat scruff and bleach white, so bright you can almost see your reflection in it. Then the plows come and churn up the earth underneath. The dirt and the boot tracks and the car exhaust mix together to make it all ash gray, almost black, and it sickens your stomach just to look at it. It happens everywhere, not just Branton, but here it's something you can count on.

But I was telling you about how it started. The ban and the notes and then the war that followed. I was telling you about Ruby Sandels getting into trouble, getting us all into trouble.

Also, just so you know, this isn't Ruby's story. She's what my chemistry teacher calls a catalyst. Something that jump-starts a reaction. The thing about Ruby, like pretty much every other kid in Branton Middle School (me being one exception), is that she was never without her phone, despite the rule against having them out in class. Nobody followed that rule. If the teacher's back was turned, texts, tweets, and ticked-off birds were flying, videos were being downloaded, villages were being raided, and walls were being posted on. Everyone did it. And if I was lucky enough to have a phone (if it ever fit into "the budget"), I would have done it too.

Which is why it wasn't unusual to see Ruby taking furtive glances at her lap during class. The problem was, on this day, she decided to do it in math. With Ms. Sheers.

Unlike Ruby "Don't *Ever* Call Me Dorothy" Sandels, Ms. Sheers lived up to her name. Sharp as a scalpel, with thin lips and dagger eyes—nothing escaped her. She wasn't like Mr. Hostler—near-sighted and three years from retirement, only really concerned with getting home and finding out who won *Dancing with the Stars*. You could come to class newborn naked and Mr. Hostler would probably just sigh and check you off the attendance sheet. Ms. Sheers, on the other hand, was a bloodhound. That didn't make her a bad teacher, necessarily. But she wasn't the sort to look the other way when she saw the flash of light glinting off Ruby's phone, or heard the nearly imperceptible click of Ruby's painted nails on the screen. She zeroed in on the desk like a sniper, then snapped her fingers and opened her hand. "Let's have it."

"Have what?"

"The phone, Ruby."

"I don't have a phone," Ruby said, sounding suddenly Dorothy-like, all innocent as she attempted to slide the phone she didn't have into her glitzy bag. It caught the edge of the pocket and clattered, much too loudly, to the ground.

Naturally, this was hilarious. At least to everyone but Ms. Sheers, who shot down the aisle and reached for it, hawklike, snatching it out from underneath Ruby's fingertips.

"Give me my phone back," Ruby said, her face suddenly flushed, lunging upward as Ms. Sheers held it out of her reach.

"You don't have a phone," Ms. Sheers reminded her. She looked at Ruby's screen and her expression changed, Jekyll to Hyde. If it was possible for a teacher to be pretty, Ms. Sheers *might* qualify, but when she looked at that screen her face transformed into something pinched and contorted, like she had just taken a swallow of rancid milk. She looked from the phone to Ruby, then back to the phone. Ruby's eyes fell to her desk, head dropping so fast you would have thought someone had tied an anchor to her chin.

"Is this . . . ?" Ms. Sheers stammered. "Did you . . . ?"

Judging by the lack of response, the rest of us could only assume *it was* and *she did*. About a half dozen students, me included, telescoped our necks to get a look at the screen, but Ms. Sheets pressed the phone close to her chest.

We all turned and looked expectantly at Ruby, waiting for her comeback. Sarcastic or apologetic, it could go either way. I've found that kids will apologize instantly if they think that it will keep them out of trouble. I know I will. But there are some times you just know an apology—even one you actually mean—won't be enough. Then it's best to just keep your mouth shut.

I'm guessing that's what Ruby Sandels was thinking, because she didn't say a word at first. Just blushed and refused to look up.

Ms. Sheers took a deep breath. "You understand we need to go see Mr. Wittingham."

Low murmurs among the class. The Big Ham. Principal Wittingham was even more hard-core than Ms. Sheers. You could sometimes feel the tremors when he shouted at a kid from behind his office door. Ruby's head snapped up.

"But Ms. Sheers, I didn't mean anything by it. It's just talk."

She knew she was in it deep. I suddenly felt bad for her. Ms. Sheers had her gorgon stare on—turn you straight to stone—the phone still pressed to her heart.

"This isn't a game, Ruby. It's one thing to violate school policy and use your phone in class, but this . . ." Ms. Sheers looked at the phone again, as if to confirm that what she'd seen the first time wasn't a trick of her imagination. Her face knotted up again and she shook her head. "This is *inexcusable*."

Which meant that whatever it was, it must have been good.

Ruby Sandels groaned and angrily stuffed her notebook into her pack. Then we watched her be escorted to the front door. "I will be back in two minutes," Ms. Sheers warned. "Take this opportunity to complete the problems on your sheet. Silently."

We all nodded meekly. Ms. Sheers closed the door and at least twenty other phones flew out of pockets and backpacks as we all tried to figure out just what it was that Ruby had done, the wonderfully terrible things that she'd said.

Behind me Jasmine Jones squealed and clasped her hand over her mouth. She showed her phone to Samantha Bowles.

(Not Bowels. I made that mistake once. Only once.) "Oh no she didn't," Samantha said, eyes wide.

Apparently, yes, she did.

And we were all about to pay for it.

I said Ruby wasn't my friend, and she wasn't. But that doesn't mean I didn't have any.

In fact, for a while there, I thought I had just enough.

Nobody is friendless. I honestly believe this. We all have *somebody*. Even the crazy lady who lives down the block from us has her pet schnauzer, though the thing is uglier than she is, with its snaggletooth and gimp leg. Even my father—an editor for an online magazine who works out of his lonely one-bedroom apartment near the beach and thinks humans generally suck—even he has real-life people who he talks to. My mother's just not one of them.

Point is, none of us is alone. We might *feel* alone sometimes, but more often than not we are just lonely. There's a difference. We aren't alone because it's basic human nature to band together. Herd mentality. We are programmed to find our people.

That's how my mother put it. Right before my first day at Branton Middle School, a little over two years ago.

We were back-to-school shopping—gathering the instruments of torture that my teachers would use to slowly bore me to death over the next nine months. I was nervous and irritable. A better word might be "snappish" (I'm a sucker for a good word). I was headed to a new school. A *middle* school. It wasn't that the classes would get harder, or that I would get lost in the labyrinth of halls, or that I might forget my combination and look derpy just standing there, aimlessly spinning the lock, though these thoughts crossed my mind more than twice.

No. What scared me most was lunch.

People talk about nightmares where they are falling or where they are trapped in a burning building or buried alive. But ask any incoming sixth grader with at least two forehead zits and a Great Clips haircut and he will tell you the prevailing image from his nightmares is standing in the middle of a buzzing cafeteria, tray in hand, desperately looking for somewhere to sit. That was what made me sweat through my sheets at night.

Forget the boogeyman; the lunch lady haunted *my* dreams.

Standing in the back-to-school section with a half dozen other kids and their parents, trying to decide between college- and wide-ruled, Mom could tell there was something bothering me. Mother's intuition. Some people might call that a good thing. I'm not one of them. It was spooky how she could read my mind.

"Don't be nervous," she said, the corners of her mouth drawn, somehow outfrowning me.

"Easy for you to say," I muttered. "You're not the one going to a new school where you know almost nobody."

It wasn't an exaggeration. I literally knew about four people who attended Branton Middle School, and I wasn't friends with any of them. My mom and I had recently moved to a new house, a smaller one, a grand total of twenty-three miles from the older, larger, more comfortable house I grew up in. It was all part of the separation, one of a thousand aftershocks that came with my parents' divorce. The old blue house with the white shutters was too much for either my mom or dad to handle financially, so she found a three-bedroom in Branton and he found that apartment in Sarasota.

That's Sarasota, *Florida*. You should be able to find Florida on the map all right. It's the turd-shaped one falling into the ocean.

"No. I get it," Mom said, dropping school supplies into our cart as I checked items off on the printout. She bought store-brand everything: pencils, pens, markers. Even my backpack was the cheapest we could find, generic black with a little pocket for the phone I didn't own. Mom's salary as an administrative assistant at a dental office didn't cover name brands. Not that I needed Crayolas for middle school. What I needed was someone to trade sandwiches with.

Mom put a hand on my shoulder and leaned close so that

nobody around us could hear. "It's hard starting over. Trust me. I know. But it will be all right. You will find your people."

That's exactly how she said it. *Your people.* Like I was a prophet preparing to gather my flock. At least she didn't say "peeps." My mother never tried to be cool. It's one of the things that made her cool sometimes.

I grunted at her anyways.

"Give me that look all you want, Eric, but it will happen. It's instinctual. Inherited from our prehistoric days. We are wired to form groups. Otherwise we would have gone extinct eons ago. It will be hard, but you'll make it."

That's another thing about Mom. She doesn't sugarcoat it for you. She tells everything straight up. And her hugs are fierce and quick, like the one she gave me just then. "It will be awkward at first, but it gets better. You find your people and you make your tribe and you protect each other. From the wolves."

"That's middle school?" I asked her.

She gave me a sad kind of smile. "That's just life," she said. Then she threw three packs of off-brand sticky notes in the cart and pushed on to the next aisle.

I stood there by the Elmer's glue display, imagining my body being ripped apart by ravenous beasts. In the middle of the school cafeteria, no less, with everyone around me pointing and laughing. Mom was smart and I loved her. But she didn't always know the best thing to say to a guy.

You find your people. Sure. But it was those wolves I worried about.

Ruby Sandels wasn't one of the people I'd eventually found, but I still felt bad for her as Mrs. Sheers escorted her out of the room. The Big Ham was surely going to eat her alive.

I knew what she said. By the end of fourth period we all did. It's not difficult. I'm pretty sure that's the whole reason the internet was invented: to make it easier to spread gossip. I know what Stephen Curry eats for breakfast. I know what the president thought about the new Marvel movie. I know how many Ping-Pong balls a man can fit inside his mouth at one time. You don't even have to know where to look. Just be patient enough and eventually somebody will tell you whether you care or not.

Ruby's message was passed around, jumping from phone to phone like a skipping stone, each of us gawking at it in turn.

The kids all knew before the parents. We probably even knew before Ruby's mom did. There was no way to take it back. You can't erase what everyone else has seen, and you certainly can't stop the gossip train once it has gathered steam and rocketed out of Branton Middle School Station. The whispering was like static in the halls.

"She actually *said* that?" Bench said with a whistle.

We were walking together to lunch, the day Ruby's phone was taken from her. It was the four of us: Deedee with his *Lord of the Rings* lunch box that wasn't retro enough to be cool yet and Wolf with his brown paper sack that was. Me wearing Bench's last pair of Nikes and a T-shirt that said *SAVE THE WHALES— THEY MAKE GOOD LEFTOVERS.* My uncle sent it to me for my birthday. He's kind of demented, but he always remembers, which is nice.

Bench was leading the way. We always let him take point.

"Technically she typed it," I said. "I don't think you'd ever hear her say those words *out loud.*" I tried to imagine Dorothy from *The Wizard of Oz* dropping the kinds of bombs that Ruby did in that text message. Some of the things she wrote would have made the Wicked Witch turn white.

"She's going to get suspended," Wolf said.

"Or worse," Deedee added.

"I still can't believe she said that about *him.*"

Bench shook his head. The *him* was a big part of the problem and one of the reasons Ruby was sure to get sent home this time. It wasn't some guy she'd had a crush on or some other kid who bad-mouthed Ruby behind her back. The *him* was Mr. Jackson. An adult. A *teacher*. He apparently gave Ruby an F on her last science test because he suspected her of cheating. In response she thumbed a long rant to her friends, calling him several choice names and saying that he could just go kiss a certain part of her backside. With three exclamation points. She only sent the text to two people, but it didn't matter. Friends have friends. The message made the rounds. Ruby was going to have a really hard time passing science this year.

"I saw Mr. Jackson in the hall. He looked bad. All sweaty and red," Deedee said.

"He always looks like that," I said.

"Yeah, but he looked like he was going to have a heart attack."

"He always looks like that, too." Mr. Jackson was not a small man, as many of the crude drawings in the boys' bathroom could attest to. He was a few hundred pounds, much of it pillowing around his center like a monster truck tire. *One* of the unfortunate F-words Ruby used in her text was "fat."

"Definitely expelled," Deedee said. "You just can't say those kinds of things. Not in school. Not about a teacher."

Actually, I wouldn't dare say some of things Ruby said about anyone. Not in any way that could be traced back to me, at least.

"Why not, though?" Bench asked. "I mean, she's entitled to her opinion, right? Like, constitutionally?"

I gave Bench a look. He wasn't defending her. He wasn't friends with Ruby any more than I was; he was only playing devil's advocate. We learned about the Bill of Rights in social studies earlier this year—from a droning Mr. Hostler. I didn't pay too close attention. Most of the amendments only seemed to matter if you got arrested, which wasn't in my foreseeable future (Mom would *kill* me), though Bench's comment made me wonder if Mr. Jackson could have Ruby arrested for defamation of character or something. Verbal abuse. Assault with a deadly text.

"The First Amendment says nothing about reasonable consequences for sending texts calling your science teacher a—" Deedee tried to muster the courage to repeat what he'd read, but it was too much for him to say out loud. He wasn't exactly a rule breaker. None of us were. We weren't total suck-ups either—we just tried to keep our noses clean. We flew under the radar. It was one of the many keys to survival. "I'm pretty sure it just keeps you from being arrested for saying what you think. Doesn't mean you can't get in trouble."

"I think she was better off keeping her opinion to herself," Wolf said from behind me.

Wolf. The voice of reason. We counted on him for that. Just like we counted on Deedee to find drama in everything and Bench to keep us from getting beat up. And counted on me . . . I'm not sure what we counted on me for.

"Mark my words—this isn't over," Deedee divined. "Somehow or another it's going to come back and bite us all in the you-know-what."

"Are you going to roll for it?" I asked. "Or are you suddenly psychic?"

"I'm telling you," Deedee said. "Stuff like this doesn't go unnoticed."

"Nothing's going to happen," Wolf countered. "Nothing ever changes around here."

I nodded, sure he was right. I'd never seen Wolf get flustered over much of anything, even the little shoves and digs that come with being in middle school, the needling comments and sidelong sneers. Wolf took them in stride, and he certainly took enough of them. Bench called him "composed," which made a lot of sense when you thought about it. Sometimes that meant that you didn't know exactly what Wolf was thinking, not if he was being quiet, which was kind of a default for him. Unlike Deedee, who might as well have billboards above his head spelling out his feelings for anyone who cared to know, which was usually just the three of us, and not always that many.

"I'm serious," Deedee said. "You wait and see. We're all going to pay for this."

Wolf gave him a playful shove as we pushed into the cafeteria, Bench and I waiting in line, Deedee and Wolf headed toward our usual seats. The same seats we'd sat in for a couple of years now. Just the four of us.

My people. The ones I found.

The ones I counted on for everything.

THE CRACKDOWN

I SHOULD STOP AND TELL YOU ABOUT THEM. THE TRIBE. MAYBE IT WILL help you to understand what happened. Maybe not. Maybe there is no explanation. Maybe my dad is right and people are just basically jerks. It certainly seems that way sometimes.

I have this theory. I call it the theory of socio-magnetic homogeny. A bunch of big words, but it basically says that people gravitate toward people who share their interests and whatnot. Band kids will hang out with other band kids. People with pierced tongues will hang out with people with pierced noses. The basketball players will clump together like cat hair on a sofa. Kids whose lawyer fathers drive heated-leather-seated sports cars hang with other kids whose lawyer fathers drive heated-leather-seated sports cars. There are exceptions, of course, but all other things being equal, you merge with the crowd that reminds you the most of you.

It's not that original, I guess. And it's mostly just common sense, but I took it one step further. My theory has to do with the people who *don't* find people just like them. These people—they find each other. And then they realize that *not* finding people like them is the thing they have in common. That's what happened to me, I think. I found the people who weren't quite like other people, and we used that difference as glue.

There were four of us. All boys. And we were all smart, or at least above the national average according to state-mandated standardized tests, so we had that too. What we *didn't* have was a tribe.

So we made one.

For me, at least, it started with Bench. Real name: Jeremiah Jones. His parents and teachers call him J.J. but we don't call each other by our real names. You can blame me for that one. Bench does sports, the big three of football, basketball, and baseball—but he's not that good at any of them, not good enough to start anyways, so mostly he just moves from bench to bench, waiting for the fourth quarter or the ninth inning, when the game is completely out of hand and putting him in won't really cost anything or alter the fabric of the universe.

The cool thing about Bench was that he didn't seem to care

that he wasn't very good; he just enjoyed being a part of the team. The other players didn't mind having him around because he was a nice guy (who also never threatened to replace them), and the coaches liked him because he was an A student and never complained. Bench was BMS's poster boy for student athletes; he brought the cumulative GPA of the basketball team up. It was good for us because being attached to Bench, the rest of us were mostly ignored by the other jocks. We didn't care that he never scored a single goal. In fact, it was probably better for us that he didn't. It's not as if the starting quarterback sat at our table.

Besides, Bench could at least make a free throw, which is more than can be said for Deedee, aka Advik Patel, the third member of our tribe. His dad is Indian, which Bench says should make him genetically inclined to love cricket, at least, but Advik prefers to fight dragons instead. Deedee is short for D&D, which is way too geeky to say out loud, even for us, but he says none of us can pronounce his real name right anyway, so Deedee's fine with him. Unlike Bench, who has an inch on me, at least, Deedee's a full two inches shorter than I am, with shorter black hair and an even shorter attention span, and he knows way too much about Tolkien and Harry Potter and Gary Gygax.

You probably don't know who Gary Gygax is, and even if you do, you probably wouldn't admit it. I don't blame you. There are some things that have to stay among your tribe.

Deedee's a polyhedral dice junkie. That's what you call those dice with so many different faces. He's got a collection of them tucked away in a wooden box shaped like a treasure chest under his bed. Clear ones and colored ones and ones that look like they've been chiseled out of marble. Little pyramids that go up to four and giant, angular eyeballs that go all the way up to sixty. I won't bother telling you what most thirteen-year-old boys keep hidden under their beds, but I guarantee you it's not dice. He also keeps one in his pocket, a ten-sider with a dragon in place of the number one. He insists it's good luck. He uses it to make pretty much all his major life decisions.

We played D&D with Deedee on the weekends—so long as Wolf wasn't out of town at a recital and Bench didn't have some kind of camp or practice (turns out I'm almost always available). Deedee was the dungeon master, of course. Bench was a hulking barbarian with too many swords. I was an elvish thief who went around stabbing everyone in the back.

Wolf was a bard. He stood in the back and played his music and tried to stay out of the way.

That's called typecasting.

Wolf is short for Wolfgang, which is short for Wolfgang Amadeus Mozart, because, as Wolf puts it, he could never pull off the nickname Mozart. Of course he can't pull off Wolf either, but we let it go, mostly because his real name is Morgan, which at some point became much more popular for girls than boys.

Nothing about Wolf looks particularly wolfish. Maybe starved-wolf-who-doesn't-get-out-of-the-cave-much—lanky limbs and freckly face and moppish blond hair that he's constantly brushing out of his eyes. What he *is*, though, is a piano prodigy. Three-time Falsin County award winner, juniors division. Wolf has been playing since he was five. Mostly classical. Some jazz. He can actually play that bumblebee song—the one that sounds like the piano itself is having a seizure. We keep begging him to put his talents to good use writing rock songs, but his parents don't believe in good music. They believe in Chopin and perfect posture and two hours of practice a day. Wolf sits on a bench almost as much as Bench does.

Except we're all pretty sure that Bench is never going to be a starting wide out for the Lions, despite all his talk of someday winning the Super Bowl. Wolf's different. Someday we are all going to go watch him play Carnegie Hall. He'll be wearing a tuxedo and white bow tie to match the keys. And the three of us will have front-row seats.

Bench, Deedee, and Wolf. The tribe. My people. Not that we couldn't have tried to fit in somewhere else. Bench had guys he knuckle-bumped in the halls from his various teams. Wolf knew people in the band. Even Deedee had a couple of kids he went to summer camp with. But there was something that drew the four of us together. We just *got* each other. It was *easy*.

We knew where we belonged.

There were others, sometimes. Nomads. People who hadn't found their tribe yet. Guys like Nips (superfluous third nipple, on the right, just below his equally superfluous second nipple) and Crash (skateboard versus car, car won), but for the most part it was just the four of us. Bench, Deedee, Wolf, and me.

My name is Frost.

Cool, right?

Trust me, it's not.

But at least it's better than Nips.

Ruby's text—seen by Ms. Sheers, and then the Big Ham, and eventually by most of the student body—was (as one concerned teacher put it) "the straw that broke the camel's back." Though, if I had to guess, I'd say the camel was pretty well dead before Ruby had her phone taken away. After all, there had been several incidents of technology misuse before Ruby's rant against Mr. Jackson. Facebook posts. Crude pics on Instagram. A whole Snapchat exchange that got two kids sent home for three days. Flame wars. Threats. At least a dozen instances of kids getting caught using their phones to cheat on tests. No doubt Principal Wittingham had hundreds more occurrences written up in his files. More than enough to fuel a crusade. Ruby's text was simply a spark.

A catalyst.

Word spread quickly outside the walls of Branton Middle School. Kids told their parents. Parents told other parents. Wittingham sent out a message to every family, calling for a school community meeting. In the span of only forty-eight hours it suddenly became clear to every teacher, parent, and administrator that cell phones—with their texts and their apps and their electric, buzzy addictiveness—were no longer just a nuisance: they represented a clear and present danger to every student at BMS.

The meeting was held. Studies were cited. Statistics were shown. Other school systems were held up as models. Turns out cell phones were to blame for everything wrong in the world. They weren't just the primary avenue for bullying, though that was brought up several times. They were also eating away at our brain cells. They were almost solely responsible for the decline in test scores in Falsin County in particular and for the failure of the American education system in general. They caused cancer. They could suck out your soul. They were the next step in mankind's eventual demise.

Forget the fact that half the adults in the room were using their phones to find even more statistics for why phones were bad for you. The point was, in school anyways, cell phones were a menace. "Confiscating them," Principal Wittingham argued, "is not simply a matter of sound educational policy. It's in our best national interest."

A vote was taken. The majority ruled. The students got no say. A new school policy was written into the student code book.

No more phones. Period.

Not in lockers. Not in pockets. Not in backpacks. They were to stay at home. If you absolutely had to bring one for emergency reasons or for use after school, it would be turned in at the office at the start of the day, placed in a labeled Ziploc baggie, and kept there until the final bell. If your parents called to tell you that your aunt Tilda slipped in the bathroom and stabbed herself in the eye with her own toothbrush, the secretary would take a message and have you called down to the office. Principal Wittingham couldn't control what was said and done off school grounds, but while we were inside the cinder-block walls of BMS, there would be no texting, calling, posting, playing, or surfing. We were there to learn. Case closed.

A few parents protested. Complained that their kids had a right to keep their electronic devices on them at all times. The administration reminded them that there was nothing in the US Constitution specifically governing the individual rights of cell-phone-carrying minors. Having a phone was a privilege.

And one that the students of Branton Middle School had finally lost.

When the vote was passed, Mr. Jackson looked like a cat that just ate a three-hundred-pound canary. Ruby just stared at her shoes. They were white Chucks, with red letters to match the color in her cheeks. Everyone blamed her, of course, though it could just as easily have been them who'd gotten caught. Afterward they went online, telling her *thanks for ruining our lives* and that she should *find a tornado and get sucked back to Oz.* A couple more eloquent students posted long messages directed at the administration, asking them to reconsider. *The Falsin County Gazette* published two pages' worth of articles about it in Sunday's editorial section—mostly in favor of the new rule.

Everyone had to get all their online complaining out before Monday, when the school's new policy would take effect and we'd all be disconnected for good.

The new rules were clearly posted on two different signs on the way in (and on several more scattered throughout the halls), informing students that any phones or tablets found in a student's possession would be confiscated immediately and the student would receive a warning. If it happened again, it was an automatic one-day suspension. After that it got even worse.

By the end of the week, seventeen kids had been suspended. The administration was in full crackdown. Ms. Sheers looked like a sniper sitting at her desk.

Not that it mattered to me, of course, because of the budget and all.

Bench and Wolf both had phones, but Bench just used his to call his father for a ride after practice and Wolf mostly used his to listen to music. The only one of us heartbroken was Deedee. He was a member of several online gaming communities and even contributed to a blog called *The Dungeon's Depths*. That first day, I could tell he was getting twitchy. He certainly wasn't the only one.

There was a mob at the front office when the last bell rang, kids pouring out of their classrooms, swarming like hornets. A few kids were knocked over. As soon as students got their phones back you could see them turtle, faces suctioned to screens. Deedee cradled his and called it his *precious*, though not loud enough for anyone but me to hear.

The bus ride home that Monday was church-service quiet, everyone desperate to catch up on everything they'd missed, even though they hadn't missed anything because none of their friends had had their phones either. I finished up my math homework while Bench surfed next to me, telling me a whole bunch of junk I could care less about. I heard the kid in the seat behind us mumble something about how unfair it was. "I can't imagine going the entire year like this," she said.

It was clear from the start that this no-phone thing was going to be a problem. The students of BMS would have to find some way to fill the void. Some way to stay connected. I just didn't know that that something would come about so quickly.

Or that we would be the ones to start it.

Screenless, I looked out the window at the flash of trees. I felt Bench's elbow in my side.

"Check this out," he said. He showed me a picture somebody had already posted of Principal Wittingham's face pasted onto Darth Vader's body, crushing a Photoshopped cell phone in his hand. "Behold the power of the dark side."

I nodded and smiled. Then went back to watching the trees.

The bus—*this* bus—was where it all started. At least for me.

This was where I met Bench.

It was the last week of August. Sixth grade was well under way and I had made zero progress finding my people, despite my mother's promise. I'd eaten my lunches by myself. Spent my classes sitting in the back. Walked down the halls trying not to accidentally brush up against anyone. I told myself I was just feeling everybody out, getting a sense of the place, but the truth was I felt cut off, stuck behind an invisible wall. Life sucked, middle school sucked, and I was pretty sure I was destined to spend the next three years miserable and alone.

Then one day this boy stepped on. Black hair buzzed to nearly bald, wearing a Calvin Johnson jersey and expensive-looking high-tops, slapping his hands on the back of every seat he passed as if he were marking his territory. I hadn't seen him before.

I stuffed my nose back into my book—reading was the easiest way to avoid making eye contact—and waited for him to go by. He shuffled past, and then he stopped, turned around, and plopped right down in the seat beside me.

"You saving this?"

I nodded, then shook my head, then tucked my feet back a little so he couldn't see the cheap shoes I was wearing. *Saving it.* Funny. Like there was a waiting list of people that wanted to sit next to me. The bus rumbled on. The boy rubbed his head and smiled. He had a really big smile. A count-all-the-teeth smile.

"Cool hat," he said, pointing at the Detroit ball cap I wore every day to school.

"Thanks," I mumbled. I made a point of turning a page of the book even though I hadn't actually bothered to read it yet.

"You like the Tigers?" the boy asked.

"It was my dad's," I explained. "He gave it to me. He used to like them. Now he likes the Marlins." Dad kept threatening to take me to a game in Miami the next time I came to visit even though I really didn't like baseball and probably couldn't name more than ten teams, the Tigers and Marlins included.

The boy looked offended. "*What?* You gotta be kidding me. The Marlins are *terrible*!" He said it with the conviction of a holy man. "I mean, they got, like, Stanton and Alvarez, but for the most part, they suck big ol' donkey turds through a straw."

"Yeah," I said. I wasn't sure why anyone would suck a donkey turd, or if it could even fit up a straw, but I could appreciate a good image when I heard one. "Honestly, I just wear it because he gave it to me."

"Naw, that's cool," the boy said. "I didn't mean anything bad about your dad or anything. Just . . . you know . . . the *Marlins*?" He shook his head. "Throw a tiger into a baby pool with a fish and see who comes out on top. That's all I'm saying."

"They're pretty big fish," I said. "I'm not sure they'd even fit in a baby pool." My father sent me a picture of a marlin that he caught on a chartered fishing trip his first year down there. It was almost as big as he was. "They're fast, too. And they have swords for noses." I suddenly realized how nerdy I sounded and shut up.

"Swords for noses?" The boy raised his eyebrows. "Man, that's got to be awkward."

I didn't know what he meant, this strange kid who just sat next to me and started talking about donkeys and tigers for no reason whatsoever, so I just stared at him.

"I mean, how they ever going to kiss another fish without stabbing 'em in the face?" He smiled all teeth again.

I snorted. I couldn't help it. Just picturing two marlins trying to make out, writhing around, filleting each other in the process. "Yeah. Guess I never thought about that."

"They'd be, like, poking out each other's eyes and stuff."

"Right."

"Not that fish kiss each other or anything."

"No. Of course not."

"Though they got the lips for it."

Then the boy made a fishy-kiss face by pressing his cheeks and working his lips up and down. He went cross-eyed in the process. It was pretty hilarious.

"You kind of *laugh* like a donkey," he told me.

I stopped laughing. I realized it had actually been a really long time since I laughed in front of anyone but my mother. She always said she loved my laugh. I think maybe she was required to, though.

"It's cool," the boy said. "Could be worse. My dad farts every time he laughs too hard. That's why nobody makes any jokes at dinner." He raised both eyebrows again to let me know he was dead serious this time. Then he stuck out his fist. "I'm J.J.," he said.

"Eric," I said, receiving the first fist bump of my middle

school career. "But most people call me Frost." Actually, most people didn't call me anything, but when they did, they called me Frost.

"Frost, huh? How'd you get that?"

I told him it was a long story, even though it really wasn't, but we were already pulling into the school parking lot. "I'll have to tell you some other time."

The boy named J.J. shrugged.

"What period you got lunch?" he asked.

And that was all it took. A fish face and a fist bump and I suddenly wasn't alone anymore. I had J.J., soon to become Bench. He lived within walking distance of my house, liked video games, and had a trampoline in his backyard. More importantly, he filled the empty seat beside me and made me laugh.

It was just the two of us for a while. We didn't complete the tribe until the sixth-grade fall field trip to Newaygo State Park, the teachers trying to squeeze in some appreciation for Mother Nature before winter bit us in the butt. We ate lunch in the grass and then set out on a two-mile trail—ninety-eight sixth graders following teachers like waddling ducklings. But Bench and I wandered off into the woods and got separated from everyone else. By the time we found our way back to the trail the herd had moved on, so we set out on our own, keeping our ears perked for barking teachers, until we ran into two other kids just as lost as we were.

They introduced themselves as Advik and Morgan. We introduced ourselves as J.J. and Frost. We agreed to stick together, working along the trails until we found the rest of the class. It only took thirty minutes, but in that thirty, and in the ten more of scolding from Principal Wittingham that followed, we clicked, just snapped together like Legos.

I'm still not sure what it was about that day, that trip, that moment. Maybe it was the four of us daring each other to pee in the Muskegon River, or Bench climbing a tree and getting his undies snagged on a branch, or Deedee claiming to have found a print in the mud that he swore came from a velociraptor. Or maybe we all just kind of subconsciously realized that there was strength in numbers. That four was better than two and two.

We rode the bus together that afternoon, talking the whole way back to school. About everything. Favorite bands. Lame movies. Best video games. Lousy parents. Worst teachers. The smell on the bus (gasoline, damp leaves, sweat). The odd fact that we had never talked to each other before even though we had a few classes together. How strange it was for us to get lost at the same time, to just run into each other in the woods like that. How Deedee's farts sounded like a dying baby elephant. How Principal Wittingham looked like he was going to pop when he found out the four of us had wandered off on our own. How none of us really liked our first names.

I remember laughing hysterically and eating most of Dee-dee's goldfish crackers. And for the first time in what seemed like forever, feeling like I was a part of something.

The next day at lunch we found each other and just picked up where we left off.

Mom was right. You make your tribe. Sometimes I hate it when she's right, but not that time.

Looking back on it, I think it had to be something like getting lost in the woods. Otherwise we might have just gone on ignoring each other. I don't want to make it out to be some big gooey, sappy thing. We didn't share the same pair of traveling pants or promise over spit shakes to be BFFs. We just kind of glommed together.

And we managed to stay that way for two whole years. Just the four of us. Pretty much perfect.

Then she came along. And the war started.

And everything came unglued.

That first Monday—after the cell phone crackdown—I went to my locker before seventh period to grab my Spanish notebook. Attached to the metal door above the combination was a sticky note. Standard yellow. From one of the packs that every student was required to buy at the start of the year for no real reason whatsoever.

It was from Deedee.

Welcome to the Dark Ages, it said.

He didn't sign it, but I knew it was from him. No one else would be so melodramatic.

That was the first one. The one that started it all, I guess.

I folded it in half and dropped it in the bottom of my locker without a second thought.

THE VARIABLE

SO, FROST.

Deedee, Bench, Wolf. Tribal names. All names we gave to each other. All except Frost. I was Frost before I ever met them.

Word of advice: if you ever get the chance to win your fifth-grade district-wide poetry competition, don't. Or if you do, try to keep it to yourself.

Because sometimes things stick. They attach themselves like burrs on your socks and they follow you. Like that story your parents always tell your friends' parents at dinner about how you got into the pantry when you were four and ate a whole box of lemon Jell-O—the raw powder, not the jiggly stuff—straight out of the package, turning your tongue bright orange and forcing them to call Poison Control. From that moment on, you know those people will never eat the stuff without laughing. You will forever be Jell-O Boy, in addition to all the other things you've become.

More often—in school, at least—it's a label, thrown out on a whim, maybe, by some kid trying to get a giggle from the kid next to him. But then it's picked up on and passed around until it becomes a part of you.

Kid Who Never Brushes Her Hair.

Kid Whose Crack Is Always Showing.

Kid with the Giant Schnoz.

Kid Who Always Gets Picked Last.

Kid Who Blew Chunks Onstage.

These are all real people, except I can't tell you most of their names. Even I know them only by what stuck. Except the Kid Who Always Gets Picked Last. That's Deedee.

If you're lucky—or at least not terribly unlucky—the thing that sticks to you will just be a nickname, and not a pathetic one.

Like Frost.

Ask most twelve-year-old kids to name a poet and they will probably tell you Shakespeare or Shel Silverstein or Kendrick Lamar. Some of them will probably say Dr. Seuss, though, like my dad says, just because your stuff rhymes, it doesn't *necessarily* make you a poet. I don't imagine a whole lot of kids would tell you their favorite poet is Robert Frost. I'm probably the only one.

I blame my father, in fact. He's the one who introduced us—me and Frost. On a tedious summer Sunday, a glass of wine in his hand, sitting across from me on the porch and handing me a copy of Frost's *Selected Poems*. This was before the Sarasota Shuffle. The Big Split. Back when my parents tried to just ignore each other as much as possible and I tried to ignore their ignoring. When the house would speak to us in creaks that we could hear because nobody else dared to speak because they were afraid of what they might say.

We sat on the porch in the backyard by my mother's bright fuchsia azaleas, just the two of us, the sun baking the grass. "I think you're old enough," he said to me with a nod, and for a moment I thought he was going to hand me his glass for a sip. Instead he gave me the book.

Some dads take their kids fishing. Or play catch. My dad wrote for a living. Just my luck.

"I don't like poetry," I said, which wasn't entirely true then and certainly isn't now. When we did the fifty-book challenge in the fourth grade I was the only one who had a volume of poetry on my list. Jack Prelutsky. But the book my dad handed me wasn't anything like Jack Prelutsky. For starters, there were no illustrations. Plus the cover looked kind of prissy, all blue-and-white flowers. I tried to hand it back, but my father just reached over and flipped to a flap-cornered page.

"Start with this one," he said. "It's one of his most famous."

The poem was called "The Road Not Taken." Dad told me to read it out loud. He wasn't the kind of father you said no to, not unless you wanted an hour-long lecture on the topic of "things that are good for you."

"'Two roads diverged in a yellow wood,'" I began, and I read it all, careful not to sound too bored, so as not to offend my father, or too interested, so as not to encourage him either. When I was finished he asked me what I thought about it.

I shrugged. "Pretty good, I guess," which is actually what I thought. I'd had to read worse stuff in school. I figured that was the end of it—it hadn't dawned on me that my dad might actually be interested in my opinion, but he told me to read it again. Quietly. To myself.

So I did. With him sitting across from me, looking out over the porch at the heavy clouds and grimacing at the birds in the maples. I read it again. And again. And when I looked back up after the third reading he asked, "How does it make you feel?"

I could feel his cloud-gray eyes on me. He wanted a real answer. He seemed to be holding his breath.

"Guilty," I said at last. Though I wasn't sure why. That was just the first word that came to mind.

My dad reached over and scuffed my hair. "It's not guilt," he said, "it's regret. They aren't quite the same." He took another sip of wine and went back into the house, leaving me and Robert Frost on the porch.

He moved out three months later.

I read all 114 poems in the book that summer. Most more than once. That next winter, with my father and mother still haggling on the phone about what to do with the house that he didn't even live in anymore, I came home with an assignment to write something for the thirteenth annual Branton School District Young Authors' Competition. It could be a poem or a short story. You could illustrate it if you wanted to. The winner would receive a medal and a fifty-dollar gift card to Barnes & Noble.

I wrote a poem inspired by Frost's "Mending Wall," my personal favorite of the 114. Frost's poem was about these two guys who meet in the middle of a field to repair this broken old stone wall that separates their properties, and it has this line, "Good fences make good neighbors," which the speaker of the poem thinks is total crap, and yet he goes on and keeps building the fence anyways. And you kind of wonder *why?* What would happen if they left the wall broken, or tore it down completely? Wouldn't they *still* be good neighbors? Would they maybe be *better* neighbors? Would they maybe be something more? Like friends?

My poem was called "The Elf's Mischief" and it began, "I

am the thing that does not love a wall." It was about all those questions. About broken walls, and whether good fences ever made for good families too.

Maybe it was because it wasn't another haiku lazily written in the back of the bus on the way to school. Or maybe the teachers who were acting as judges had fence issues of their own or divorced parents or both, because I won. Pretty much the only time in my life I've won anything.

The day after the awards ceremony my name was called over the morning announcements at school. The teacher made me show everyone the medal and then asked me to stand in front of the class and read the poem out loud. The other kids asked if they could have the gift card. Without even thinking, Mrs. Beck said, "We now have our very own Robert Frost."

Boom. That was it. One comment from my fifth-grade teacher and I became someone else, the junior poet laureate of Falsin County.

That same night that I earned my new nickname, my mother drove me to the Barnes & Nobles in Portage, about an hour away, to spend my reward. I bought her a Frappuccino and spent the rest on comic books. As we passed the sign welcoming us back to Branton, sitting right out in the middle of an empty field, I thought about my father and Sarasota and Frost and how there were actually a whole buttload of fences out in the world, but most of them were invisible. Deep thoughts for an eleven-year-old, I guess, but reading Robert Frost all summer after your parents split will do that to you.

When I got home I called my father to tell him about my victory and what the kids were calling me at school, but he wasn't there.

I didn't bother to leave a message.

I told you the whole thing started with Ruby Sandels, and in a way it did. But it was another girl who got the most attention.

Her name—her *actual* name—was Rose. Like the delicate flower. Though "delicate" is not the first word I would use to describe her. I know most of it—the war, the notes, the thing with Wolf—probably would have happened regardless. But without her it would have gone so much differently.

She came the same week that the school's ban on cell phones took effect, the same week Ruby was allowed to return to school after her suspension, the same week that my father wrote me an email telling me about the trip we were going to take next summer to Cape Canaveral. At least it wasn't to Miami for a ball game—space shuttles and giant rockets were more up my alley.

Rose Holland came that week and everything changed.

There's a famous Alfred Hitchcock movie called *The Birds*.

It sounds like a documentary, but trust me, it's not. In the movie all the birds in this small California town go all avian apocalypse and start attacking people—plucking out eyes, blowing up gas stations, pecking everyone to death—just about the same time that this one woman shows up. Whether or not she's the reason the birds attack isn't entirely clear. It could just be a fluke. Or maybe there is something about this lady that makes the birds batty. I watched the movie with Bench, who conked out about halfway through after muttering for an hour straight that any movie without at least one CGI character was bound to be boring. I watched to the end, though. I wanted to see if the woman was going to make it out of the town alive or if the birds would get her.

I won't spoil it for you, just in case, but I will say that sometimes somebody shows up in your life and throws everything out of whack. Or just happens to show up the moment the out-of-whackness starts.

I wasn't thinking about *The Birds* when Rose Holland appeared at school though, the day after the Great Confiscation. At the time I was thinking about algebra. I had a quiz in second period—the dreaded Ms. Sheers—and had barely bothered to study. And then here comes the new girl, already six weeks into the semester. In two-plus years I had finally gotten comfortable with my surroundings. I knew who I could copy off of and who to avoid in the halls. I had the people I high-fived and the people I nodded to, and the people I slunk right by (which was still most of them). Then here comes this unknown. That's what I saw when I looked at her: not the girl from the bird movie, but a variable. Person X.

Capital X, because if there was one thing you instantly noticed about Rose Holland, it's that she was uppercase. Not big around, like Mr. Jackson or like Sean Forsett, who looked kind of like a beach ball with limbs glued to its sides. Not even overweight. Just big. More squared than rounded, like she had been constructed of cinder blocks. Of course this was middle school: I was used to taller girls. But most of the girls at Branton who were tall were also skinny, like stretched taffy. Rose Holland was tall and wide. Muscular, like Bench. I figured she was an athlete. Volleyball maybe. Or soccer. She'd make an excellent goalie. Practically impenetrable.

Yet she walked through the hall the same way all of us did on our first days, with her eyes on the tiles below her feet. Her frizzled brown hair, lighter than mine, hanging over her face like a veil. Dark jeans and a black sweater that could probably fit two of Deedee. You could hear the sound of her boots from a mile away.

"Who's she?" Bench said, standing beside me.

"Who knows," I replied.

"She looks like she can hit. Linebacker material."

"Be careful," I told him. "She might replace you."

Bench didn't have an answer to that. I glanced at the new girl again, noticing everyone step out of her way only to give her a long second look after her back was to them. You'd be tempted to tell them *Take a picture, it'll last longer,* except, of course, nobody had their phone on them anymore. Already there were whispers trailing after her, though, and you could tell just by that brief walk down the hall that she was going to have a tough first day. I muttered a short prayer for her under my breath.

"I'd stay out of her way, if I were you," Bench remarked.

I snickered, though it was really more of a grunt as I pictured this new girl bowling over everyone in the halls, leaving smashed Play-Doh versions of them stuck to the floors with only their eyes bugging out. It wasn't really funny, but I'm a sucker for a good image. The new girl disappeared around a corner looking lost. I shut my locker and headed to first period with a promise to catch up to Bench later.

I met Wolf and Deedee outside the door to English. Wolf looked exhausted. "Long night?"

"George and Martha were at it again," he said.

George and Martha were Wolf's nicknames for his parents. He says he got the names from an old movie he saw once about this couple that is always arguing. His parents' real names were Todd and Trina.

That's something Wolf and I had in common: front-row seats to the failing-marriage show. Except where my parents mostly refused to talk to each other, his parents never shut up. His dad hadn't moved out of the house yet. I figured it was only a matter of time, but Wolf said it would never happen. His parents would never split. *That* would require them to *agree* on something. Strange thing was, I actually kind of liked Wolf's parents, from the little time I'd spent with them. They seemed like nice people and they seemed to like me. They just didn't like each other. Made you wonder how they got stuck together in the first place.

"You want to talk about it?" I asked. I knew the answer already, but I asked anyway.

"What's there to talk about?" Wolf said. "I just wish they'd let me move down into the basement. It'd be quieter at least."

"But what about the piano?" I asked.

"Yeah. We'd have to move that too."

We ducked into class and found our seats, Deedee on one side, me on the other, Wolf in the middle where he belonged, all of us ignoring the dirty looks from the three boys who sat behind us. Normally you'd get a comment from one of them, a completely unoriginal "here comes the dork patrol" kind of thing, but today we managed to slip by. Mr. Sword finished scrawling something on the whiteboard and humming loud enough for the whole class to hear. Wolf leaned over and told me it was classical. Beethoven's Pastoral Symphony. I told him no self-respecting eighth grader should know that. Mr. Sword turned to us and started taking attendance.

He had just worked his way down the roster when the variable burst into the room.

"Sorry I'm late. Got turned around," she said. Her face was red, flushed from running or embarrassment or both. Her eyes, I noticed, were deep blue, like her jeans. She filled the doorframe completely.

"It's all right, Rose," Mr. Sword replied. He turned to the rest of us. "I'd like to introduce our new student. Everyone, this is Rose Holland."

The girl put up a hand self-consciously. It was that moment. That terrible, blood-freezing, ashy-mouthed moment when you suddenly realize that sixty eyeballs are fixed on you, deciding what to do about you, where you fit in. I gave the new girl a smile, just a small one, to let her know we weren't so bad. She didn't smile back.

"Rose comes to us all the way from the Windy City."

"I'm surprised the wind could carry her," somebody— probably Jason or one of his friends—whispered from the back of the room. Okay. *Most* of us weren't so bad.

"Excuse me?" Mr. Sword said sharply. Whoever it was didn't bother to repeat it. Mr. Sword turned back to the doorway. "You can take any open seat, Rose."

I looked around. There were three empties. One of them was on the other side of me. She took the one closest to the door and I felt a twinge of relief. It would have meant something—her coming all the way across the room just to sit next to me. Maybe not to her, but to everybody else.

"This week," Mr. Sword said, already moving on even though most eyes were still on the new girl, "we will be starting our unit on Elizabethan drama. Raise your hand if you are already an expert on drama."

Half the students groaned and raised their hands, some of them pointing to each other. I nodded to Deedee, encouraging him to raise his hand too, but he just gave me a dirty look. I noticed Wolf was still looking at Rose. Her eyes were fixed on the front of the room.

"The rest of you are lying, then," Mr. Sword told us. "*I* think most of you create more drama in one day than Shakespeare could imagine in a lifetime. But when he did it, at least, it was all in good fun."

To prove his point, Mr. Sword launched into a lecture on Elizabethan theater, which was actually pretty boring until he described how actors would fill animal bladders with sheep's blood and keep them beneath their stage clothes so that they would explode in a gruesome display during fight scenes. Sometimes, he said, if you were one of the lucky ones sitting up front you'd get some of the blood on your clothes too. He called it the sixteenth-century splash zone.

"Sheep's blood?" Christina Morrow said with a grimace. "Gross." She pronounced the word as three syllables. Guh-roh-ohss.

"I think it's cool."

I looked at the girl by the door, cheeks still pink, eyes still fixed on Mr. Sword. All the girls sitting near Rose Holland recoiled, wrinkling their faces. Beth Strands even scooted her desk over an inch. Mr. Sword made a motion for Rose to elaborate.

"No. I mean, it's really creative. Like special effects," Rose added. "Before there was even such a thing as special effects."

"And the audience would agree with you, Ms. Holland," Mr. Sword said, smiling. "All that gore helped to account for the theater's popularity. It wasn't a good drama if somebody didn't get stabbed, hanged, or poisoned by the end. Preferably all three. The audience was always out for blood."

People were still eying Rose. A couple of the girls in the back started whispering, no doubt about her—what she said, how she looked, her clothes, her hair. Deedee scrawled something on a yellow sticky note—he had a stack of them sitting on his desk. He handed it to Wolf and I leaned over to see.

Guess things haven't changed much, the note said. Deedee glanced sideways at the new girl. I smiled. Wolf didn't.

No blood yet, just dirty looks. If Rose noticed the reaction of the people around her, she didn't seem to care. Or maybe she was just good at ignoring it. Not an easy thing to do.

I told myself to stop looking at her, just in case she got the wrong idea.

THE PROMISE

THE ROUND TABLES IN THE LUNCHROOM HAD SPACE FOR FIVE chairs—six, if you crammed, but most tables didn't bother to cram. Only the tables with the most popular kids were crowded.

We only ever used four. We formed a perfect square, somehow meeting at the corners.

Deedee and Wolf met all the way back in elementary school—spending their recesses together, avoiding pickup kickball games and hiding behind the slides from bigger kids, trading Pokemon cards and splitting Oreos—but middle school jammed us together. Together we knew a little bit about just about everything. Bench had kissed a girl not on a dare. Deedee had visited Paris and India and had pictures of himself grinning in front of the Arc de Triomphe and the Taj Mahal.

Wolf had hiked down into the Grand Canyon—though he said all he remembered was his parents arguing about who didn't bring enough water. He'd also been stung by a jellyfish. I'd been to Disney World and already had my wisdom teeth pulled. Together we had already broken most major bones—legs, arms, fingers, toes, collar, ribs.

We filled in each other's gaps. We sometimes completed each other's sentences, but usually with burps and other gross sounds just to annoy each other. We spent most of our time together hanging out after school, playing video games, watching ridiculous videos, or seeing how many Sour Patch Kids Wolf could chew at once without drooling. Sometimes we'd grab a ball and play H-O-R-S-E in Bench's driveway (he always won), or take our bikes and ride down to Mr. Twisty's, our favorite soft-serve ice-cream place, where you could mix in whatever candy you wanted and where half of my summer allowance went. But most of the time, if we weren't battling hordes of Deedee's demonspawn, we just hung out and talked.

Not like, *talked* talked. Nothing serious. Just regular talk. About *stuff.* YouTube videos and homework and other kids. The lamest superpowers in the world (male Wondertwin's bucket of water trick, hands down) and how to best make weapons out of rubber bands and paper clips. If you were having a thoroughly craptastic day, you'd be allowed to vent using all kinds of words that would never get back to your parents. But I wouldn't say we really talked about *feelings* or whatever. It was okay to *have* feelings, just so long as you kept them mostly to yourself, which was fine by me.

Sometimes we talked about girls, but not often. More like how you talk about presidents and movie stars, with a kind of guarded detachment, careful never to admit too much. Not that we didn't know any—girls, that is. Bench especially had a few he made a point of saying hi to in the halls and Deedee had several he admired from afar. Just that as far as our crew went, it was always just us boys. And there was kind of this unspoken promise that it would stay that way. Just us. Forever.

I know what I'm doing. I'm trying to justify what happened. How I acted. How we all acted, but me especially. You're not going to buy it, though. Because it wasn't just that Rose Holland was a girl, and that's no excuse anyways.

It's that she was who she was. And we were who we were.

And there had always, ever, *only* been four.

I didn't see Rose in either of my next two classes. I heard her name whispered once or twice. I figured it was none of my business so I tried not to listen.

Right before heading to the cafeteria for lunch, I stopped by my locker to find another note from Deedee stuck to the door.

The fourth one that morning, counting the one in English. All, presumably, from the same yellow pad. This one just said *Breadsticks!* Underneath was a smiley face, just in case the exclamation point didn't give it away. Deedee only got school lunch on breadsticks day. He still showed up with his *Lord of the Rings* lunchbox, but he ignored the sandwich that was packed inside. He was a garlic fiend, and the butter the lunch ladies slathered those sticks in could slay a coven of vampires.

I stuck the note to Deedee's forehead five minutes later as Bench and I sat down at our table. "If you leave me any more of these, I'm going to start demanding that you take my calls and fetch me coffee," I said.

"He stuck one to my locker too," Bench said.

Wolf held up six fingers.

"He wrote you *six* notes?"

"One of them just had a drawing of a whale on it," Wolf said.

"It was an airplane. I was bored in math. Excuse me for sharing." Deedee peeled the sticky note from his forehead. "I would text you, but . . . you know . . ." He held up empty, phoneless hands. Day Two of the Great Confiscation had gone only slightly better than Day One, with only one student—Becka Peachman—practicing a form of nonviolent protest and going limp in the hallway, having to be dragged to first period by her armpits. In his phone's absence, Deedee was making do with what he had. "They make us buy four-packs of those stupid things at the start of every year and we don't need them for any of our classes, so I figured why not put them to good use?"

"I think we need to define what qualifies as 'good use,'" I said.

"*And* teach you how to draw," Wolf added.

Bench elbowed me and I followed his eyes to the end of the lunch line. Rose Holland was standing there, tray in hand, surveying the landscape again. I felt bad for her. I'd been in that same spot. I watched as she approached the closest table of girls, then noticed Beth Strands from English—the one who'd scooted her chair away—look up. She must have had a nasty look on her face, because Rose immediately steered around and wandered toward the corner. That was Beth's superpower—she could wither you with a glance. The Witherer. Some people were just like that. There were quite a few empty tables, though. Rose would find a place to sit. I turned back to Deedee, who was telling a story about a kid in band who got caught with his phone. He panicked when the teacher came in and tried to hide it in his tuba.

"Sounds like something you would do," I teased.

Deedee pretended to be offended. "I play the trumpet, remember? A phone wouldn't fit." Deedee played in the school band mostly because his parents insisted on it. Wolf refused to play in the school band on the grounds that they sucked—though he would never tell Deedee that. Honestly, they sounded like a herd of dying giraffes being chased by a pack of howler monkeys.

Deedee wadded up his sticky note (*Breadsticks!*) and flicked it across the table. He was aiming for me. Instead it landed in my applesauce cup.

"Two points," Wolf said.

"Actually, the other side of the table is three-point territory," Bench corrected.

"It was a lucky shot," I said, picking the dripping wadded yellow ball from the cup and flicking it back. This is what lunchtime usually looked like for us. Building towers out of milk cartons. Stuffing vegi-straws up our noses. Flicking things at each other. "You couldn't do it again in a million tries," I dared. It was a safe bet. Deedee made Bench look like Cam Newton most days.

"Fine. But if I do, I get your last breadstick," he said, pointing at my tray. I agreed. Most of the time I ended up giving him one anyway.

Deedee lined up the wadded ball of paper, closed one eye, and gave it another flick. This time it sailed high and wide, up over my shoulder. I heard it hit something with a little wet slap.

"You got me."

Deedee's face went ash white, which was kind of remarkable, given his Indian heritage. I jerked around to see Rose Holland standing beside our table, looming over us, her tray sporting only a package of cheese-and-peanut-butter crackers and a chocolate milk. There was a splotch of applesauce on her black sweater the size of a quarter, like a gunshot, just below her shoulder.

"Oh. Oh man. I am *so, so* sorry," Deedee blathered, suddenly bug-eyed, trying to shrink behind his lunch box, probably afraid of that carton of milk being smashed over his head, which is exactly what somebody like Jason Baker or Cameron Cole would do. But Rose just looked at her sweater and shrugged, then rubbed the spot of sauce in with her thumb.

"Got it at a garage sale," she said. "It's seen worse."

She was standing between me and Wolf and I could see now that the sweater was frayed at the bottom, her jeans worn at the knees, the laces of her boots equally ragged at the ends. She was even more imposing up close. Rose looked at the only empty chair at our table then back at her tray.

I flicked my eyes around the room, trying not to be obvious. There were still plenty of empty seats. In fact there was an empty table three down from us. That's probably were she had been going when she got hit. Deedee and his terrible aim.

"You're in my English class," she said, looking at me first,

59

holding her tray close. "Three of you, anyways. And you and I have history together." She glanced at Bench. "It's J.J., right?"

Bench nodded, lips tight. It was the face he used whenever other people's parents tried to talk to him, a half smile barely hiding its phoniness. He looked over his shoulder at a cluster of tables full of other eighth graders twittering away. Deedee watched the pseudo-nacho-cheese congeal in his plastic cup. I looked at the empty chair. *Don't say anything,* I thought to myself. That's how it worked. *Don't say anything one way or another and you don't have to take responsibility, one way or the other, and everything goes on like normal. She will just keep walking.*

Wolf thought differently, though. He gestured to the empty chair.

"Wanna sit with us?"

Deedee coughed. Or choked. I couldn't tell which. I suddenly became aware of all the sounds in the lunchroom. The cling-clang from the kitchen. The scrape of chairs along the floor. The constant buzzing of a hundred voices talking at once. I held my breath, waiting for the new girl to realize that Wolf was just being polite—because that's the kind of person he is— and to do the equally polite thing and decline the offer. A casual *No thanks, some other time maybe.*

"I thought you'd never ask," Rose said.

She set down her tray and pulled out the chair.

Suddenly we weren't square anymore.

The strangeness of it hit me. Like how sometimes you're on the bus taking the same exact route that you've taken a hundred times before, with every coffee shop and neighborhood sign memorized, but you look up and you are certain that the bus has taken a wrong turn because everything seems unfamiliar, and it takes you a moment to get your bearings. Bench and I looked at each other. For two years we'd sat at the same table together. Never once had a girl sat down next to us. But Rose Holland didn't seem to care. She settled into her seat and proceeded to unwrap her crackers, the crinkle of the package much louder than it should have been. I tried to read Wolf's face, to see if he thought he'd miscalculated, if his plan to do the right thing had backfired, but he didn't give anything away, just went back to eating his lunch, maybe even smiling a little.

Deedee, on the other hand, couldn't stop staring.

"Um . . . you know it's breadstick day?" he mumbled after ten seconds of awkward silence, as if confirming that there was something abnormal about a girl who didn't like garlic-butter-soaked lumps of bread stretched to look like some grandmother's gnarly fingers.

"I'm on a strict diet," Rose Holland explained. She had a raspy sort of voice. It seemed to fit her.

"Of peanut butter crackers?" Deedee asked.

"Of foods that stick to the roof of your mouth," she replied, stuffing in the first of the crackers. She chewed in slow motion, it seemed, as if she were afraid of making too much noise, then wiped her mouth with the back of her hand. Maybe she was nervous too. We all watched silently, like a girl eating crackers was the most fascinating thing we'd ever seen. Finally Rose cleared her throat and leaned across the table, the package in her hand.

"If you want one, all you have to do is ask." She thrust the crackers at each of us in turn.

I blushed and looked down. Bench looked away as well, taking an interest in conversations at other tables that he couldn't even hear. Deedee fiddled with his milk carton. Only Wolf managed to find the words "No thanks." But even he could sense it. I could tell. The disruption to the natural order of the universe. After another twenty seconds of awkward-as-walking-in-on-your-dad-shaving-naked-in-the-bathroom quiet, Rose set her crackers down, leaned back in her chair, and let out a sigh.

"Okay," she said. "I'm guessing you're all new to this 'girl at the table' thing. How about this: I promise that I won't bite or give you cooties or whatever else it is that you all are flipping out over. I won't talk about my hair or blather on and on about celebrity heartthrobs or all the girls I hate, because, frankly, I've only been here for three hours, which isn't quite enough time to hate anybody yet. I won't discuss brands of moisturizers or lip gloss or use the word 'crush' in any kind of nondestructive capacity. And in return, you can stop looking at me like I'm some deranged lunatic. How does that sound?"

Rose Holland smiled and I noticed the freckles on her nose, so light and small, not like the constellations on Wolf's cheeks. Her eyes really were kind of pretty. Not that I would ever say such a thing out loud. To anyone. Especially not her.

Surprisingly, Deedee was the first to speak up.

"We don't really talk to girls," he admitted. "I mean, we *can* talk to them. Just not . . . you know . . . *about* them to them . . . not that we do . . . talk to them. Not usually . . ." His voice trailed off.

"Don't listen to Deedee," Wolf said. "He lives in his own little fantasy world. We are perfectly capable of talking to girls."

Then he proceeded to not say anything else.

I fiddled with my last breadstick.

"It's really not that hard," Rose said. "We're just like you, only smarter."

It was a joke. At least I was pretty sure it was a joke. But I was too nervous to laugh.

"You know, just talk about whatever you normally talk about. Stuff you're interested in. Like, what do you do? What's your *thing*?" She looked at me when she said it.

Our thing? Our thing was sitting here by ourselves. Being goofy and not self-conscious. Our thing was not having anyone ask us what our thing was, because, frankly, nobody else cared what our thing was, so we could do it, our thing—whatever it was—without worrying about it. "Um . . . ," I said.

"Er . . . ," Deedee added.

"Well," Wolf said finally, "Bench here plays, like, fifty-seven different sports."

"Three," Bench said curtly, finally snapping back to attention.

"And he doesn't really play them so much as encourage others to play them," I added, which earned me the sharpest sideways glance from Bench.

"So you're a cheerleader?" Rose prodded.

"He's a looking-at athlete," Deedee said.

Bench started ripping off little pieces of breadstick, squeezing the grease between his fingers then dropping the mangled nubs to his tray.

"It's cool," Rose said. "I happen to like male cheerleaders."

This seemed to embarrass Bench even more. He pointed his

finger across the table. "Deedee here thinks he's the lord of the ring."

Deedee wrapped his arms around his lunch box, drawing it close to his chest.

Rose's eyebrows shot up. "You like Tolkien?" she asked.

"*Yeah?*" Deedee ventured. "I mean, kind of but not really . . . all that much . . . *maybe?*"

I laughed, only because I knew he had a shelf full of *Lord of the Rings* action figures and a replica of Sting hanging above his bed. But no—not all *that* much. Rose leaned closer to him. "Who's your favorite character?"

Deedee looked down at his lunch box, at the picture on the lid. "Aragorn, probably. You know. If I *had* one. If I was, like, *really* into it. Which I'm not . . . really . . . into it."

He also had a giant framed map of Middle Earth on his wall.

Rose nodded. "Yeah, Aragorn's cool. Reluctant, brooding king and all that. But personally, I like Gollum."

"Wait . . . the weird slimy guy who eats fish guts?" Bench dropped what was left of his breadstick, looking disgusted.

Rose shrugged. "What can I say? I have a soft spot for the tortured and misunderstood." She smiled at Bench—a genuine smile, not a sarcastic one. He didn't return it. "And what about you two?" She looked back and forth from Wolf to me.

"I like short hairy men," I said. "So it's Gimli for me all the way."

Rose laughed, coughing cracker crumbs across the back of her hand. It was the first time I'd made a girl laugh that I could remember. It felt weird. "I meant what are you *interested* in. J.J. here plays sports. . . ."

"It's Bench," Bench said irritably.

"Right. Sorry. And . . . Deedee, is it?" Deedee nodded. "He's all about the swords and sorcery. So what about you? What's your deal?"

Wolf spoke before I could beat him to it. "Frosty here is a poet."

"I'm *not* a poet," I insisted. "I wrote *one* poem. Wolf here is an actual piano prodigy. He's won, like, a million competitions."

"Only eleven," Wolf corrected.

I looked at him, impressed. I didn't know it was that many. Seems like something I should have known, though.

"Frosty . . . like the snowman?" Rose asked, eyeing me.

"It's just Frost," Bench corrected again.

"Frosty's better," she said. She stared at me as if she expected me to agree with her. Or was challenging me not to. I felt warm all over, but uncomfortably so. For a moment I was afraid she could read my mind.

Bench pushed his tray toward the middle of the table and leaned over on his elbows. I could tell he was irritated. "What about you? What do you do? What's your *thing*?"

Rose didn't flinch. "What do you *think* I do?" she shot back.

We all glanced around the table.

"Softball?" I said with a shrug. It was either that or wrestling.

"Lacrosse?" Deedee guessed. Rose shook her head at each of us.

Wolf snapped his fingers. "I've got it. Professional turkey wrangling."

Rose snapped her thick fingers right back at him. "*So* close. It's wombats, actually. And I don't wrangle them. I groom them for professional wombat breeding competitions."

"Really?" Deedee asked, eyes wide. It took him a moment. It sometimes does with him. "Oh."

"No, seriously. You have to play *some* sport," Bench insisted. "Or work out or *something*. I mean . . ." He didn't finish the sentence. He didn't have to.

I held my breath, waiting for Rose to take offense. To grab her tray and excuse herself, go sit down at one of the empty tables, but she shrugged it off.

"Nope. No sports. Though now that you mention it, I've recently considered taking up ballet."

67

Silence.

Were we supposed to laugh? You couldn't tell by her sudden stone-faced expression, taking each of us in, maybe even daring us to. I tried to imagine her on the stage, doing a pirouette or a *pas de bourrée*, but instead I got an image of her lifting Deedee up and twirling him above her head, then dropping him across her knee, snapping him in two WWE style.

"I'm totally kidding," Rose said at last, breaking the silence. "Seriously? I mean, could you even *imagine* me in a tutu?"

Wolf shrugged. Deedee giggled nervously. I shook my head—a little too emphatically, maybe—then looked at the clock on the wall and calculated how many more minutes until the bell rang.

"Ballet," Bench snorted.

Rose Holland polished off another cracker in one bite and brushed the orange crumbs from her sweater. "To each their own," she said.

And for probably the third time since she sat down I became conscious of all the other students in the cafeteria who seemed to be looking our way, almost certainly getting the wrong idea.

After lunch Rose said she'd see us around. Her tone was casual, like she hadn't just contributed to twenty of the most uncomfortable middle school lunch minutes in human history. Or more like she knew she had and she just expected us to get over it.

"That girl is funny," Wolf said after she'd left.

"Yeah," Deedee agreed, though he didn't seem too sure. I looked at Bench.

"She's different," he said.

I couldn't begin to get a handle on what all he meant by that. It was impossible to disagree with, though. There was something extraordinary about Rose Holland. I couldn't put my finger on it yet, but Deedee gave it a shot.

"I mean, who doesn't like breadsticks?" he wondered out loud.

"To each their own," Wolf echoed. I wasn't quite sure what he was thinking either.

"Not really into it?" Bench said, eyeing Deedee. He was probably picturing that map of Middle Earth too.

Deedee reached into his back pocket and pulled out a thin stack of sticky notes. He quickly sketched out a stick figure wearing a football helmet and holding a set of pom-poms and handed it to Bench. On the top he'd written *Go Team!!!* Bench promptly crumpled it up and stuffed it down the back of Deedee's shirt, then threatened to find some real pom-poms and stuff them somewhere else. They tussled a little, until Bench got Deedee in a headlock and noogied him into submission.

They were just horsing around, I knew, same as always, but part of me wondered if it stung a bit, us teasing Bench in front of her. For a moment I considered the possibility that maybe he liked her—this new girl—and that's why he'd gotten embarrassed.

I'd find out soon enough.

THE NUDGE

OKAY. I LIED. THAT DAY AT LUNCH, WHEN ROSE HOLLAND ASKED me what my *thing* was. I told her I'd only written one poem, which isn't true.

One poem earned me my nickname. But I've actually written hundreds.

I keep them in a notebook under my bed, like Deedee and his box of dice. It's nothing special, just your regular spiral-bound notebook, college-ruled, with a navy blue cover. I fill the pages late at night when I'm supposed to be asleep. The real Frost supposedly wrote his poems in an overstuffed blue chair. I write mine by flashlight, belly down on my bed with my feet in the air.

I don't bring the notebook with me to school because there

are certain people—certain *types* of people—who would take one look at it and find a way to use it against me. I realize most kids wouldn't care. Some of them would even think it's cool. It's the few who don't—who read way too much into a thing—those are the ones who will make your life miserable. Kids who wouldn't know a heroic couplet if it was tattooed on their forehead but who would take writing poetry as an excuse to be mean. Kids who would steal it, tear out the pages, and read them out loud in class. Tape them to the bathroom mirrors. Use them to stop up the toilets.

They would come up with other nicknames for me. Names worse than Frost. Names that start with *P*, and "poet" wouldn't be one of them.

Some things are better kept to yourself. I don't share my poems with anyone. Not even Bench or Wolf or Deedee. Not because I'm afraid of what they would think. I mean, we play Dungeons & Dragons. It's hard to be embarrassed when it's the four of us. I just prefer not to share. We all need something that's ours. A thing that we know absolutely about ourselves that others can only guess at.

One day, I think, when I'm good enough, I will pull the notebook from its hiding spot beneath the mattress and open it up for others to see. I will sound my barbaric yawp, as Mr. Sword calls it, over the rooftops of the world. But I'm sure as sushi not doing it while I'm in middle school. I'm not an idiot.

I know what words can do.

Deedee broke out the sticky notes again in art class later that afternoon. We were sketching still lifes of plastic fruit that had been set on the front table—taking the fake perfection of the glossy apple and golden-tinged banana and making them imperfect again through our rough, wobbling lines. It struck me as odd, making a copy of these copies, but real fruit would have rotted before we ever got around to finishing our drawings. Sometimes it's better to fake it, I guess.

I was sketching the bunch of rubber grapes when Deedee peeled off the top note from his pad and gave it to me. Passing notes had nearly gone extinct back when everybody snuck their phones into class. But only two days into the ban, the furtive art of note passing had experienced a resurgence, and teachers were probably wondering if it wasn't better before when it was just screens being tapped and not elaborately folded sheets of paper being shuffled under desks like some gossipy game of telephone.

Deedee stuck his Post-it to my sketch when Mr. Stilton, the art teacher, wasn't looking.

What was that all about? the note said.

I knew what he meant. He meant Rose Holland crashing our lunch.

Guess she just needed somewhere to sit, I wrote back. It was the simplest explanation. It obviously wasn't the one Deedee was looking for, though. As soon as I handed the sticky note back to him he began to scrawl across it.

Yeah, but why us?

That was the better question. Because she has a soft spot for the tortured and misunderstood? Because she knew somehow, instinctively, that Wolf would ask her to? Because I smiled at her in first period, even though I tried to keep it just a polite kind of thing, like how you smile at your waiter when he refills your glass, and not a hey-just-feel-free-to-come-plop-right-down-at-our-lunch-table-if-you-feel-lonely kind of thing.

Or maybe she thought we were the cool kids and she was looking to score popularity points by being seen with us.

Yeah. That *had* to be it.

I pointed to Deedee's pack of sticky notes and snapped my fingers until he pulled a few off for me. I had no idea where mine were, probably stuffed in my locker somewhere. There was absolutely no talking allowed in art; Mr. Stilton said it "disrupted the creative energy flows that emanated from each artist's soul." We weren't even allowed to whisper. I used my charcoal pencil, filling the top yellow square. *Maybe if you hadn't shot her with an applesauce wad,* I wrote.

Deedee scrawled something quickly. He just held his note up for me to see.

Not my fault. I didn't ask her to sit.

I wrote just as quickly.

I didn't ask her either.

Deedee scribbled and flashed another note.

Do you like her?

I shook my head vehemently. Gut reaction. He shook his head back and continued writing.

No. Not like that. *I mean, would you want her to sit with us again?*

Again? Like tomorrow? I hadn't really thought about it. I assumed it was a one-time-only thing. Rose Holland was getting her bearings. Window shopping. Tomorrow she would sit some-where else. Then somewhere different the third day, and so on, until she found her people. Because that's how it worked.

We weren't her people. She had to see that. We were at maximum capacity. Once was fine, but I couldn't imagine her really fitting in. She *was* funny, sort of, and you kind of had to admire the gutsy way she just inserted herself, but she stuck out. She drew attention to herself, and that was a problem. Because who you sat with mattered. Who nodded to you in the halls. Who saved your seat on the bus. Who signed the back of your yearbook. It all meant something.

Do you want her to? I wrote back, handing the sticky note to Deedee, but he didn't reply, partly because Mr. Stilton was making the rounds, polished shoes clicking against the floor, inspecting our handiwork. It didn't matter, though. Deedee's silence was answer enough. Sometimes the truth was hard to admit. My mother was the one who taught me that if you can't say something nice, don't say anything at all, which goes a long way toward explaining why the house was so quiet in the last few years before Dad left.

Mr. Stilton stepped up behind me and looked at my sorry-looking sketch with its lopsided banana. "Nice work," he said. Which is pretty much all he ever said, whether you were a junior Picasso or some kid who couldn't even make a straight line.

Maybe his mom had told him the same thing once.

When we left art, Deedee got nudged. Hard enough that he winced and dropped his backpack, rubbing his shoulder where he was hit. Noah Kyle got him, leading with his shoulder, though he had to stoop a little to get a good shot.

There are other names for it. A bump. A check. A brush. At BMS we called it a nudge. When someone—usually someone bigger than you, or in Deedee's case, always someone bigger— steps into your path and slams into you, catching you on the arm or the shoulder, preferably the one your backpack is slung across so that it gets knocked off. Better still if you're holding some-thing—a bottle of Gatorade, or a stack of books—something you can spill or scatter, to multiply the embarrassment factor, so that the rest of the students standing around you clap at your apparent clumsiness or even take pictures (before the Great Confiscation, anyways) as you bend down to gather your things.

Nudging is a fact of middle school life. It's inevitable, like puberty and armpit stink and lame assemblies. You just learn to live with it. It's better than getting tripped and probably a heck-uva lot better than getting hit. I wouldn't know about that—I had never gotten in a fight—but I'd been nudged a dozen times, maybe more. Some of them were by accident, other kids honestly not looking where they were going. Most of them weren't.

Some kids you can see it coming. You can track the shift in trajectory, the other kid working the angle to guarantee impact. Sometimes they even smile at their friends before it happens. A premeditated shoulder slam. It's not a big deal. It's not like you've been shoved into a locker or had your head stuffed into the john. It's marking territory. Good fences make good neighbors. You just pick up your books and move along. It's not something you tell your parents about. It doesn't bear a remark of any kind. *It was just an accident.* That's what you tell yourself.

Sometimes they would mock-apologize, the girls more than

the boys. Make a big production out of it—"Oh, I'm *sooo* sorry. Did you get in my *way*?" That was the real insult. They made it *your* fault you got nudged. Your fault for being invisible, for not stepping aside.

Wolf didn't get nudged much, not that I saw, anyway. More often he got dirty looks or snide comments from the kids who sat behind us in class. Deedee was an easy target for nudging, though. His size was a big part of it. A stiff enough shoulder could actually send him spinning. And the drama. Watching his face contort, seeing his cheeks burn. I'm pretty sure some kids nudged him just to hear him say "Hey, man, knock it off," in that nasally whine of his.

Fortunately, nobody ever nudged Deedee—or any of us—when Bench was around. But Bench wasn't always around.

We stepped out into the hallway after art and headed toward the last period of the day when Deedee suddenly spun sideways, his backpack slipping off of his left shoulder, his math textbook tumbling out of it along with a bunch of papers. "Hey! Watch it!" he squealed.

Noah Kyle twisted his head, turned down his bottom lip. "Whoops. I didn't see you down there." Beside him, Jason Baker laughed. They were the usual suspects. Noah. Jason. Cameron Cole. A few others. Kids we'd been through the past two years with. Kids whose shoulders we were used to. Kids whose laughs we could identify with our eyes closed. Some of them had been nudging Deedee since elementary school. Though they certainly weren't the *only* ones, they were at least the most reliable jerks in the school. Cameron once "accidentally" dumped his orange juice down my back in the sixth grade. And Jason seemed to be gunning for Wolf for over a year now, whispering things by his ear in class, flicking paper wads at his back, though in true Wolfish fashion he'd just shrug it off. Deedee was a different story.

I bent down and helped him gather his stuff. "You okay?"

"Yeah. Whatever," he said, sniffing and stuffing his papers back into his math book. He looked down the hall, the opposite way of Noah and his friends, not wanting to look me in the face either. Then he stood up with a deep breath and reshouldered his pack. "C'mon," he said.

Just a nudge. Though Deedee walked a little slower than before. And kept between me and the wall the rest of the way just in case. No doubt he was imagining a Balrog bursting through the tiled floor, picking up Noah Kyle and crushing him in its fiery fist.

Or maybe that was just me.

After the last bell I went to my locker to grab my books before meeting up with Bench and heading out to our bus. On days when he didn't have practice—which weren't many—we at least got to sit together on the way home.

When I got there I found another yellow square of paper stuck to the door. I figured it was from Deedee—some little quip or stupid drawing, maybe of Deedee skewering Noah on the tip of a sword. As I got closer, though, I realized the note wasn't from him at all. It didn't have a name, and I didn't recognize the large, looping script, but I knew immediately who wrote it. I looked around to make sure nobody was watching, then peeled the note from the door, folding it twice and shoving it in my pocket.

Thanks for lunch, it said.

And beneath that was a drawing of a snowman.

I went to go find Bench.

THE FISH

THE DAY BENCH ALMOST GOT US ALL KILLED WAS THE DAY I KNEW we were inseparable, that he'd always have our backs.

It's no exaggeration. I really did think we were about to die. Or at the very least, be beaten to sacks of bloody mush. I can still remember being called names while dodging through a playground full of little kids. I can still remember the look of terror on Deedee's face, the same look he got when we made him watch *Jaws* for the first time. Can still remember the bigger of the two kids nearly chasing after me, then tripping, planting his face in the mulch.

But mostly I remember Bench telling me he'd pay me back.

It was this past summer, before eighth grade. Unseasonably cool enough that we all wore hoodies with our shorts. We were at Freedom Park, Branton's most popular stretch of green, complete with a plastic playground and a field big enough to fly kites in. We'd met up because our parents collectively kicked us out. Bench was back from whatever athletic camp his parents had shipped him off to. Wolf had just returned from a music competition in Grand Rapids. Deedee was desperate to start a new Dungeons & Dragons campaign—there was talk of succubae—but the cloudless sky and our parents' nagging forced us to the park instead. Wolf brought Capri Suns. Deedee brought leftover naan to munch on.

I brought the soccer ball.

None of us played soccer, unless you count my brief stint on the worst team in the 7–8-year-old division six years ago. But Deedee was literally incapable of catching a baseball, and we were tired of shooting hoops in Bench's driveway. Deedee could run, at least, almost as fast as Bench, and if the ball happened to roll in front of his foot he had a better than fifty-fifty shot of kicking it.

Unfortunately he still didn't have any aim. So when he shanked his first shot of the afternoon well to the right of the trees we were using as goals, it sailed into a group of high school kids, knocking over a can of Mountain Dew, making me wonder if we shouldn't have taken Deedee bowling instead.

There were four of them sitting in a circle. Two guys, two

girls, probably juniors or seniors. Wolf said they looked like they were his brother's age. Maybe his brother even knew them. Deedee's shot bowled over the soda and the ball came to rest by one of the boys—a tall, blond kid with gelled-stiff hair and a too-tight shirt. He grabbed the ball and stood up to face us.

Deedee apologized, of course, though he was too far away for the kid to hear his mumbling. The three of us came and stood beside him. Wolf held his hands out, gesturing for the ball back.

The boy holding it looked at the girl in the grass beside him—a *watch this* glance if I ever saw one—then he twisted and gave my soccer ball a tremendous kick, smashing it clear the other direction, another fifty yards, easy. Payback, I guess. I started to go after it when I felt Bench's hand on my arm, stopping me.

"Hey!" he called out.

The high school kids looked over at us. Bench took a couple steps toward them. "Hey!" he said again. "That's our ball."

"Then go and get it," the boy who kicked it said. The girl sitting beside him brought a hand to her face, embarrassed, but the other two kids just smiled at each other.

Bench wasn't smiling though. He had his game face on. The one he always wore despite never playing when it mattered. He was still walking, getting closer and closer. We followed, afraid to let Bench go by himself, but a step behind. "You're the one that kicked it over there," he said. "*You* go get it."

The boy shook his head. "You're lucky I didn't cram it down your throat." His friends stopped smiling. I suddenly felt a pain in my stomach. This wasn't like getting nudged. These kids were a lot bigger than us. And strangers. In school there were rules. There were people watching. At least most of the time.

I wasn't the only one concerned. Wolf leaned over, speaking softly. "Bench. It's all right, man. Let's just get the ball."

Bench shook his head. "But that guy's a jerk. It was an accident. Deedee didn't mean to."

"All right, he's a jerk. The world's full of 'em. Let's just go get our ball and go."

Wolf pulled on Bench's arm. Bench resisted at first, but with the second tug his feet pulled loose and we dragged him across the field to where the soccer ball sat. I bent over and picked it up, all the while watching the two older boys watching me, part of me burning at giving them the satisfaction. Nothing worse than knowing you're right and somebody else is wrong and still being on the losing end. "Let's just go back to my house," I said, suddenly wanting to be anywhere else.

I figured that was the end of it.

We started walking toward the playground where our bikes were racked, the swings and slides full of carefree kids, little ones who didn't need a tribe yet because when you're five, everybody's a member. I kept stealing glances at the cluster of high schoolers off to our left now—the blond one had his back to us, but one of the girls was still looking our way. We'd have to pass by them, but not close. Not close enough to matter.

Bench reached over and grabbed the soccer ball from my hands.

"I owe you a ball," he said.

"What?"

"Get ready to run," he added.

Before any of us could say anything or reach out to stop him, Bench veered left, taking just enough steps to ensure his accuracy. Then he hurled the ball as hard as he could—one-handed, baseball-style, right on the mark. It rebounded off the back of the bigger boy's head with enough force to nearly knock him over. I could actually hear it bounce off the kid's skull. A strangely satisfying *thump*.

The next thing I heard was Bench's voice, screaming, "Go! Go! Go!"

We tore through the grass, all four of us, Wolf, Deedee, and me out in front, Bench catching up quickly, waving us on like Indiana Jones fleeing from a pack of angry natives. One look behind me confirmed that both of the teenage boys were on their feet in pursuit, cursing at us, demanding that we *get back here*. My shoes skidded in the mulch as I ducked under slides and bridges, heading for the bike rack, thankful that none of us bothered to chain up. I glanced again just in time to see the one who'd kicked my ball go down, slipping to avoid running over a toddler, getting a mouthful of mulch. Bench was right beside me, grinning like an idiot. "Did you *see* that?" he said.

I didn't have time to yell at him or tell him how stupid he was and how we were about to be murdered in the middle of a playground. Or what a great throw it was, and maybe he should try out for quarterback. Or to even ask him why he did it. But I didn't need to ask him that. You make your tribe. You protect each other from the wolves. We hopped on our bikes and kicked off, careening into the street and pedaling as fast as we could from the two screaming teenagers swearing to hunt us down and kick our butts, though they weren't that polite in their terminology.

We rode all the way back to my house without stopping and collapsed in the front yard, laughing and gasping for breath. Deedee made the moment appropriately geeky by saying "Feel the wrath of Garthrox the Barbarian!" Wolf ripped up a handful of grass and threw it at him, starting a grass war that would leave bare patches in the lawn, but I didn't care. We'd just experienced the thrill of escaping annihilation. Bench was the hero, of course, but we were all in it together.

Afterward we lay on our backs, heads nearly touching, making a plus in the middle of the yard. Bench was lying to my right.

"I don't believe you," I said to him.

"Just glad I didn't miss," he said back.

"They had it coming," Wolf said.

Bench smiled, sort of proud of himself, I guess. I never saw that soccer ball again. And Bench never got around to replacing it. But I knew from that moment on what we counted on him for.

It wasn't until that next day, the Wednesday after the Great Confiscation, that the sticky notes became a *thing*. Not the fad that it would blossom into, or the monster that it would eventually become, but it was definitely *a* thing. It was just *our* thing.

It started with Bench this time, leaving dumb jokes on all three of our lockers. Mine was *Why wouldn't the man carry the grizzly on his back?* The answer, found on the folded-over flap at the bottom: *Because it was unbearable.* The ones he left for Deedee and Wolf were even worse. But it was all right. I was glad to see that nothing had changed. Bench was still Bench. We were still us.

Then there was the note Deedee stuck to my backpack as we passed in the halls, showing a stick figure stabbing some other poor stick figure in his skinny stick back with a smaller stick—a gentle reminder that we had promised him we'd go dungeon diving this weekend. We always agreed to play reluctantly, made it out to be an act of kindness, us coming over to his house and nerding out with him. If we protested long enough, he'd make his mom stock up on Red Bulls and pizza rolls before we came. I think she was just happy her son had other kids to hang with. She'd probably buy us caviar if we asked. I confronted Deedee with the note and told him that Ceric the Elvish Rogue preferred Pringles with his demon slaying. He said he'd look into it.

There was also the sticky note from Wolf, folded into fourths and passed to me in English that morning while Mr. Sword was detailing the difference between tragedy and comedy. Apparently tragedy claimed that life was full of pain and suffering moving inexorably toward death, and comedy said life was ridiculous and people were pretty much fools who sometimes stumbled upon happy endings. They both sounded about right to me.

I took Wolf's note and unfolded it in my lap.

Do you mind if she has lunch with us again?

I looked over and Wolf poked his chin at the door. Rose Holland hadn't moved closer to us, even though there was still an empty seat beside me. Today she had on an oversize plaid button-down shirt, untucked, and the same dark blue jeans and black combat boots as the day before. It looked like maybe she'd raided her father's closet for something to wear—and her father was a lumberjack. She'd waved to us when she came in, but hadn't looked my way since.

I held Wolf's note and stared.

"In a tragedy," Mr. Sword continued, "the hero struggles against his inevitable fate, so it is naturally a losing battle. But in a comedy, he is often the victim of chance or coincidence, so even in his folly he can still somehow do the right thing."

Wolf raised his eyebrows at me.

I shrugged. I wasn't sure what to say, wasn't sure what he *wanted* me to say. Either answer, yes or no, seemed like it could cause a problem. Wolf didn't seem satisfied with my noncommittal shrug, but before he could write another sticky note, Mr. Sword swooped down on us, placing his hands on my desk.

"So how about it, Mr. Voss? Do you see yourself as the hero of a tragedy, or a comedy? Are you fated to let your pride lead to your inevitable destruction, or are you simply a fool being toyed with by forces beyond your control?"

I didn't like either option, really. I glanced at Wolf and then back at Mr. Sword. "Um. I'm pretty sure I'm just part of the chorus," I said.

Apparently it was a good answer, because Mr. Sword laughed and let me off the hook.

"And a good thing, too," he said. "They are usually the only ones still standing at the end." Mr. Sword went back to lecturing the class. Wolf let his question drop.

I tried not to watch the clock above the door.

Wolf's question was answered three periods later when I walked with Bench to the cafeteria. I realized then why Wolf was even asking. He wasn't seeking permission; he was just seeing how I felt about it. He'd already made up his mind.

There they were, Rose and Wolf sitting next to each other at the otherwise empty table, laughing like a couple of lunatics. Like old friends.

Beside me, Bench grunted out a "Really? Again?"

I got behind him in line and we snagged our spaghetti and weaved our way through the maze of tables. I sat down next to Deedee, who had snuck in while we were getting our food, forcing Bench to take the other empty seat—the one on Rose's right. Her tray had one of those fruit-filled snack pies on it, along with three celery stalks and a carton of milk. I wondered how the celery fit in with her stick-to-the-roof-of-your-mouth diet. Maybe she had a secret jar of peanut butter in her pocket to dunk them in.

Bench scooted his chair over, deliberately giving himself extra elbow room, putting him closer to me. Rose didn't seem to notice.

"Wolf was just telling me about the time all four of you nearly blew your own lips off," she said. Bench raised his eyebrows. Deedee chuckled at the memory, though it really wasn't all that funny, not even in a looking-back-on-it-now kind of way.

"We didn't almost blow our lips off," I said. Though I guess we could have. We got a little singed, at least. Last summer— after the soccer-ball-to-the-head incident—the four of us tried to make our own dynamite. Not because we had anything in particular to blow up, save for a couple of Wolf's old models that he didn't like anymore. More because we were bored and couldn't think of anything dumber to do. It bothered me a little, Wolf telling Rose these kinds of things already. Not that our summer shenanigans were top secret or anything—though homemade bombs weren't exactly the kind of thing you wanted to brag about in school—just that Wolf didn't make a habit of going around telling stories. He liked to keep things to himself. It was another thing I thought we had in common.

"A shoe box of leftover fireworks and your mom's stolen lighter are a dangerous recipe," Wolf said.

"We needed a longer fuse," Deedee remarked. I studied Deedee's face. He didn't seem that put out that there were five of us again, but it's not like he would have told Rose to get up and leave. He popped open his lunch box and fished out his food like it was any other nonbreadstick day.

91

"We needed some brains," Wolf corrected. "I mean, whose idea was it to split open three hundred Black Cats and empty the contents into a toilet paper roll and set it on fire anyways?"

The idea had been mine, actually, though I didn't care to admit it. It hadn't turned out as spectacular as I'd hoped. I was imagining proton torpedo blowing up the Death Star. It was mostly just loud and smoky. Our lips remained firmly attached to our faces, but the black smudge could still be seen on my driveway. Nothing quite gets out stupidity, not even bleach.

"Small town," I explained. "Long summers. And the public pool's always too crowded."

"You four need more hobbies," Rose said. Bench grunted and dug into his spaghetti. He seemed to be intent on finishing his food in record time. He hadn't said a word since we'd stepped out of line.

"Speaking of hobbies," Wolf said, "did you know Rose is a professional orgamist?"

"Origamist," Rose said. "And Wolf is exaggerating. I've only recently gone semipro. Here." She dropped the celery stalk she had been nibbling at and took the napkin off my tray without even asking. I watched her fold it in half. "Pick an animal. Any animal at all."

"Me?" I asked, wondering why I'd been singled out. I was

supposed to be part of the chorus. I looked at Bench, who refused to look up from his food. I tried to think of something creative, something challenging. Something impossible. "Komodo dragon," I said.

Wolf snorted. "Really, Frost?"

"She said any animal."

"It's all right," Rose said. "I've got this. One Komodo dragon, coming right up."

The four of us sat and watched. Even Bench stopped scarfing his bowl of spaghetti, looking at Rose Holland over the top of his fork. She worked quickly, her hands moving almost as fast as Wolf's when they danced up and down his piano keys, impossible to follow. Fold and crease and fold. Press and crease again. I watched something taking shape, though I couldn't make it out at first.

"Voilà," Rose said after twenty seconds or so, handing my reshaped napkin back to me.

I held it between us for a moment. I'm sure I looked confused.

"It's a fish," I said.

"Nope. Komodo dragon," she said.

I held it up. "Really? Because it *seriously* looks like a fish." It was definitely a fish. It may not have had a sword for a nose, but it was certainly no Komodo dragon.

Rose leaned across the table, her face suddenly close to mine. "Honestly, Frost. Where's your imagination?" Her breath smelled like celery and cinnamon gum.

"It's a very nice fish," Deedee said, snatching my napkin-fish out of my hands and arcing it up and down through imaginary currents. He swam it up to Bench and pretended to tickle his cheek.

Bench wrapped a fist around it, crumpling it and then dropping it to his tray.

"Fish murderer," Deedee scoffed. Bench shrugged.

"Do one for me," Wolf said, snatching the napkin off of Bench's tray this time and handing it over before he could snag it back. "An elephant."

"No problemo," Rose said. Fifteen seconds later she handed Wolf another fish.

"You forgot the trunk," he said. Then he took a stray strand of spaghetti from my plate and smooshed it against the fish's nose, where it dangled.

"Perfect," Rose said. She turned to Deedee. "How about it? What'll it be? A kangaroo? An armadillo? A three-toed sloth? Just name it and the Fabulous Folding Rose will make it for you."

But before he could answer, Josh Penn, a kid with a buzz

cut and a habit of scratching his armpits in class, stuck his head between Bench and me and whispered, "Evan Smalls is running the Gauntlet."

"When?" Bench asked, finally finding a conversation he wanted to be a part of. "Today?"

Josh nodded. Scratched. "Four o'clock."

"Why?" I asked, but Josh ignored me. It was a stupid question, anyway. The why was superfluous. Probably somebody had dared him to and he didn't want to wuss out. Maybe it was an argument. Maybe just a challenge. Maybe it was a bet. It didn't matter, not to the people watching. What mattered was that Evan was going to run. I glanced around the lunchroom, but I didn't see him anywhere. Josh Penn moved on to share the news with the next table, spreading it the old-fashioned way in light of everyone's phones being kept prisoner in the Big Ham's office.

"Evan Smalls," I repeated. I knew him. We weren't friends, obviously, but I had nothing against him. Nothing that would make me want to see him break his neck.

"He's going to kill himself," Deedee said, echoing my thoughts. His voice was matter-of-fact. Like it was a forgone conclusion.

"Excuse me, but what the heck is a gauntlet?"

Deedee looked at Rose as if she had an alien crawling out of her throat. "You're joking, right? You mean you've never *heard* of *the Gauntlet*?"

Rose put up her hands in protest. "All right. First off, you don't have to say it like that. You're not Han Solo talking about the *Millennium* freaking *Falcon*. Secondly, I just moved here three weeks ago, and I didn't get a chance to finish *Frommer's Guide to Exploring Podunkville, Michigan*, before I came. Is this some kind of stupid dare thing?"

"Pretty much," Wolf said. "With an emphasis on the stupid." Wolf had never been a fan of the Gauntlet. I believe he once used the phrase "immature, idiotic, macho load of bullhockey" when describing it. He was in the minority, though. The rest of us knew better.

"It's the place where legends are born," I explained. "It's basically this gigantic hill, completely covered with trees, and you walk your bike to the top and then try to ride back down as fast as you can, no brakes, without flipping or kissing bark. Deedee's right. It's completely suicidal."

"So you just ride down the hill?" she asked.

"Yeah. But it's called 'Running the Gauntlet.'"

"And this is what you guys do around here for fun?"

"Not us. We make bombs," Wolf said proudly.

"And play Dungeons and Dragons," Deedee added. I think maybe he surprised himself by admitting that, because he started sucking on his juice box to keep from elaborating.

"And that boy came around and told you, why? So you can go and *watch*?"

I nodded. Wolf shook his head.

"I only watched once," Deedee said. "Remember Kyle Ralston?"

I remembered. Kyle's nose was still crooked, and the scar on his leg where the bike's gears bit into him earned him lots of second glances in gym class. Kyle had made it two-thirds of the way down. The farther you make it, the bigger the impact. Momentum is a killer.

"I'll be honest . . . it sounds kinda dumb," Rose said.

"It is," Wolf echoed. The two of them shook their heads at each other.

Bench dropped his fork onto his plate. "Well, *I'm* going," he declared. He turned to me. "You'll be there, won't you?"

Suddenly I was on the spot. I squirmed in my seat, sensing Bench boring holes into me on one side, and Wolf's sharp green eyes on me from the other. A simple enough question, except it wasn't simple it all. Bench was challenging me, and somehow I couldn't back down, not in front of everyone. Not in front of Rose.

"What? Pass up a chance to watch someone plow into a tree at forty miles an hour and possibly crack their skull open? Who wouldn't want to see that?" I said halfheartedly.

I didn't return Wolf's stare, or bother to look at Deedee, either. I did glance over at Rose, just to see if I could tell what she was thinking, but there was no reading her expression.

I did know one thing, though. When Bench punched me playfully on the shoulder after I agreed to go with him to watch Evan Smalls try to kill himself, it hurt a little.

Bench picked up his tray and said that he was finished and that he needed to go get something from his locker before next period. "We'll meet up after school, all right?" He was speaking to me. Only to me.

I gave the most imperceptible of nods.

As he walked away, Wolf waved to him, but Bench's hands were so full he didn't wave back.

THE GAUNTLET

MIDDLE SCHOOL IS A MINEFIELD. DECIDING WHO TO LIKE AND NOT like and who to follow and who to ignore completely. Worrying that you're going to trip while walking down the hall and sprawl all over the floor like a beached starfish. Wondering if you should raise your hand when the teacher asks a hard question and risk exposing your nerdiness for the sake of a few bonus points. Taking every sideways glance as a message, trying to crack the code. Every day you're bound to do something that gets you noticed by the wrong people. Every day you're bound to step somewhere you shouldn't.

I know all about minefields—actual, honest-to-god-explosives-buried-in-the-dirt minefields—from my crazy uncle Mike, the one who gave me the whale shirt for my birthday. He served in the army straight out of high school and did two tours on the bomb squad. His official title, I guess, was explosive ordnance disposal specialist, but his buddies gave him the nickname Pinky. He spent most of his time over in Iraq for Round Two, as he called it, helping to detonate and disarm land mines and IEDs—improvised explosive devices. Like a toilet paper tube full of gunpowder only more complex and a lot more dangerous. It was an IED that gave my uncle his nickname. It actually blew off three of his fingers, but the surgeons managed to reattach two of them. Sometimes things stick, and sometimes they don't. Uncle Mike told me all about it. In incredibly gory detail.

I could sit and listen to my uncle's war stories for hours, partly because they expanded my vocabulary—he only censored the language when Mom was around—but also because they kind of put things in perspective. My uncle has seen bombs capable of leveling buildings, taking out a whole city block, though he says that's nothing compared to the one time he had to babysit me as an infant and I blew out my diaper. (He called me a biological WMD—weapon of mass destruction—and told me that one diaper was the reason he never got married and had a kid of his own, though I suspect there were others.) He'd seen things I'd never seen and hoped I'd never have to see, and he said he didn't have a whole lot of patience for people who didn't know a good thing when they had it.

Sometimes I wondered if he didn't mean my parents.

Uncle Mike used to come visit a couple times a year before my dad moved away, and when he did he'd tell me about all the things he'd seen blow up.

The last time I saw him was four years ago. Mom and Dad hadn't spoken to each other in a while, and I swear it was so cold in the house you could see icicles hanging from the windows in June. On the second day of the long weekend Uncle Mike came outside to finish his beer, and found me bouncing a tennis ball off the garage.

"I know what you're doing," he said with a sly grin, stepping off the porch and coming toward me. He wore long sleeves, even in the summer. Said he'd gotten accustomed to having every square inch covered.

"I'm playing catch," I told him. I was only nine at the time. I hadn't met Bench yet. I had sort-of friends, but no tribe, and I was used to spending time by myself. I lobbed the tennis ball against the garage door again, but my uncle was faster than me and snatched it before I could. He held the ratty old thing up between us in his four-fingered hand.

"*You* are staying out of the way," he said.

I didn't know what to say, so instead I took the ball from him and started chucking it again. In some ways Uncle Mike was the exact opposite of my father. He didn't care for books. He liked big crowds and loud gatherings. He was a people person, which he said was unusual for someone who spent most of his working hours by himself, trying not to get blown up. He actually tried to get along with my mother—made a pretty constant effort—which was another big difference between him and Dad. But there was one thing he and Dad had in common: neither of them was afraid to lecture me about life, whether I wanted them to or not. I took it better coming from Uncle Mike. It didn't sound like a lecture. It just sounded like two guys talking. Besides, he was immensely cool in a yeah-I-got-my-finger-blown-off-in-combat kind of way.

"It's all right. I get it," he said, standing beside me, taking a sip from his can. "It's the safest thing. You walk down a road and you see a wire poking out of the dirt, you stop walking, you back the hell up, and you call EOD." Uncle Mike liked to use acronyms. He was full of them. I suspected he was full of a lot of things. Nobody could have *that* many stories. "You take cover, clinch hard, and cross your fingers, but you stay out of the way. Sometimes there are no RSPs."

"RSPs?" I stopped bouncing my ball.

"Render safe procedures. Whatever you gotta do to make sure a bomb doesn't hurt somebody. You know—don't cut the black wire or whatever crapola they teach you in the movies. But sometimes there's really not much you can do. Nothing but trigger the thing and stay out of the way and try not to get hurt. You know what I'm saying?"

I wasn't sure. "Coming from a guy with nine fingers," I said, tossing the ball again. Thunk. Bounce. Catch. Thunk. Bounce. Catch.

"I said *try*," he said, intercepting my ball again. "You don't always get out in one piece." He bounced it as hard as he could against the pavement with his pinkiless hand, a fly ball for me to catch. Unfortunately the sun temporarily blinded me and I lost track of it and it bounced down the driveway and into the street. My uncle and I both watched it, sort of daring the other one to go after it.

In the end we just left it there, resting by the curb, and sat together on the porch instead, him nursing his beer and me chugging a Coke, both of us listening to the nothing coming from inside the house, me wondering what kind of man decides he wants to disarm bombs for a living and my uncle probably wondering the same thing.

But some things, I guess, you can't shy away from. Some things you just have tackle head on, whether it's safe or not. Even if it means losing a part of you.

Evan Smalls was running the Gauntlet at four, which meant I needed to get home and grab my bike if I wanted to make it out to Hirohito Hill in time to meet Bench.

That's what everyone called the Gauntlet when nobody was careening down it: Hirohito Hill. At least that's what kids long before us called it, and it stuck. I'm not sure it even has a real name. I don't even know who owns the land—the town, I guess. Or maybe it's just been in somebody's family for generations and they've forgotten about it. There are no signs saying KEEP OUT, though there probably should be.

Not that it would stop us. There's not much that would stop thirteen-year-old boys from trying to kill themselves in an attempt to prove how cool they are. Maybe barbed wire. Maybe high voltage. But probably not. The rules would just be different. Legend says that the hill was named after the emperor of Japan during World War II. The same emperor who encouraged his pilots to nose-dive into battleships and aircraft carriers. They could have called it Kamikaze Hill, I guess, but then you wouldn't have the alliteration. I'm sort of a sucker for alliteration too.

You'd think it would be the kind of thing you'd grow out of. An idea you packed up after elementary school, along with your glue sticks and your Yu-Gi-Oh! cards. But not in Branton. In Branton, the Gauntlet is an institution. As integral to our way of life as Mr. Twisty's, Stockbridge's statue, Fredo's greasy pizza parlor, or Mustache Mick, the homeless guy who begs for loose change outside Andy's Bar on Tenth Street and has a big, black broom curtaining his mouth. Every kid in Branton had given Mick at least a dollar and shelled out two fifty for a jumbo slice at Fredo's. And everybody had seen at least one kid try to tackle the Gauntlet. It was our proving grounds. Our Octagon. Our Hunger Games. A giant, tree-studded hill, overgrown and wild with brush and ivy. There was no easy path down. The slope, Deedee once calculated, was at least fifty degrees (I know better than to question his math). It took you three minutes to walk your bike up it. You could make it back down in twenty seconds, provided nothing stopped you, but something always stopped you. There was no single straight-line path. To navigate, you had to turn, and turning on that kind of slope going that kind of speed was tricky to do once, let alone the dozen times you would need to in order to dodge the trees and reach the bottom intact.

I'd never *ridden* the Gauntlet, but I'd run down it on foot a few times. That was slightly safer; when you feel like you are going too fast you can just whip out an arm and lasso one of the thousand trees that threaten to pulverize you, anchoring yourself to it. But even running down you run the risk of tripping over a root or getting tangled in the underbrush, splitting your head open on a rock or twisting your ankle. On a bike you're almost better off just closing your eyes and hoping for angels to guide you.

In the whole history of Branton Middle School—more than

fifty years—there were probably only a dozen kids who had made it to the bottom of the hill in one piece. All of them had long since graduated, their names recorded in whispers, passed down from kid to kid, generation to generation.

None of them were named Evan Smalls. He was going to crash, no doubt about it. That's why everybody was here. They wanted to watch.

I met Bench at the base, standing in the field of clover and spent dandelions where everybody just pitched their bikes in a great big pile. I was early—Evan hadn't even shown up yet—but there was already a crowd. Lots of people I knew, but Bench was the only one I was friends with.

"Beat ya," he said when he saw me. "I'm guessing they didn't change their mind?"

Wolf and Deedee, he meant. Maybe Bench thought they would call at the last minute and say they were coming. But Wolf was probably rocking Chopin, and Deedee was probably locked in his room polishing his dice and drawing up maps for our Saturday-night session. I didn't tell Bench how close I had been to not coming myself. How awkward I felt with both him and Wolf staring at me at our table.

He seemed to know what I was thinking, though. "Man," he said. "Lunch today."

"Yeah," I said.

"Weird."

"So weird," I repeated, not sure if we were using the word the same way. It had certainly been uncomfortable. But then the origami thing had been kind of funny. "Komodo dragon," I mumbled.

"Yeah. What was up with that, anyway?"

"If I would have known, I would have just told her to make me a fish."

Bench grunted. "Something tells me Rose Holland is gonna do whatever she wants to, no matter what you say." Those words mashed together seemed to form a compliment, but it didn't really come off that way. "And her and Wolf. He didn't even ask. I mean, that's *our* table."

I didn't tell Bench that Wolf *did* ask. Sort of. He just didn't ask Bench. Maybe he knew what the answer would be. "It's just lunch," I said, sensing the tension in Bench's voice. Suddenly I wasn't sure I wanted to talk about it anymore.

"Yeah, I know, but did you see the looks we were getting?" he asked. "And not just today. Yesterday too. Some of the guys I practice with, you could just tell what they were thinking."

I tried not to think about what they were thinking. I told myself I didn't care. I didn't have guys who I practiced with.

But I had Bench, and he obviously cared. "It's kind of hard to blame them," he continued. "I mean she is kind of—well, you know . . ."

She is what? The unfinished sentence hung between us as we started up the hill, daring me to fill in the blank. Rose was a little odd, I guess. She didn't dress like most of the other girls at school. Didn't act the same way. In two days I hadn't seen her in the hall with anyone besides Wolf or one of the teachers. She was new. An outsider. Someone who'd never even heard of the hill we were currently walking up or seen anyone ride down the other side. She obviously stuck out.

"It's not just how she looks," Bench added quickly, seemingly reading my thoughts again. "I heard her mom's crazy, and nobody has ever even *seen* her dad."

"You sure know a lot about her," I said, maybe more suggestive than I meant to.

Bench stopped and gave me a hard stare. We were nearly at the top of the hill now where everyone else had gathered, clustered in their own tribes. "People say things, Frost. You know that."

Yeah. I knew that. Sometimes the things they say get back around to you. Sometimes they don't. But you know they're out there.

"I'm not suggesting I have anything against her personally. I just don't know if she should sit with us all the time. Things were just fine before, right?"

I stood in front of him and thought of all the ways I could respond. I *could* say that it's only been twice so far, which hardly counts as "all the time." I *could* say it wasn't his decision to make; there were four of us at the table. I *could* say that it shouldn't matter who she sat with, or who we did. I could throw his own words back at him and say that Rose Holland was probably going to do whatever Rose Holland wanted to do.

But he wasn't wrong. We were just fine before.

"Okay," I said. I wasn't entirely sure what I was saying okay to. I was just ready to stop talking about it.

"All right," Bench sighed.

Up on the hill the crowd of onlookers started to buzz and Bench and I craned our necks to see Evan walking his bike up. He was joined by Jimmy Reese, his best friend and wingman. You needed to bring someone with you when you ran the Gauntlet. Someone you could trust to call 911, if it came to that, and to lie to your parents for you or make up some excuse. Someone to help push your mangled bike as you limped back home. Bench and I stopped talking and followed the blob of fifty or so kids to Evan's chosen launch spot.

Everyone attempting the Gauntlet picked their own takeoff point. There were some that were considered better than others, but there was no single entry point into the dense wooded hillside that gave a person a better shot at making it. "Did you ever find out what this was even about?" I asked, nodding toward the doomed boy and his bike.

"Evan and Mikey V. have been talking trash, apparently trying to impress Alicia Raymond. They have a bet that if Evan makes it down, he's got to pay Evan fifty bucks."

Fifty bucks. Hardly seemed worth risking your life. Of course I once watched my parents argue for three days over whose turn it had been to empty the dishwasher, so I'm probably not the best judge of what is and isn't worth fighting for. People had risked the Gauntlet for less. I looked around for Mikey V. and spotted him at the edge of the crowd, arms crossed. He seemed pretty confident he'd hold on to his money. I wondered if Alicia Raymond was even here.

Evan Smalls sat on his bike and peered down the hill, probably mapping his course, or just trying to find the courage to lift his feet. He wasn't wearing a helmet. It was tradition. The kids who ran the Gauntlet forty or fifty years ago didn't wear them, so kids today didn't wear them. Convoluted logic. Like saying you shouldn't wear sunscreen because your grandma never bothered.

There were no speeches. No bequeathing of material possessions. Jimmy and Evan bumped fists. "Good luck, man." It was the only thing anybody ever said. Evan hitched a huge breath and then hunkered down over his handlebars. The crowd hushed, each of us silently counting down in our heads. Three. Two. One.

We have liftoff.

He didn't need to pedal. The pedals were just a place to keep your feet. Gravity did all the work. Evan Smalls careened down Hirohito Hill on an orange-and-black Huffy, undulating over the rutted terrain. I thought about my uncle and what he would say about this—except there were no render safe procedures for the Gauntlet. There was the top of the hill and the bottom of the hill and a thousand ways to get mangled in between.

I found myself holding my own sweaty hand and saying a little prayer for Evan as he dodged one tree after another. He wasn't a friend or anything—it's not like we ever hung out—but he'd never nudged me or called me a dweeb or a loser either. *Please let him make it,* I whispered. *Let him get to the bottom.*

But the bloodthirsty gods that watch over Hirohito Hill don't take requests.

Evan had barely gotten halfway when his pedal clipped a tree, causing him to jerk the opposite direction. He sideswiped an even bigger tree and wiped out, shielding his head with his forearms and using his right shoulder to absorb most of the impact as he flipped, the crowd of students at the top of the hill flinching in unison, fists to their mouths. The bike twisted and slipped out from underneath him, the busted gear assembly sawing through his sock and into his ankle, leaving a jagged gash. He lay there, sprawled out in the dirt, entangled in the metal tubes and springs of his ride, rolling and wincing and holding his right arm as several kids, including Jimmy, made their way to him, none too quickly, afraid they would take a tumble down the hill themselves.

Bench and I stood at the top and watched. Even from where we were you could see Evan's face squinched in pain.

"Nasty," I said.

"Yeah."

"Is that blood?"

"I think so."

There wasn't a lot else to say.

A small crowd of students had gathered around Evan now and were helping him to his feet. To his credit, he didn't cry, even as he limped the rest of the way down the hill, Jimmy guiding the bike with its busted tire and slipped chain behind him. It would probably cost fifty bucks just to get the bike back in shape. Not to mention he'd have to explain to his parents where he got the huge yellow bruise that was no doubt going to blossom across his shoulder. It takes a while, sometimes, for things like that to show. A bloody sock you could just toss in somebody's bushes on the way home. But the bruise would sneak up on him in the middle of the night, and somehow, his parents would find out, and he'd have to make some excuse, because parents weren't allowed to know about the Gauntlet. Like most things kids do that they probably shouldn't: if the adults found out, they would put a stop to it.

The show was over. Bench and I headed back down the gentler side of the hill toward our own bikes.

"You think you'll ever try to ride it?" Bench asked.

"For fifty bucks? No way." Probably not for a girl either. Even if I thought running the Gauntlet would impress one of them long enough to like me, which was doubtful.

"For anything, then?" Bench asked.

I stopped for a moment and tried to think of something that *would* be worth it. Hypothetically, I would do it for a thousand dollars. Or maybe five thousand. I'd do it if I could end world hunger. Or if my life depended on it. Or if somehow it might get my parents to just talk to each other again. But for the reasons that kids normally tackled the Gauntlet? I shook my head. "You?"

"I don't know," Bench said. "I guess if my rep was on the line, you know? I wouldn't want people talking smack about me, saying I wasn't up to it."

Bench's reputation. Sometimes I forgot any of us had one, but I guess if one of us did, it would be him. I wondered what people he meant. If there were certain ones he was thinking of.

"I mean, how hard could it be, really?" he said. "Keep your head up. Keep your eyes forward. Don't let go. Oh. And try not to crash."

"Well, when you put it that way . . . no. I still wouldn't do it," I said.

Try not to crash. It sounded like sage advice.

If only it were always that easy.

That night, after Mom managed an epic fail at eggplant parmesan and had to order takeout, I finished up my homework and checked my email. I was one of the few kids I knew who still bothered with it (e-mail, not homework, though I knew a lot of kids who didn't bother with that either), mostly because I didn't own a phone of my own and Mom put the kibosh on social media accounts until I turned fifteen—though I had one that she didn't know about.

There were the usual messages. Hot twenty-four-year-olds in

the Branton area looking for a date. A pill that would help me with the urination problems I didn't have. Kohl's was having its fourteenth biggest sale of the season. Delete all. Amid the junk, though, one message caught my eye: from hollandrose42@gmail.

Apparently I wasn't the only one who preferred email over texting. I opened it.

There wasn't much in the body of the message, just a subject line that said, "Thought you might like this," and a link underneath. She signed it simply *Rose*.

I paused, wondering first how she'd even gotten my address, and second (and more important) why she decided to use it. I wasn't the one she was laughing with at the start of lunch today. And yet here she was sending me a message.

I remembered what Bench told me back at the hill. People say things. They *see* things. They jump to conclusions.

I actually looked around idiotically to see if anyone was watching, though the only other person in the house was my mother and I could hear her in the kitchen scraping burned egg-plant from the pan. I clicked on the link, my palm sweaty, and found myself directed to a website teaching viewers how to fold origami animals.

Or, more specifically, an origami Komodo dragon.

It was actually a thing.

First take your sheet and fold it lengthwise. Then pull down the top two corners. . . .

I smiled at no one in particular as I watched the video one time through. I went back to the beginning and reached in my jeans pocket for the sticky note, the one from Bench with the joke on it (*unbearable*), and did my best to follow along, but my square was too small, and what I ended up with looked a lot more like Evan Smalls all crumpled and tangled in his bike than a Komodo dragon.

I threw it in the wastebasket underneath my desk. Then I spotted the other sticky note clinging to the side of my monitor. The one with the snowman on it.

Thanks for lunch.

I couldn't just ignore her. It didn't seem right. I hit reply.

Maybe I should just start with a fish. ☺

My cursor hovered over the send button, finger poised over the mouse, reading that one sentence, over and over, making sure I hadn't said anything I hadn't meant to, which would have been hard given the fact I'd only used eight words. I even fretted over the emoticon—considered the one with the winking eye, but that would definitely give the wrong impression. And that was the *last* thing I wanted to do.

I clicked send and stood up to go brush my teeth but paused over the keyboard, refreshing the inbox once, then again, standing there for thirty seconds, a minute, two. Just to see if, by chance, she was online right at that moment and had gotten my reply.

And if she would write me back.

THE REVOLUTION

THE NEXT DAY, THE STICKY NOTES GOT AWAY FROM US.

Nobody knows if it was Ashley P. or Ashley W. who stuck first. We weren't even sure it was an Ashley, though the odds were good—there were eight of them in our school, and five of them were popular enough to take it to the next level.

Working backward, it had to have been someone in one of those groups. The North Facers. The Under Armour Jock Squad. The Weekend Shopping Spree Brigade. Somebody higher on the ladder than us. Otherwise it wouldn't have caught on. We weren't trendsetters. We weren't even trend followers.

And yet someone noticed. Someone saw us sticking our little yellow squares to each others' lockers and thought it was a good idea, or at least thought *they* could turn it into a good idea. A sneaker is just a sneaker until LeBron throws his name on it. Then it's worth a fortune.

"Look over there," Deedee said, meeting me before the bell with a half-eaten granola bar and wide eyes. It was the fourth day after the Great Confiscation and students were still noticeably bitter. A petition was going around that was supposedly headed to our congressman, asking him to intercede and somehow overthrow the school board's decision—as if he gave a flying fart what happened at BMS. I didn't even know who our congressman was. Probably Francis B. Stockbridge VIII.

Deedee squirmed and pointed, but seeing Deedee excited about something was hardly cause for alarm. He practically peed his pants at movie previews. "Look where?" I asked.

Deedee pointed even more emphatically. I didn't see anything. At least nothing out of the ordinary. A bunch of kids moping their way to first period. Everybody trying to wake up.

"Amanda Shockey dyed her hair purple again?"

"No. Not there. *There*. On the locker."

I scanned the row of blue lockers across the hall. They all looked the same, except for one that was dented from when one of the football players tested out his new helmet by running headlong into it. And the one with the square of paper stuck to it, too far away for me to read. "You mean the note?"

"Yeah, *the note*," Deedee said. "Don't you know whose locker that is? That's Missy Upton's."

Missy Upton the cheerleader. Deedee would know. He knew the lockers of most of the cheerleaders. Just because we didn't talk about girls or to them or to them about them or about them to them didn't mean we never thought about them or even stared at them sometimes.

"I saw six others as I walked in this morning. Don't you see what this means?"

"It means Missy Upton hasn't been to her locker yet?"

"It means," Deedee said, sticking his granola bar in my face, "that we've started something. Like a sticky note . . . thing. A communications revolution. Like Alexander Graham Bell inventing the telephone."

Deedee was delusional. I put a hand on his shoulder. "Whatever, man. We need to get to class."

"You don't believe me."

"It's one note on one locker. That hardly qualifies as a revolution."

On the way, though, I saw a kid whose name I couldn't remember leave another sticky note on another locker, a lopsided heart in swirly black marker. It had initials on it and an arrow shot through the center. Since when did pierced vital organs become a symbol for love?

"See, I told you," Deedee said, tugging on my arm.

I shrugged. It *was* kind of weird—people besides us using sticky notes like that. But no weirder than the two sixth graders who were trying to snort chocolate milk up their nostrils on the bus that morning. Middle school was a breeding ground for random behavior. "Just a coincidence," I said.

I spotted two more notes before we even made it to class.

We also passed Evan Smalls, his right wrist wrapped tight, limping with every step. I thought about telling him he had a good run at least, except there was nothing I could say that would make him feel better about lip-smacking a tree trunk. I settled for a nod instead.

I stepped into Mr. Sword's class to find my seat taken. The one beside Wolf. The one I'd sat in since the first day of the year. Rose stood up as soon as she saw me.

"I was keeping it warm for you," she said as I came over. Wolf laughed and I wondered if this was some kind of joke at my expense. I looked around and saw a few other students watching us. Jason Baker had his tongue in his cheek, one eyebrow cocked—supervillain facial accompaniment to the phrase *Well, well, what have we here?* I just ignored him. I was sure I would hear about it later.

As she passed me Rose whispered in my ear, "Try not to melt."

Try not to melt. Keeping it warm. Frosty the Snowman. I got it.

I sat down slowly and watched Wolf watch Rose head back to her usual place by the door. Cameron Cole whispered something to Noah Kyle behind us. There was zero doubt in my mind that it was about me. I told myself I didn't care.

"We were just talking," Wolf said.

I nodded. My seat actually was warm. I was about to ask what, exactly, they'd been chatting about when Mr. Sword bustled in with a big stack of paperbacks and started passing them down the rows. The class immediately hushed, not because we were being polite or anything, but because the man was wearing a toga. You could see his usual sweater and pant combo on underneath, but it's still the sort of thing that gets a class's attention.

"It's Shakespeare time," Mr. Sword said with way too much enthusiasm. The collective groan could probably be heard clear in the other wing of the school.

The copy of *Julius Caesar* landed on my desk. The picture on the cover at least looked promising. Bloody daggers and a dead body. Still, I could think of about 147 other writers I'd rather spend the next two weeks with. Supposedly Mr. Sword taught *Julius Caesar* every year. Maybe it was mandated in the curriculum. Or maybe he just liked it that much. He *did* own his own toga. Deedee leaned over to Wolf and me. "Caesar dies," he said.

"Don't need to read *that* now." I slapped the book against my desk with mock irritation. The cover—and ancient history—kind of spoiled it before Deedee could.

"I read the SparkNotes already," Deedee continued. "They all conspire against him and stab him over and over again. But it's all right because all the people who murder him end up killing themselves in the end."

"You're right," I said. "That makes it all better."

Wolf didn't say anything. I had no idea what he was thinking or if he was even listening. He laughed, and I realized that he was reading something scrawled on a note that he'd hidden in his lap beneath his desk. Judging by the handwriting I guessed it was from Rose. Back at the front of the class, Mr. Sword started in on the history of Ancient Rome—necessary background for understanding what we were about to read. He put several names on the board. Julius Caesar. Marcus Brutus. Gaius Cassius Longinus.

"*Gayus Long*inus? Seriously?" Cameron whispered.

"I think it's pronounced Guy-us, moron," I heard Amanda Shockey say. That girl almost always had a book in her hand, though hardly ever the one Mr. Sword assigned. She also didn't care much what anyone else thought. I was tempted to give her a high five. It was always nice when guys like Cameron were called out . . . not that it ever stopped them. To prove my point, Jason Baker put his hand up.

"Yes, Jason?" Mr. Sword said.

"Yeah. Weren't the Romans . . . you know . . ." He made a wishy-washy hand gesture. "I mean, the guys at least, didn't they prefer . . ."

Over my shoulder I could see he was having a hard time keeping a straight face. Beside him Noah Kyle snorted, trying not to laugh. Mr. Sword gave them both a puzzled look. "I'm not sure I understand."

Jason lowered his head and slumped in his chair. "It's all right. Forget it."

Mr. Sword paused for a moment, jaw working back and forth, maybe deciding if he should press the issue. Instead he took a deep breath and continued with his lecture on the expansion of the Roman Empire and Caesar's rise to power. I only paid half attention, trying to see what was written on the note Wolf was reading. That's when I saw Jason lean over Wolf's shoulder. Most days they were interchangeable, Jason and Noah and Cameron, at least as far as I was concerned. You figured one of them would give you a hard time, but couldn't be sure who. But with Wolf it always seemed to be Jason.

"When in Rome," he whispered. "Am I right, *Morgan*?"

Wolf just kept reading, but I saw his face turn red. He folded the note in half and tucked it away.

"Knock it off," I snapped. Jason leaned back in his chair,

grinning. Mr. Sword was eyeing us so I faced forward again, glancing sideways at Wolf to make sure he was okay. He stared at the front of the room, fists in his lap.

Mr. Sword held up his copy of the play and asked us, "So are you all ready to get bloody?" Judging by the lukewarm response, the murmuring, and the yawns of first-period English, the answer was "not really."

But it didn't matter whether we were ready or not. This was Shakespeare.

Getting bloody was in the script.

Over the next three periods, multiple sticky note sightings confirmed Deedee's suspicion: we really had started something. Not on purpose, of course, but the ripple effect was undeniable. The yellow notes sprouted like weeds.

It wasn't completely out in the open yet, though. Most of the notes were still passed under desks, or palmed and transferred via high five. Some were left on backpacks or attached to shoulders in passing. I saw two traded in English. Another four in social studies under Mr. Hostler's nearsighted eyes. Saw quite a few more posted in the hallways. Most of them were innocent—smiley faces and questions about weekend plans. This wasn't the start of the war so much as the buildup of arms.

I did spot one "PLANT FOOT HERE" with an arrow

pointing buttward, attached to the back of Winston Ferman, a kid perpetually teased for being two grades ahead in math. I was going to tell him what was sticking to him, but by the time I'd made up my mind he'd already turned the corner. The note would probably fall off on its own before anybody followed its instructions anyway.

Not surprising, there was a note on my locker as I went to drop my books off before lunch. It had Deedee written all over it.

¡Viva la revolución!

I tucked the sticky note in my copy of *Julius Caesar*, figuring it would make for a fitting bookmark, then met up with Bench on the way to lunch.

"Did you see?"

"See what?" he asked.

"All the sticky notes. They're showing up everywhere."

"I saw some." Bench's tone was clipped, preoccupied.

"Deedee thinks we started something," I pressed.

"Deedee believes in UFOs and government mind control," Bench reminded me. In other words, you couldn't always believe everything Deedee wanted you to. We walked down B Hall and I searched for a single sticky note to point out to Bench, but of course by the time you get around to showing somebody something, it's always gone.

We got to the cafeteria and I started in but stopped when I

realized Bench wasn't right behind me. He was standing in the entrance, as immovable as Francis B. Stockridge.

"Get in there, you big furry oaf, I don't care what you smell," I coaxed. You can never go wrong with Wookiee humor, but Bench shrugged me off. He actually brushed my hand off his shoulder.

"It's all right. You go on. I'm not hungry," he said, his voice flat.

I turned up my hands—universal gesture for *what gives*. This was Bench. The same kid who once bet me he could eat fifteen dollars' worth of Taco Bell in one sitting, costing me two weeks of allowance and him a record number of trips to the bathroom. He was always hungry. I looked back over my shoulder, finding our table by the wall.

Three seats were already filled. I'm no Winston Ferman, but I could do this math.

"Seriously? You're not coming to lunch because of *her*?" I kept my voice low. Suddenly this had become one of *those* conversations. The kind you don't want other people to hear. Bench shook his head and whispered back.

"I told you. I'm not hungry. I think I'll just get a pass to the computer lab or something."

"Dude—it's twenty minutes. You have to eat. Besides," I added tentatively, "she's not that bad."

It was as far as I was willing to go, at least with Bench. I wasn't about to defend Rose's honor or anything. I wasn't anybody's champion. I just wanted him to come sit with us, like he always did. But he was having none of it. He pulled me aside, out of the doorway, out of view. "You don't get it," he said. "The other guys . . ." The other guys again. Maybe the ones on the team, the ones *he* warmed seats for. "They call her 'Moose.'"

I craned my neck around the door and looked across the filling tables at Rose Holland, at least three inches taller than Wolf. Shoulders you could park a car on. And that face. Those eyes, large and luminescent. If faces were states, she'd be Montana and those eyes would be full bright moons.

Moose. I didn't want to, but I could see it.

"*I* never said it," Bench explained. "I mean, it's not like I got anything against her really, it's just, you know. When people talk like that . . ."

I could hear it in his voice. It wasn't just Moose. They said other stuff. Worse stuff. Bench didn't want to tell me, and I didn't want to ask. Or part of me did, but I knew I would just feel worse for knowing. Other kids brushed past us, squeezing through the door into the cafeteria. Bench gave me a pat on the back. Or maybe it was a shove. "I'll catch up with you later." And before I could argue with him any more, he turned and started back down the hall.

I waited in line by myself.

"Where's Bench?" Deedee asked when I finally took the seat next to him. I suspected they saw us at the doorway, and I wondered if they registered Bench's hesitation, the traded whispers, his unexpected retreat.

"He said he wasn't feeling well," I lied. "I think he might go to the nurse's office." I looked at Wolf. He was studying me, trying to unpack all the stuff I wasn't saying, so I examined my grilled cheese instead, the waxy orange oozing between two pieces of soggy bread. Suddenly I wasn't that hungry either. Everything felt out of place. Mismatched. Like when you accidentally put the wrong shoe on the wrong foot. We were a square again, but with the wrong corners.

I could tell they sensed it too. Even Rose. Awkward. But more than that—it felt like a betrayal, being here without him. I pushed my oily sandwich away. "I can't eat this," I said.

"That's why I pack my lunch," Deedee said, peeling the skin from his tangerine.

Rose waited a moment, then slid her package of pecan swirls across the table, along with a crooked, hopeful smile.

I looked around to see if anyone was watching. A few faces looked away quickly, though I could have been imagining it. "Do these stick to the roof of your mouth?" I asked.

"If you chew them long enough they do," she answered.

I took one of the pecan swirls and nodded. My way of saying thanks without having to say it. Then Rose turned and asked Deedee for his lucky die.

I shot Deedee a look. He told her. When did he tell *her*?

"What for?" Deedee asked, anxious. He hardly ever took the ten-sider out of his pocket at school. Only when a major decision called for it, and even then he rolled it in secret, under his desk into the palm of his hand, or in the corner when nobody was watching. He had enough to contend with without also being "that dweeb with the dice."

"What do you think?" Rose asked. "We're going to play a game. That's what it's for, isn't it?"

"He also uses it for getting dressed in the morning," Wolf said. "Judging by that awful sweater, I'd say today he rolled a two."

"For your information, my mom picked this out for me," Deedee said before realizing that was even worse. He reluctantly fished out his ten-sided dragon die and stealthily slid it across the table. "Fine. Here. Just . . . you know . . . be careful."

Rose nodded. "Your secret's safe with me," she said. She started whispering so that I had to lean across the table to hear her. "All right. So here's the deal. I'm gonna roll. If it comes up evens, I'll tell you something you didn't know about me. Like a kind of a secret thing. But if it comes up odds, then I get to pick one of you—any one of you I want—and you have to do the same."

Immediately I thought of Bench and how he would never go for this. He'd call it childish or stupid just to get out of playing it. Maybe that's why she was doing it now. Because he wasn't here to say no.

"This is just Truth or Dare," Deedee said. "With a die. With *my* die."

"And without the dare," Wolf said.

"In that case, I dare you to play," Rose said.

I'd never played Truth or Dare before. I assumed it was the kind of game you played at parties, and I never went to parties. I did play spin the bottle once, on vacation in North Carolina with my second cousin and two of her friends. It ended regrettably with an unexpected and ill-timed burp, made worse by half a bag of Cool Ranch Doritos. I spent the rest of spring break avoiding my second cousin. "Wait. What happens if we *don't* tell you something?" I asked.

"Come on, guys," Rose prodded. "Remember what Shakespeare said? 'Screw your courage to the sticking place'?"

"To heck with that," Deedee remarked, but Rose had already rolled the die on a napkin to muffle the sound, keeping it quiet and close.

She rolled an eight. Spotlight on her. She looked at the

number and shrugged. I wasn't sure I wanted to hear whatever Rose was about to tell me. Not that I would share it. Not that it would get out. Just that sometimes it was better if you kept your secrets to yourself.

"All right. Are you ready for this?" she said in her husky whisper. "My real name isn't Rose . . . it's *Rosalind*."

"Rosalind?" Deedee repeated. "Like the bakery?"

"That's Rosalyn," Wolf said. "Rosa-lind with a *D*." He turned to Rose. "And that's not much of a secret."

"Nobody around here knows it," she scoffed. "That makes it a secret."

"I pooped four times yesterday," Deedee said. "Nobody knew that either. Doesn't make it a secret."

"I wish you'd kept it one," I said.

Rose smirked. "I was named after my great-grandmother. But Rosalind sounds so eighty-year-old-woman, don't you think? So I shortened it."

"Yeah. Rose doesn't sound old-womanly at all," Wolf joked.

"Nobody asked you." She slapped him on the shoulder and he didn't even flinch, which was odd because Wolf wasn't fond of being touched. Maybe she didn't know that about him yet. The thought gave me a strange feeling of satisfaction—all the things I knew about Wolf that she didn't. Rose pinched the die and gave it another spin. I feigned disinterest, taking another bite but watching out of the corner of my eye.

Three.

Her eyes circled the table, stopping on me. I stopped chewing, a glob of pecan roll melting to mush and sticking to the roof of my mouth like she promised. Then she snapped her head to the right. "Deedee."

"Me?"

Rose nodded. "You have to tell us something," she said. "Something *nobody* at the table knows. And *not* having anything to do with your bodily functions."

I figured that was going to be pretty tough—the nobody-knowing part. Deedee and Wolf had been friends for years. I couldn't imagine there were too many secrets left between them.

"All right. Something you don't know. Okay. I've got one." His voice went to a whisper. "I actually *like* tapioca pudding." He said it like it was top-secret CIA intelligence.

Wolf shrugged. "All nerds like tapioca pudding."

"That's not true," Deedee spluttered. Wolf looked at me.

"It's true," I confirmed. "Of course I can't stand the stuff myself."

"Because you're not a nerd," Wolf said. Deedee gave us both

a dirty look, but then he shook his head and smiled. I glanced back toward the door, thinking I might catch Bench peering through the glass, spying on us, but he wasn't there.

"Ignore them," Rose said to Deedee. "You eat whatever your nerdy little heart desires. But I'm afraid your answer doesn't qualify. We need something juicier. Something we can use against you when you run for mayor later in life."

I laughed, picturing Deedee as mayor, passing laws with a roll of his dice—*It's a seven. No public school this year.* Deedee thought it over, then a pained look passed over his face. "All right. But you have to promise not to tell anyone. If my parents find out . . ."

We promised. Deedee's parents were the nicest of our lot. His dad was like an Indian version of Santa Claus, thick silver beard, jelly-belly and all, and his mom knitted potholders for every teacher in the building every year for the holidays. If there was something Deedee was afraid to tell them, it had to be good.

"I cut the whiskers off of my cat once," he mumbled.

Wolf sprayed a little milk on his tray. "You did what?"

"I was six," Deedee confessed. "And I had just read in *Discovery Kids* or something how cats use their whiskers to help them sense what was around them, so I wanted to test it. You know. Like an experiment."

"You dewhiskered your cat?"

"Only on one side," Deedee explained.

"That's horrible," Rose said.

"And hilarious," I said. Then I saw the look on Rose's face. "But also so, *so* horrible."

"What happened to the cat?" Wolf asked.

"Well, he ran into things for a while. But eventually the whiskers grew back and he was fine."

"That's cat abuse," Rose said.

"We aren't here to judge, *Rosalind*," Wolf said. "Just roll the die."

"Fine—just don't ever come near me with a pair of scissors," she warned. Rose rolled again. Seven. I felt for sure I was next, but she turned to Wolf instead. "Your turn."

Wolf crossed his arms in front of him. "I don't have any secrets," he said matter-of-factly.

"Everybody has secrets," she insisted.

"Tell her about the time you caught your house on fire microwaving a can of SpaghettiOs," I prompted. I was there. He managed to find the opener and get the lid off, but he didn't bother to take them out of the can. We learned a valuable—and fiery—lesson in radioactive metallurgy that day.

"She already knows about that," Wolf said. Which made me wonder when, exactly, the two of them found time to talk so much. She'd only been here for three days. They had to have talked outside of school. Maybe they texted. Maybe he actually called her. Maybe that's how she got my email address.

"All right. Here's one," Wolf said. "When I was four, my parents abandoned me at the grocery store. They were arguing—"

"Breaking news," I interjected.

Wolf nodded and continued. "Right? And I guess I got distracted by the candy in one of the checkout lanes. They made it all the way to the car before they noticed I was gone. When they came back, I had already eaten two Kit Kats and was unwrapping a Baby Ruth, and nobody at the checkout was paying the slightest attention."

"Were you scared?" Rose asked. Her voice was suddenly serious. Much more serious than when she found out Deedee's cat lived without half of his whiskers for a while.

"Are you kidding?" Wolf said. "A four-year-old with no parents and all the chocolate he could eat? I wish they'd left me there for good."

Nobody said anything for a moment, then Wolf reached over and nabbed the die from Rose's hand, rolling it before she could snatch it back. Four. We all stared at her, waiting.

"Doesn't count," Rose said. "I have to roll it. It's my game. I invented it."

"It's my die," Deedee said.

"And it's a four," Wolf insisted. "So spill it."

Rose's shoulders slumped. "All right. Fine. It's another name thing. I bet you can't guess what they used to call me in elementary school?"

And suddenly there it was, Bench's voice in my head. I pictured the antlers. The flaring nostrils. The big, melancholy eyes. I nearly blurted it out. *Moose.*

Deedee shrank in his seat—maybe he'd heard too. Or maybe he'd heard other things. It couldn't be that, though. She was from Chicago. There's no way something like that could have followed her all the way here.

"I'll give you a hint," Rose said, then she rubbed her cheeks vigorously with her hands, smiling real big so they stretched and puffed.

"Chipmunk Cheeks?" Wolf asked.

"Close," she said. She rubbed again and I watched the sides of her face pink up like two giant strawberry muffins. I had it.

"Rosy Cheeks."

Rose pointed. "Score one for the snowman, who, so far, has managed to escape the penetrating inquisition of the all-knowing die. You can bet you're next."

She snatched Deedee's lucky die back from Wolf and gave it a spin in her tray, the dragon doing pirouettes, Deedee shifting to block anyone not at our table from seeing it. I held my breath, hoping for an even number. Not that I cared to hear any more of

Rose's names. I was just afraid of what I might say.

The die came up nine. Rose put out a hand as if she was asking me to dance.

Then the bell rang.

"I guess you're off the hook," Rose said.

But the look in her eyes suggested otherwise.

Looking back on that first lunch without Bench, I wonder what secret I might have shared. What I might have admitted to. I'd never cut the whiskers off a cat, but I'd said and done plenty of things I wasn't proud of. I wonder if I would have made a confession.

That's what a secret is. It's a confession in disguise. Well, sort of. The whole power of a secret is in the keeping—the power of knowing something that nobody else does. But the whole point of confession is letting go. You're supposed to feel better afterward. Like the weight has been lifted and your soul is suddenly free to fly or whatever.

But what if it isn't? What if, after telling someone, you feel just as bad as you did before, except now everybody *else* knows? And you can see it in their eyes as you walk down the hall? Your secrets staring right back at you? Wasn't it better, sometimes, to not say anything at all?

I'd made a habit of keeping things to myself.

I think back to that lunch, and Bench walking away, and Rose Holland rolling that die, and the bell ringing, saving me from having to make something up. Because if I'd had to say something true, at that very moment, it would have had something to do with her, and the things *they* were saying about her, and what it was starting to do to us—to the tribe. And I would have ended up admitting something about myself too.

And yet, the thing I remember most from that game isn't being saved by the bell, or the guilty look on Deedee's face when he told us about the cat, or the mischievous grin on Rose's face every time she rolled the die, so eager, it seemed, to tell us everything about her.

It's Wolf. Shrugging nonchalantly that moment his own number came up.

Insisting that he didn't have any secrets to tell.

THE BOMB

THERE'S THIS OTHER POEM BY ROBERT FROST THAT I LIKE A LOT, about the end of the world. It's only fifty words or so, but you can do a lot with fifty words. Heck, you can do a lot with just one or two. I should know.

The poem's called "Fire and Ice," and it basically asks if the world will end with the planet turning into a giant ice cube or with us all being burnt to a crisp. I guess it just assumes the end is coming regardless and maybe we'll at least get to choose how we bite it, like the Ghostbusters did when they picked the Marshmallow Man. Most of the time when I picture the end of the world, it's like the first one: fire and brimstone, explosions and collapsed bridges and everything up in smoke. Then again, I've seen a lot of alien invasion movies.

Except I know that most things don't end in a big fireball. They just wither and fade, like a leaf curling brown at the start of winter only to be crunched under your foot.

Or like when your parents spend their last year not talking to each other, spending all their time in separate rooms.

Toward the end, Mom usually slept on the couch in the living room instead of the guest bed, and I'd sometimes wander downstairs to the kitchen late on a Saturday night to find her staring at a book but never turning the pages. She'd ask me if I was okay, if I needed anything. I was sort of afraid to tell her yes. I was even more afraid to ask her the same thing back.

Some say the world will end in fire. Some say ice. That's how Bobby Frost puts it. Truth is, things rarely end so suddenly. And you definitely don't get to choose.

And when it does finally come to an end, it totally sucks, whether you saw it coming or not.

That afternoon I was supposed to meet Wolf to discuss the apocalypse. It was for a grade.

Mr. Hostler had paired our social studies class up earlier that week and given us each a major twentieth-century war/calamity/ atrocity/human rights struggle to research and report on. He pulled them out of a hat, one of those black bowlers from a time when wearing hats was part of dressing up, and we unfolded them and read them to each other. The Great Depression. School segregation. The AIDS epidemic. A whole bowler full of misery and pain. By the time we finished drawing, everybody in class felt oddly fortunate to have been born in the twenty-first century, with its terrorists, global warming, mortgage crises, and standardized tests, though it's even more depressing to realize things haven't changed that much.

Wolf and I drew second-to-last and got the nuclear arms race. It could have been worse. At least we would get to read about bombs. Still, all I knew about the arms race was that it was the US versus the USSR, which I was pretty sure stood for "United, something, something, Russia." Wolf knew that there was something called the Bay of Pigs, which he guessed was where the Russians kept all the Americans they captured but also sounded like something you could order off the menu at Bob Evans. We also both knew that we were the only country to ever use atomic weapons on anyone, which didn't seem like something to be proud of.

It wasn't enough to fill a posterboard, though, so Wolf agreed to borrow his mom's laptop and meet me at You Old Smoothie's after school. Bench had practice that afternoon, so I didn't have anyone to ride the bus home with anyway.

Besides, I didn't mind hanging out with just Wolf. In some ways, he was the easiest to just be with. With Deedee you hardly ever got a word in, and with Bench you sometimes had to pretend to be interested in some of the same things he was interested in, like batting averages or fantasy football rankings. But Wolf and I knew how to just shut up and chill.

Except it wasn't just Wolf waiting for me outside Smoothie's.

Rose was wearing a green army jacket with big pouch pockets and her hair pulled back. She and Wolf stood next to the entrance looking and laughing at something on Wolf's phone. She spotted me and waved me over.

"Hey there, Snowman. Wolf said you guys needed help with your social studies project."

Wolf smiled like it was some genius move on his part, inviting her along, like having Rose Holland's assistance gave us the edge we needed to win the Pulitzer Prize in Middle School Historical Research Projects. I stuffed my hands in my pockets as a mild sign of my dissatisfaction. "I'm pretty sure we can handle it," I said. "This is Mr. Hostler's class. Write down a few facts, slap a picture of a mushroom cloud underneath, and you're gold."

Rose crossed her arms. *The better to challenge you with,* I thought. "Do you even know what Star Wars is?" she asked.

I *derred* her. Out loud. "Derr." I couldn't help it. It was more than she deserved for what might be the most ignorant question asked of a thirteen-year-old boy ever.

She *derred* me right back. "Not the movie, dinglefart. The

143

plan to put lasers into outer space to shoot down nuclear missiles. Do either of you know who Mikhail Gorbachev was?"

I wasn't sure how I felt about Rose Holland calling me a dinglefart. It didn't seem like the kind of thing you call someone you've only known for less than a week. If Cameron or Noah had called me that I would have thought about punching them. I wouldn't have *actually* punched them, of course, but I would have fantasized about it. I'm sure they'd called me worse behind my back. And I *know* Jason had said worse about Wolf. "Gorbachev. Isn't he the bad guy in *Iron Man*?" I guessed.

Rose shook her head. "I'm definitely going to need a shot of ginkgo biloba for this." She turned and went inside. I grabbed Wolf by the shoulder, holding him back.

"Why is she here?"

Wolf brushed my arm off, the same as Bench had done before. "I invited her. She's smart. Smarter than either of us. Did *you* know about that Star Wars thing?"

"No. But I'm pretty sure Mr. Google does," I said. And how did Wolf know how smart Rose was? Were they comparing grades now?

"She just wants to help," Wolf said. "Besides. I don't think she likes hanging out at home much. Her dad works late and her mom sleeps most of the day. Sometimes you just have to get out of the house, you know?"

Wolf stared me down. He knew exactly what to use against me. We both went through periods when home wasn't the cheeriest place on earth. Now that I had two different homes a thousand miles apart, it wasn't so much a big deal for me, but his drama was still all under the same roof. "Besides, with her help we are guaranteed an A."

"We're already guaranteed an A," I said. Still, I nodded and followed Wolf inside. Rose was already at the counter, ordering. She paid for her and Wolf's drinks and offered to pay for mine, but I said no. I might sport a ten-dollar backpack and Bench's old sneaks, but I could swing three bucks for a strawberry-banana juice. Besides, judging by the hand-me-down clothes and the scuffed boots, Rose Holland didn't have wads of cash to throw around either.

We found a table in the corner by the fireplace and sat and sipped our drinks and worked quietly for a while, mostly reading online articles about Ronald Reagan and Fidel Castro and ICBMs, occasionally sidetracking to watch humorous videos of cats on treadmills or music videos from bands Wolf said we had to like. Every few minutes I would pan the room, looking for someone I knew. Kids from school. Anyone who might make a note of me being here. Of the three of us here together. There were a couple of other kids our age, and some older, but nobody from BMS.

And Wolf was right. Rose was smart. Scary smart. Knew exactly what we should be looking for. She said it came from having a lot of time to read. She used to live within walking distance of the public library back in Chicago, she said, and was there every three days checking out something new. The librarians took to calling her "Worm." Short for bookworm, I guess.

Worm. Moose. Rosy Cheeks.

Wolf. Deedee. Bench. Frost.

She had almost as many nicknames as we did put together.

Over the course of two hours I learned that our government spent billions of dollars on giant, rocket-propelled instruments of death that they would later just throw away. I learned that Salt I and Salt II were not at all what they sounded like. I learned all about Gorbachev, though he still reminded me of a villain in a superhero movie.

And I learned that there was something about Rose Holland, something that I guess Wolf had already seen in her but that I was just starting to. A kind of surety. I think it was her laugh—high-pitched and a little annoying, but always full and loud, never clipped short, never held back. I hadn't really noticed it at the lunch table where the din of a hundred conversation-starved middle schoolers could drown out a nuclear bomb test, but there in the restaurant she made no attempt to stifle it, not even when other people turned and gave her looks. It was a determined laugh. Totally in-your-face. And it was growing on me.

After an hour and a half of research (or maybe thirty solid minutes of research and an hour of goofing around) we called it quits, having gathered enough information to fill six poster-boards if we'd wanted. Wolf asked Rose if she needed a ride home.

"I don't live far," she said. "I'll walk. It's no problem."

Then she gave Wolf a quick hug, chin barely touching shoulder, but still a hug. I'd been friends with Wolf for two years and I'd never seen him hug anybody, not even his parents or his older brother, Simon. I figured he was just the type who didn't want to get too close to people. Same as when he started wearing his shorts and T-shirt underneath his street clothes on gym days to avoid being in the locker room longer than necessary. It fit with his personality. Closed off. Quiet. Untouchable.

Yet here Wolf was, standing on tiptoe to make the hug even. Rose turned to me and smiled. I kept my hands at my sides just in case. "See you guys tomorrow," she said.

"Yeah. See ya," I said.

I watched her leave, circling around the smoothie shop and growing steadily smaller. Wolf found a spot on the curb and texted his mom to come pick us up.

I sat down next to him and studied the cracks in the street, the dark, hard, bubbly patches from last year's road construction, the plumes of coughed exhaust from passing cars. A man and a woman passed by with elbows locked, bumping into each other, smiling. It was a little sickening. I'm sure Wolf noticed it too.

I waited for him to start talking, say something about that afternoon, and Rose, and the hug, and all that. Or maybe about lunch and Bench. But instead he said, "Did you see all those notes today?"

"Yeah." You really couldn't miss them by the afternoon. There were probably twenty in the hallway by the end of the day. Maybe thirty. Most of them were stupid, hardly worth reading—though that hadn't stopped me. Like sneaking a peek at someone else's diary. You feel bad, but not bad enough to quit.

"It's catching on," Wolf said. He was starting to sound like Deedee.

"If you think about it, it's no different than people posting stuff online or sending a text. Except this just wastes more paper."

"And you don't always know who's saying it." Wolf's glassy green eyes focused on the tin roofs of the building across the street. I wondered if he was talking about Rose. Maybe he'd heard about her nickname too.

"I guess so," I said.

Wolf drew an imaginary picture on the curb with his finger, tracing and retracing patterns only he could see. "It can't be easy for her," he said. "Coming to a new school. Being on the outside."

"I don't know," I said. "We did it."

"And it wasn't easy," Wolf countered. "Still isn't, some days. Besides. I had Deedee and you had Bench. And it didn't take us *that* long to find each other." He finished his imaginary drawing and then erased it with his foot, kicking the loose gravel. I could tell by the look in his eyes that something was gnawing at him. It wasn't as easy as it was with Deedee, but every now and then Wolf would let his guard down.

"You ever think about starting over completely? Like, going to a whole new school and being somebody different?"

I squinted at him. It was an intense out-of-left-field kind of question. But I guess sitting on a sun-dappled curb after learning about the end of the world for an hour can put you in that kind of mood.

"There's always high school," I said. "One more year."

"Right. Branton High. Go Cougars." Wolf made a less-than-enthusiastic yay-rah fist pump. "Don't tell Deedee I said this, but I think their band sucks even worse than ours some-how. And they don't even *have* an orchestra."

"Yeah—but their meat loaf is supposed to be excellent," I said.

"Great. Something else to look forward to."

Wolf and I had talked about this before. Neither of us was really looking forward to high school. More work, more stress, and the same jerks who gave us a hard time here would follow us there. The only saving grace was that we would all go together. "It might not be that bad," I said.

Wolf didn't buy it. "It won't be any different. Same kinds of kids. Just more of them. It's still Branton."

I wasn't sure what to tell him, what it was Wolf wanted to hear. I pictured my father, leaving late at night, heading south to the ocean that he later told me was calling his name. "I don't think you can ever start over. Not completely," I said. "You can't stop being you."

"That's what Rose says," Wolf muttered. "Except *she* says it like it's a good thing."

"Yeah, well, maybe she doesn't know you as well as I do," I joked.

Except maybe that wasn't even true. Just because you eat lunch with someone for two years and drink out of the same soda and drag them on a skateboard behind your bike, that doesn't necessarily mean you really *know* them. There was a lot about Wolf that I didn't know.

One thing I was starting to realize, though: he liked Rose; maybe not in that way, but they had obviously clicked. And when you like something, you get upset when someone else doesn't. You take it personally. I know how I'd feel if I asked Wolf to read some of my poetry and he hated it. Maybe that's why I never showed him.

"She is pretty smart," I said.

Wolf shielded his eyes from the sun and smiled. "I told you."

"Smarter than you, anyways," I added. "At least about Star Wars."

Wolf laughed, shook his head, and leaned back, lacing his fingers behind his head, staring past the streetlamps and the awnings up into a sky spotted with one brushstroke of a cloud. "Kind of strange when you think about it—how close they were to blowing each other up. One button away from wiping out the whole freakin' world."

I leaned back next to him.

"Yeah. But they wouldn't really have done it. I mean, nobody's *that* dumb."

Wolf looked at me and I knew he actually had some names of people in mind who might just be.

But he was too nice to say them out loud.

THE SWORD

SOMETIMES, THINGS STICK. LIKE FROST ON A WINDSHIELD OR chewed-up pecan rolls to the roof of your mouth. And it's annoying. Especially when you can't get rid of them.

Other times, though, they catch fire. Like a too-short fuse leading to a toilet paper roll full of gunpowder that you've sprinkled inside.

And then they explode.

It happens all the time. Stupid dances. Catchy pop songs. Videos of people acting like total fools. Things you wouldn't expect. The right person finds it, likes it, favorites it, tweets it, endorses it, gives it four stars, two thumbs up, and then it just spreads. Like an avalanche. Like the common cold.

Like a nuclear arms race. First one bomb. Then two. Then

hundreds. Then thousands. Piled up in silos. It's called "prolif-eration." That was the fancy name given to the building of all those nuclear missiles sixty years ago—I know because I read all about it while sipping juice in the middle of a smoothie shop, sitting across from one of my best friends and somebody who looked to be on her way to becoming his best friend.

That's what happened with the sticky notes. They prolifer-ated, went viral. In a matter of days they went from something only we were doing to *the* thing to do. By the end of the week, we knew it was big. And not just because every third or fourth locker you saw had a note attached. It was the color change. The notes weren't all yellow anymore, which meant students weren't using the ones they'd been forced to buy for school. They were going out and *buying* new pads of sticky notes. Blue and hot pink and neon green, the color of cartoon toxic waste. Different sizes, too. Long rectangles. Arrows. Some shaped like hearts. Appar-ently they make sticky notes shaped like poo. I saw one outside the gym.

The notes jumped the social fences. Preps and nerds, goths and floaters, popular, not so popular, rich kids, poor kids, all the in-between kids, everyone was writing them. Literally overnight they were everywhere. *¡Viva la revolución!*

The biggest clue came as we walked into Mr. Sword's class on Friday and saw the blank Post-its, standard yellow, sitting on our desks. There was also a quote on the board from Albert Einstein. It said: *Two things are infinite: The universe and human stupidity. And I'm not sure about the universe.* I thought about Wolf and me sitting on the curb outside the smoothie shop talking about the potential end of the world.

"Who can tell me what an 'aphorism' is?" Mr. Sword said once we'd all settled down in our usual spots.

"Isn't that when the blood in your brain explodes?" Samantha Bowles guessed. I had seen her reading a note when I walked in, eyes wide at whatever gossip was scrawled on it.

"That's an aneurism, but thanks for playing. Yes, Marianna?"

"It's a bug that eats trees."

"You're thinking of aphids. But again, nice try."

Mr. Sword was already out of hands to call on. "An aphorism is a pithy or witty saying," he continued. "Like a little kernel of wisdom wrapped up in a single sentence. We might think of them as quotes, except they are designed to say something deep and true about the world, and not all quotes do that."

"Like 'Life sucks and then you die,'" Noah Kyle suggested.

"Or 'Girls drool, boys rule,'" someone else chimed in.

"*So* lame," Amanda Shockey said. Her hair was purple today.

"How about 'May the Force be with you,'" Max Conners offered. I kind of liked Max.

"Even more lame."

"It's 'lamer,'" Mr. Sword corrected. "And no. Aphorisms go a little deeper than that. They speak to something universal about the human condition. They *can* be humorous, and often are, but they should always make you think. They should be true in some way."

"So they're like memes," someone said.

"I guess. In a way. Though most of what you'll find on the internet is obnoxious or downright cruel."

"The truth can be cruel sometimes."

I glanced over at Wolf, a little surprised. He wasn't much for speaking up in class. He fiddled with his blank note, sticking it to his desk and then peeling it off, over and over again.

"And *that*," Mr. Sword said, pointing at Wolf, "is much more like an aphorism." Then he went to the board and started writing furiously. "I've noticed that you all have taken to posting little messages for each other—no doubt in response to our recent change in cell phone policy. I've actually read a few of them. And while 'Liam Hemsworth is hot' may sound to some of you like universal truth, I hardly think it qualifies as a profound thought that requires sharing. Therefore I think it's worth taking a time-out from Caesar's plight in Ancient Rome to think about the power that language can have. After all, the Romans ate aphorisms for breakfast."

"Eww," Marianna said. I'm pretty sure she was still thinking of aphids.

"So here's your assignment," Mr. Sword continued. "You have ten minutes to think of your own original aphorism—some witty little revelation that you can fit on that three-inch-square sticky note in front of you. Write it down and I'll come around and approve it. Then, after class, I want you to find someplace in the school to leave your message. Someplace where your aphorism will get the attention of the people who would benefit most from reading it. This is your chance to change someone's perspective—to teach them something about the world in twenty words or less."

A hand went up behind me. Mr. Sword pointed.

"You're kidding, right?" Cameron said. "No offense, Mr. Sword, but this is kind of stupid. Doesn't matter what we write, somebody else is just going to come along and toss it in the trash. What's the point?"

"The point, Mr. Cole, is that *all* of us have something meaningful to share," Mr. Sword shot back. "Maybe you're right. Maybe most of these notes will simply be thrown away, but if just one of you writes something that strikes a chord and gets another person thinking, then I think it's worth it, don't you?" He turned back around and took up his chalk. "I'm putting a few more examples on the board—just to get your pistons firing. But don't just quote something you've heard your grandmother say. Tap into something you know about yourself, something you've realized about the way the world works. Don't make it *too* personal—I don't want to see anybody's name on any of these—but they can come from a personal place."

There was another chorus of protest. I watched Mr. Sword continue writing for a minute, scribbling one saying after another in his sloppy script, covering the board.

He who knows does not speak; he who speaks does not know.

Freedom is the right to tell people what they do not want to hear.

The early bird gets the worm, but the second mouse gets the cheese.

The pen is mightier than the sword.

"Unless you're trying to slay a cave troll," Deedee murmured. I instantly conjured an image of writing-utensil-wielding hobbits plunging Sharpies into the backs of orcs, except instead of blood the bodies spilled ink. Mr. Sword snapped me out of it.

"You are going to put this out in the world for others to see. You can write something provocative. Something challenging. Something passionate and opinionated and even, potentially, dangerous. But keep it clean. Don't write anything that would get you in trouble."

I watched Deedee furiously erase what he'd already written. Mr. Sword went back to his board.

I stared at my sticky note. *Something deep.* I thought about the notebook tucked under my mattress at home, full of secret poems written over the past three years. There was probably something in there that would work. In the course of fifty verses surely I'd said *one* meaningful thing.

As soon as Mr. Sword's back was turned I felt a kick in the back of my chair.

"You should be good at this, right, Frost?" Noah Kyle whispered, snickering.

"Yeah, *Frost.* Let's see what you've got." Jason Baker arched up out of his seat, trying to look over my shoulder. I covered my note with both hands even though I had nothing written yet and cursed my fifth-grade teacher all over again.

"Back off," Wolf said in a hushed voice, turning and glaring at both of them.

Jason cocked his head to the side. "I'm sorry, was I even talking to you?" He leaned in close to Noah. "I think I offended his boyfriend."

A stern whip-around look from Mr. Sword was enough to drop Jason back in his seat. "Eight minutes," he warned. I entertained a brief image of Jason and Noah being mauled by a pack of starved lions in the middle of the Colosseum in front of a cheering crowd—too much Roman history, I guess—then turned back to my blank note.

Around the room there was a lot of pencil tapping. Sitting by the door, Rose had both fists clenched around clumps of hair. I looked at Wolf's desk. He seemed to be finished already, his paper flipped over so I couldn't read it. I stared at my own blank square and tried to think of something worth sharing with the rest of the world. Something profound. The world had plenty of problems—like people who kicked the back of your chair and wouldn't leave you alone—but nothing I could say was going to change any of them. Mr. Sword called two minutes. I scribbled something down.

He who laughs last laughs longest, but he who farts loudest gets the room to himself.

Maybe true, but not exactly insightful. I erased it. Pressed the end of my pencil to my nose. I glanced behind me in time to see Cameron Cole attaching his Post-it note to his forehead. It said *I'm with stupid* and had arrows pointing in every possible direction.

"All right. Time's up," Mr. Sword said. "Make sure it's legible. There's no point in sharing your wisdom with the world if the world can't read it."

I had nothing. So I just wrote the thing that seemed most true to me at that moment. Something I'd been thinking about for the past couple of days. It barely fit on the yellow square and I had to scrunch the letters at the end.

"Okay. Go ahead and share what you've written with one other person in class. Ask them what they think. How does it make them feel? Angry? Wistful? Optimistic? Meanwhile I will come along and make sure everyone's nugget of wisdom is appropriate. Mr. Cole, I can already tell you that yours is not."

Cameron peeled the "stupid" note from his head and started to erase it. I gave Wolf my note with a shrug. "I couldn't really think of anything," I told him.

He read it, then stuck it back to the edge of my desk. "It's good," he said. "In fact, I can think of a few people in this room who should read it." He didn't need to name names.

Mr. Sword appeared beside my desk and held out his hand. He read my note, whispering to himself. "'If you only listen to what others say, you'll never hear yourself think,' That's pretty good, Eric." Then he looked across at Wolf, who held his note up, half folded, as if he were embarrassed to share it. Mr. Sword's expression changed as he read it. He frowned slightly, then nodded thoughtfully and handed the note back to Wolf.

"Couldn't have said it better myself."

Wolf took his note, then gave it to me. We had both been

thinking kind of the same thing. But Mr. Sword was right: Wolf had said it better.

Deedee leaned over and showed us his. It said, *The truth is just a lie we all agree to believe in.*

"What does that even mean?" I asked.

"I have no idea," Deedee said. "My first one was about floaters, though, so this is a definite improvement."

Mr. Sword finished his inspection, giving almost everyone his stamp of approval, and went back to the front of the room and told us it was time to get back to Shakespeare, so that we could appreciate someone who really understood how to use language.

When English was over we all filed out the door, sticky notes in hand, ready to cover the world in our bits of wisdom. Rose waited for us in the hall. She showed me what she'd written. *A beautiful mind is worth more than a pretty face.*

"Tell that to Liam Hemsworth," I said.

"Or half the kids in this school," Deedee seconded.

"I plan on it," Rose said. "In fact, I think I'll stick it right outside the cafeteria for maximum exposure." She looked at me. "Where are you going to put yours?"

I shrugged, glanced around, then stuck my note above the water fountain just outside Mr. Sword's room. It seemed as good a place as any. Deedee said he was going to stick his outside the gym, "To give people something to think about while they're getting pummeled with dodge balls. What about you, Wolf? Where's yours going?"

But Wolf had already tucked his aphorism away.

"I'm just going to hang on to it for a while," he said.

Throughout the day, notes continued to pop up everywhere. Not just on lockers. On bathroom stalls. On teachers' doors. On windows and display cases. There was one on the fire alarm that said, *In case of emergency, run like hell*—though that one didn't stay up long. There was another on the first stall of the boys' bathroom that said, *Toxic Waste Site, Proceed with Caution*. There were dozens more. One posted outside Computer Lab A warned of a *Nerd X-ing* and had a picture of a stick figure in glasses. Another outside the band room said the same. The one outside he teachers' lounge said, *Warning: Zombies Spotted in Area*. It didn't stay up long, either. Cameron Cole was right (as much as I hated to admit it): a lot of the notes were removed almost as soon as they were posted. But not all of them.

Some were clever. Others were just dumb. Then there were the ones from Mr. Sword's class. You could tell because the words often filled the whole square and most of them made you want to vomit in your mouth. Things like *A stranger is just a friend you haven't met yet* and *There's no Band-Aid for a broken heart*. Per Mr. Sword's instructions they were all anonymous, but you could sometimes tell who they were from, if not from the handwriting, then from the message itself.

I recognized the one attached to Jason Baker's locker instantly. I'd read it once already. I even stuck around long enough to see Jason show up and peel the note free, crumpling it into a marble-sized wad and dropping it on the floor. I waited till he was gone before I went and picked it up and read it again to myself.

Words are ghosts that can haunt us forever.

I put it in my backpack, thinking the person who wrote it might want it back. That he might find a better place to put it. Getting a message through to some people was like trying to hammer a nail through a concrete block with your forehead. It would take something more than a few words penned on a sticky note to get Jason Baker's attention. In his case, the sword would probably be mightier.

I forgot all about the note by lunch, though, and it stayed in my backpack. Bench skipped out again, saying he had to talk to Coach Mallory about something; he didn't say what and I didn't ask. Instead I sat between Deedee and Rose and we played another game where we tried to see who could keep a corn chip in their mouth the longest without crunching it. I was the first one out.

Rose won handily. She seemed to be in a good mood, smiling and laughing and teasing Deedee mercilessly, but Wolf seemed distant, mouth tight at the corners, his rectangle of pizza untouched. It wasn't until just before the bell rang that I found out why.

"Are you even going to show them?" he asked.

Rose shrugged. "Show them what? It's no big deal." The suddenly serious look on her face—almost like a warning to Wolf to keep his mouth shut—suggested otherwise.

"What's no big deal?" Deedee asked.

With a roll of her eyes, Rose reached into her pocket and pulled a Post-it free, sticking it to the middle of the table for the rest of us to see.

"I found it inside my math book. Somebody must have slipped it in there while I wasn't looking. It's nothing. Seriously. There are so many worse things." She stared at Wolf, who stared right back, the two of them silently continuing some conversation they'd already started.

Deedee and I looked at the note. It obviously wasn't one of the ones from Mr. Sword's class. There were no words aside from her name. No signature. No way of knowing who wrote it. But the meaning was clear.

The war had begun.

THE CATCH

A LONG, LONG TIME AGO, OR SO THE STORY GOES, SOME GUY named Adam was lounging around the garden nibbling on a fig when the Powers That Be told him he should start naming everything he saw. So he did. He went around putting labels on everything: you're a cow, you're a tree, you're an ant, you're a snake, and so on. It was the easiest way to start making sense of the world.

He probably didn't know it, but he started a trend.

In middle school, everybody gets a label. It's important. It makes it easier to spread gossip, to choose seats in the auditorium during school-wide convocations, to decide who belongs where.

I was a nerd, tapioca or no tapioca. We were all nerds. The whole tribe. I wrote an award-winning poem once, which I guess made me a lifetime member. Deedee was in all accelerated classes and sometimes bragged about his 136 IQ. Not to mention the whole Gary Gygax thing. Even Bench was all aces across the grade book. We all earned our badge in one way or another. But only one of us was a genius.

Truthfully, Wolf was closer to Amadeus Mozart than I would ever be to Robert Frost. I'd heard him play, a dozen times from the hallway right outside the door of his family's living room, holding my breath so he didn't know I was there, because as soon as he saw me, he stopped. As if somehow his talent was something he still wanted to hide, even though everyone in the entire school knew how good he was. For most people, it's *all* they knew about him. Morgan Thompson: piano prodigy. But most of them hadn't ever heard him play.

He never made a mistake, at least not one that I could hear. Maybe he just knew how to hide them, move past them so quickly that nobody noticed. Playing the piano isn't like writing poetry. You can't edit. You can't go back and erase. If you stop and start over, people will know. They will say to themselves, "Well, it was good, but it wasn't *perfect*." Nobody knows what the first draft of Frost's poems looked like except for Robert Frost. When he showed them to the world they were just how he wanted them.

Listening to Wolf was like reading Robert Frost. I would stand outside the door, my steps muffled by the Thompsons' brown carpet, my eyes closed, dizzy with jealousy because he was still just a kid. We were all still just kids. Kids were supposed to make mistakes.

I'd never actually heard him perform in front of a crowd. I'd never been to any of Wolf's recitals. I would have gone if he'd asked me—we all would have—but he never asked. He only spoke of them after the fact, and then only when one of us noticed the new ribbon or trophy on the cherrywood mantel in his living room. They weren't stashed in a closet like my *You Showed Up!* soccer trophy. Wolf's accolades were on prominent display, visible from the foyer of their three-story house. You could see them through the prominent bay window that protruded like a blister from the front. It was a shrine. Blue ribbons and cold metal and dust. Two or three times a year Wolf would grab his sheet music and march off to conquer one competition or another, returning with another trophy for the shelf.

Ask Wolf how he got so good and he'd tell you what you'd expect to hear: practice. And in a way that's true, I guess. You have to *want* to practice that much. And Wolf did. But I think he did it mostly to please his parents. To give them something that they had absolutely no choice but to be happy about.

I can appreciate that.

I sometimes picture him up there at one of those recitals, everyone in the audience in stiff, scratchy black clothes, programs folded in their laps. I sometimes wonder what it was like for him under those blinding lights. Dressed in his suit, his eyes closed, body swaying, fingers dancing, the audience breathless, the music haunting. I wonder if he ever secretly wished I had been there for him, to cheer him on.

I feel guilty about it. Or maybe it's just regret. I'm not sure I quite know the difference yet.

I'd never been to a single one of Wolf's recitals. But I'd been to every one of Bench's football games.

And they were all ugly.

It was the lone Friday game of the season, and this time it was under the big lights—or at least bigger than usual. The Branton High Cougars were away, so the Fighting Falcons of Branton Middle School had the high school field, which meant that the three hundred or so people who usually came to watch the middle school game were scattered among bleachers that could hold two thousand. Everybody could sit close to the action.

Only we didn't.

I waited for Deedee and Wolf by the gates as usual, then we paid our two bucks and went to find a seat. I pointed to an empty section about three rows up and started that way when Wolf stopped me. "Not there," he said. He looked up the stairs. "Let's go sit at the very top this time."

I looked back at the spot he'd turned down and noticed what I hadn't at first: Jason, Noah, and Cameron clumped together on the row below that. They were all huddled over Jason's phone, laughing at something completely idiotic, no doubt. I obviously lingered too long. Cameron looked up and saw me, then elbowed the other two.

"Look. It's the Roman legion," Jason said, which was hilarious, apparently, at least to the three of them. Jason proceeded to give some kind of salute, like he was karate chopping the sky. "Hail, Caesar!" he cried. More laughter.

Wolf gave him a gesture back, much less obvious but more to the point, hand pressed close to his chest in case any of the adults were looking.

"What was that all about?" I asked. I'd seen Wolf blow Jason and company off a hundred times, but I'd never seen him *flip* them off before.

"Who cares?" Wolf said, turning back around and heading up the bleachers.

I followed Wolf and Deedee up the steps to the very top where you could hear the flags snap. It was chilly, the kind of cold you don't really notice until someone puts a mug of warm cider in your hands and you realize how stiff your fingers are (and not just the middle ones), how the first sip stings your lips. The night was clear though, star-studded, and it felt good to be out in the sharp autumn air, the smell of hot dogs and fresh pop-corn and wet leaves. I sat next to Deedee, who sat next to Wolf, our butts nearly freezing to the metal bench.

It was the fourth game of the season and the Falcons were 1–3, already an improvement over last year's 0–11. Unfortunately, according to the roll on Deedee's die, we were expected to lose again. According to everyone else you talked to, we were expected to get creamed.

"Will we at least score a touchdown?" I asked, and Deedee rolled for it. There was no chance of anyone seeing him all the way at the top, but he still kept the dragon hidden in his palm. He rolled a two, which meant a 20 percent chance. That seemed about right. I looked over at Wolf, who seemed preoccupied with the crowd. Except he wasn't looking in the direction of Jason Baker's spiky blond head. He was looking for someone else. "Did she say she was coming?"

"Who?"

"You know who."

"I'm not looking for Rose necessarily," Wolf said. "I'm just browsing."

It was a good word. It might make a nice line of poetry. *Browsing the crowd for someone worth the price of a conversation.* I knew I'd never remember it though.

"Let's see if any of the cheerleaders will screw up their

somersaults," Deedee said. He rolled. Seventy percent chance of cheerleader wipeout. At least that gave us something to look forward to. Not that I wished embarrassment on anyone in particular. Just that anyone falling on their rear was funny.

Wolf was still scanning the crowd for not-Rose-necessarily. It wouldn't have surprised me to see her lumbering up the steps to join us. In the span of one week, Rose Holland had not only navigated her way into our lunch table, she seemed to have stuck a harpoon in Wolf's side and reeled him in. I still wasn't sure what was up between the two of them, but I was glad to see Wolf out here with us, cheering Bench on.

Wolf's phone buzzed. He laughed at something, then sent a quick reply.

"Was that her?"

He nodded. "She says she's sorry she couldn't make it, but football's not her thing."

I thought back to Rose's first day, standing with Bench in the hall, watching her part the crowd. *She'd make a good linebacker.* Down on the field three little kids were chasing each other around. A referee shooed them away.

"I wouldn't exactly call it *our* thing," Deedee said.

The voice came on the speaker and began announcing the teams, starting with the visiting North Westchester Wildcats. We booed and told them just how much they sucked (so much that they were going to put Dyson out of business, said Deedee, earning him the award for lamest trash-talker of the night). The few adults closest to us gave us dirty looks, but they were still several rows away. A couple of weak, sputtering fireworks announced the home team's arrival. We stood and cheered as the Falcons took the field. Deedee pointed. "Is that him?"

It was a little hard to tell. We'd sat too far up to be able to pick Bench out from the crowd. So we waited for the starters to put their helmets on and huddle up. Bench was easy to spot once he'd assumed his customary position—number 80, sitting by himself on the end. The opposing team looked a lot bigger than us, galumphing across the field like a crash of rhinos.

"At least if it's a blowout, Bench'll get a chance to play," Deedee said. The ref blew the whistle. The Falcons fumbled the kickoff, giving the visitors the ball at the fifty.

"Yeah. There's always that," I said. I sat and watched with my hands tucked between my knees.

It wasn't a blowout, though. By halftime the score was only seventeen–zip, which was better than I thought it would be. Deedee's die was right about the lack of home team touchdowns. Then, during the halftime show, one of the cheerleaders fumbled through her flip and planted in the grass, laughing and shaking her head.

"The die rolls true," Deedee said, doing his best Gandalf

imitation, though I couldn't remember the white wizard ever saying that. Deedee's dragon was two for two so far, though. I was about to ask it what my mom's chances of winning the lottery were (she got one ticket every week), but on the ensuing kickoff the Falcons ran it all the way back for a touchdown, proving the die wrong. The crowd whooped and hollered. We banged on the bleachers. Deedee celebrated by buying us a bag of popcorn to split, careful to take the stairs all the way on the end so that he didn't get too close to where Jason and company sat. Wolf sent Rose updates on his phone. Or maybe he wasn't texting her about the game at all. Another touchdown at the end of the third put us within three. It was close.

Number 80 sat on the edge, helmet in hands, waiting, like always. "Definitely not going to play now," Deedee said. There was too much at stake.

At least we could tell him we came, I thought. That we were all pulling for him. All three of us. At one point he turned and looked at the crowd and Deedee and I waved, but he must not have seen us because he didn't wave back. Deedee finished off the last of the popcorn, then finished off the last of my Sprite. The score stayed the same through most of the fourth quarter, with neither team making any progress. With two minutes left we were forced to punt, still down by three.

"That's it," Deedee whined. "Game over. Seriously . . . why

do we even come to these things? I can watch Bench sit on his butt at school if I want."

Except not anymore, I thought. *Not at lunch anyways.* I didn't say it though. Just cheered halfheartedly for the losing team.

The Falcons kicked the ball. The Wildcats' player fielded it at the forty. Returned it ten yards. Then twenty. It looked like he might break free and put us out of our misery. The rest of the Wildcats were on their feet.

Then, the kid dropped the ball. Or maybe it was wrestled away from him. Either way, it squirted free, ping-ponged off a dozen hands and feet before getting buried under an avalanche of jerseys. Whistles trilled. Referees rushed over to the pile. Deedee muttered to himself, "We didn't get it. There's no way we got it. We never get it."

The mountain of players slowly peeled away, and a kid in a white-and-blue uniform popped up, holding the football like he'd just found gold.

The crowd exploded. The Branton Middle School Falcons had possession with a little over a minute left and sixty yards to go.

I looked at the home team sideline. Bench was standing with his teammates, cheering the starting offense as it ran back on the field. The first play, a run, went nowhere. Then our quarterback, a kid named Trevon Miller, who everyone called Tre, took the snap and made a quick completion in the middle of the field, hitting one of his receivers for ten just as the kid got blindsided, steamrolled by two Wildcats slamming him to the ground.

There was a hush. The kid who caught it didn't snap right back up. The Falcons called their last time-out with twenty seconds on the clock while the assistant coach helped the kid limp off the field. The shook-up receiver waved to show he was all right.

"You don't think . . . ," Deedee said, fishing in his pocket, but he didn't have time to roll for it. We saw Coach Mallory point. Saw number 80 jab his thumbs at his chest. Deedee and I started to holler. Wolf put away his phone.

Bench was off the bench.

I scooted to the edge of the bleacher as number 80 lined up in the slot on the right. Just about everyone below us was standing, the crowd's screams failing to fill the cavernous stadium. I spotted Bench's parents leaning over the bottom rail, his father clapping his hands above his head.

Tre called for the snap, dropped back, sidestepped a defender, scrambling, buying time. The seconds ticked. Down to eighteen. Rolling right. Another missed tackle. Fifteen. Looking all over the field. Twelve seconds. Desperate. His receivers were all covered. Two red jerseys for every white.

Except for the one.

In the middle, as open as the Pacific Ocean. The other two

receivers were blanketed along the sideline, but there was Bench at the twenty, putting his hand up, calling for the ball. Nobody was covering him. He had somehow slipped through the cracks. Even from way up at the top of the stands I could sense the quarterback's hesitation, but there really was no other option. Tre pulled the trigger.

The ball flew out of his hands, a torpedo tearing toward Bench, a flying brown prayer launched into the sky, and I thought, there's no way. No way he catches it. Because that's not how the universe works. Movies, maybe, but not real life. Not for people like us. Not for the outliers. The benchwarmers. But I'd been wrong before.

By magic or magnetism or just sheer luck, it dropped right into Bench's waiting hands and nestled there, perfect.

There was half a second, maybe less, when I swear Bench looked down at the ball in disbelief. Then he started to run.

The defense, suddenly solving the equation, tried to converge. Some were taken out by blockers. Others were too far away to get there in time. But one closed in, had the angle. He went for the knees, determined to bring Bench down and end the game, but number 80 leaped, legs brushing against outstretched fingers, hurtling over the would-be tackler. He left the kid grasping and spinning in the dirt behind him. Rumbled down to the ten. Then to the five.

The night split with the whistle's shrill cry. The ref thrust his arms into the air.

Four more pathetic fireworks briefly lit up the field. Fans started dancing and jumping in the aisles. Deedee turned and gave me a high five. "Un-freaking-believable," he said, which kept me from having to say it. Because it really was.

And in the midst of it all stood Bench, alone in the end zone. Unable, it seemed, to let go of the ball, even to spike it. Until his teammates mobbed him, crushed him, swallowed him whole. I looked to the scoreboard for confirmation, because sometimes you need to see it in writing.

Branton Middle School Falcons 20. North Westchester Wildcats 17.

Wolf stood beside us, shaking his head. "That's it then," he said, and even though he was smiling, his voice wasn't quite. If anything, he sounded a little disappointed.

Almost as if he'd seen it coming.

We pushed through the crowd on our way down to the field, hoping to get a chance to see him at least, to say congratulations, but Bench was already lost in the sea of white jerseys. They actually lifted him up and carried him, two dozen hands propelling him halfway across the field, away from where we stood. We could have gone down by the locker room, I guess, waited outside for a glimpse of the night's hero, but Wolf said, "We're never going to get his attention now," and led us back to the front gate instead.

He was right, of course, but I still wish we had the chance to say *something*. In two years Bench had never had a moment like this one. Never. This was his poem. It was his fifty-dollar gift card.

"Some catch, huh?" Deedee said. "Did you think he was going to drop it? Because I kind of thought he was going to drop it."

I shook my head. "I knew he'd catch it," I lied. All around us we heard people, mostly adults, murmuring about what a terrific play it was. Someone asked, *Who was that kid?* and I almost told them, but I fumbled with what to say—J.J.? Bench? My best friend?—so I ended up not saying anything. We walked through the gate and stood out in the parking lot. The cold had gone from nipping to gnashing. I shoved my hands under my armpits to keep them warm.

"You know," Wolf said, "you never see them carry writers like that."

I gave him a strange look. "Huh?"

"Writers. You know, like famous ones? They'll do a reading

or something, and when they are done everybody will just clap politely and that's it. They don't come over and lift the guy up and parade him through the bookstore on their shoulders. Or surgeons. You never hear about a team of nurses surfing a heart surgeon out of the operating room. And why not? He just saved a man's life. He *should* be carried around. Not to take anything away from Bench, but all he did was catch a ball."

I wasn't sure what he was getting at. "Sure, but could *you* have caught that ball?" I asked.

"No. But I bet Bench couldn't get through four measures of Chopin's Mazurka in A Minor either."

Wolf took out his phone again and started texting his parents for a ride. Deedee called his mom. Mine was already waiting for me in the parking lot. I could see the white Civic flashing its lights at me, like some kind of Morse code. She waved to the three of us as we walked closer.

"We're still on for tomorrow, right? At Wolf's house?" Deedee asked as I opened the door. "You guys promised. I've got a whole new campaign lined up. There's zombies and everything."

I assured Deedee that Ceric the Elf would not let his fellow adventurers down. Then I waved good-bye to Wolf, who gave me a nod. He was still looking at his phone, a huge grin on his face. Maybe it was too much popcorn and soda, or just the excitement from that last play, but my stomach was rolling.

"So how was the game?" Mom asked as I buckled in.

I thought about it for a moment. "We won," I said, as if the fireworks didn't give it away.

"That's good, right?" Apparently the tone of my voice was a little off.

"Good? Oh. Yeah. It was a great game. Probably the best I've ever been to."

She looked at me, pressing me for more, but I just looked out the window. I didn't tell her how Bench, the first friend I made in middle school, a kid she'd baked brownies for and taken to amusement parks—how he made the game-winning catch. I don't know why. Maybe I felt like it was one of those had-to-be-there things. Or maybe because it wasn't my moment and I didn't feel like I could do it justice. I wasn't a good enough poet to put it into words.

Or maybe, like Wolf, I felt like this was the start of something. And I was nervous about what came next.

Because things like this didn't happen to guys like us.

That night I dreamed I won the Nobel Prize for Literature.

I have no idea what the Nobel Prize looks like, but in my

dream it resembled the Stanley Cup, a glinting metal behemoth nearly twice my size with handles on the side. It had my name—my real name, Eric Voss—engraved along the base. I was the first middle school kid to ever win, absolutely unheard of, though that didn't stop the two women in silver bikinis from kissing me on the cheek as they handed me the trophy.

There, standing and sweating under the auditorium lights, I gave a speech. I thanked my dad for introducing me to Robert Frost and my mom for pretty much everything else. I thanked my friends for believing in me. Then I stood and waited for them to come up and carry me, to lift me on their shoulders and parade me through the audience and out into the lobby. I scanned the crowd, but I didn't see the faces of anyone I knew.

Instead all I could see were notes. A thousand blank squares of paper where heads should be, filling the auditorium in a sea of yellow.

That's when I spotted her. Rose. Standing in the balcony, dressed like usual in flannel and jeans. Hers was the only real face in the crowd. Her eyes seemed even brighter than the stage lights and her mouth was twisted into that punch-line smile. She looked completely normal, except for the pair of antlers that protruded from either side of her head, branching into fuzzy nubs.

No one else seemed to notice the antlered girl standing in the balcony, the blank yellow faces staring straight ahead. I just stood there, paralyzed as she climbed up onto the ledge, standing on the edge in her giant bare feet. She spread her arms wide.

"Catch me," she said.

And then she jumped.

THE RULES

BENCH'S FAVORITE COLOR WAS ORANGE.

This is probably not something I should know. Maybe if we had been friends since kindergarten or were a couple of fourth graders swapping one of those secret-password journals you can find in the bargain section of the bookstore. But it's not something that just came up naturally in conversation. Until I went into his bedroom for the first time and saw his tangerine walls and his blinding bright orange bedspread, making me wonder how he ever managed to get to sleep at night.

I know other things about Bench. Things that even his parents probably don't. Like he's a little ashamed of his dad because Mr. Jones used to be a runner—track and cross-country—and now he carries a serious gut and can barely huff it a mile. I also know Bench is still terrified of letting his dad down, which is one of the reasons he tries so hard to get straight As and make it onto every team. I know that it takes him twice as long to get through a book as me. I know that he has an irrational fear of his teeth falling out due to the fact that when he was little, his grandmother's dentures accidentally came loose and dropped into her potato soup. I know that he hates it whenever Deedee shouts, "For the Shire!" which is more often than necessary.

And I know now that even though he never came out and said it, even though he always seemed cool about it, he never liked his nickname.

Because let's face it—nobody wants to spend their life just sitting around, waiting for their chance to get into the game.

We were playing at Wolf's this time.

His dad was gone all weekend for a conference, which meant the house would be quiet for a change. We usually played at Deedee's, but Wolf pointed out the injustice of making Deedee's parents foot the bill for snacks every time. Everything they say about teenage boys and their appetites is true. We once polished off an entire family-sized pack of Oreos in one night. Forty-eight cookies, minus the crumbs on Mrs. Patel's linoleum. Deedee was the only one who couldn't keep his dozen down, scrambling for the toilet to make a deposit.

These were the kinds of stories we kept to ourselves.

I showed up to Wolf's early, eager to get out of my own house and away from Mom, who was on the phone with the lawyer, discussing alimony. She and Dad never talked to each other directly. They would email or text if absolutely necessary. She had no problem yelling at her lawyer though, so I said I'd just bike the three miles to Wolf's house. When I got there his mom was trying to finish raking the front yard before it got dark. Hardly any leaves had fallen yet, but Mrs. Thompson was finicky about her lawn. Every hedge perfectly trimmed. Every tree pruned. The grass had those diagonal mow lines that you usually only see on golf courses. She asked me how I was doing, how was school, the usual.

She asked about Mom. She didn't ask about Dad. Nobody ever asked about Dad.

I had hoped that Wolf would be practicing so that I could listen, but I spotted him in the garage instead. He was working on a plastic model of the battleship *Arizona*—the one that you could still see sunk at Pearl Harbor. I could smell the glue from the doorway.

Piano was Wolf's passion, but he was almost as obsessed with those plastic kits. When he wasn't stuck to his bench pounding out Beethoven, he was snapping pieces together, making sports cars and fighter jets that would take up the shelves in his bedroom—the ones that didn't need to hold piano awards because those were all downstairs. He had Mustangs and F-15s and a German U-boat. He had a model of the *Star Trek Enterprise* and the Apollo lunar module. I remember the first time he showed me his room. It was like walking into a museum, with fighter planes hanging from the ceiling and an aircraft carrier (also called the *Enterprise*) extending past both sides of his dresser. I'd never built one of those kits before—I would have glued my fingers together. Besides, I didn't have Wolf's patience. The first time I accidentally broke something off I'd probably just toss the whole thing in the trash.

"Deedee texted. He's on his way," Wolf said, sensing me standing there.

I nodded and walked around the garage until I spotted Wolf's brother's moped, half covered in black tarp. Everybody's known for something. Wolf's older brother Simon was known for that bike. A TaoTao 150cc, cherry apple, given to him as a consolation prize the same time Wolf got the shiny black Baldwin sitting in the living room. Simon had just started middle school at the time, and Wolf said that everyone thought the moped was the coolest thing ever. Then Simon went to high school, with juniors and seniors who drove things on four wheels that could actually hit the speed limit, and the moped suddenly wasn't so cool anymore. Which explained why it sat in the corner of Wolf's garage.

"Your brother ever planning to sell this thing?" I asked.

Wolf shook his head, fidgeted with a rudder. "Are you kidding? He still loves that bike. He says I can have it when I turn fourteen. Provided I give him a hundred bucks. He still lets me ride it sometimes, though. If I clean his room *and* put away his laundry."

I lifted the tarp a little. The bike looked like it was still in good shape. I'd probably clean Simon's room for a chance to take it around the block. "Does he ever let you take it out on the highway? You know, open her up? Full throttle?" I didn't even know if you could "open up" a moped.

Wolf laughed. "Dude, full throttle on that thing is about fifty—and that's if you're going downhill. Uphill you still have to hop off and walk it." He carefully put a radar dish in place, stepped back to admire his work. "Did you hear anything from Bench?"

He said it casual, like he didn't care about the answer either way. Maybe he didn't, but I doubted it. It had been my job to call Bench and make sure he knew about tonight. It was three hours before he called me back. "He said he couldn't make it. He's going out to dinner with his family to celebrate last night's game."

"The catch," Wolf said.

"The catch," I repeated.

The catch had actually made the paper. Local sports page, local paper, and only a two-paragraph article, but Bench's name was mentioned. *A miraculous forty-yard catch and run by Jeremiah Jones, coming off the bench to seal the victory for the Falcons.* I was sure his parents had already clipped it and framed it. I kept our copy of the sports section just in case.

I sensed there was something else Wolf wanted to say about "the catch," but instead he just screwed the cap back on the glue and began putting the rest of the unused pieces back in the box. The battleship was still only half finished. It was in need of more guns and a whole lot of paint, but it looked pretty good. Wolf's work always did. "His loss," Wolf said. "I'm sure we can tackle anything that pathetic excuse of a dungeon master throws at us."

"Just for that I'm adding more zombies."

We both turned. Deedee stood in the driveway, an overstuffed Avengers backpack threatening to topple him backward. "Your mom says that if we bag those leaves we get pizza."

I smiled and nodded. I'm not sure what Mr. Thompson's problem was. Seemed to me like Mrs. Thompson knew the way straight to a man's heart. We went out to bag leaves.

Afterward Wolf's mom ordered an extra-large pepperoni and

189

promised to leave us alone for the rest of the evening, retreating to her bedroom to enjoy some "quiet time," which Wolf translated for us as reading mystery novels and stalking people on Facebook. We thanked her for the pizza and promised not to break anything.

"How's it going?" I whispered to Wolf as his mother padded upstairs.

"She's been happy today," Wolf said with a shrug. "I like it when they're happy, even if it's only one at a time."

I didn't bother to say that with me it was always one at a time. He was right, though. A happy one was better than a miserable two. Most days.

While we waited for the pizza, Deedee unzipped his pack and pulled out the library of manuals he'd brought, complete with maps and traps and cardboard tokens representing everything from zombie rats to vampire lords. He unloaded a small hoard of dice that skittered across the table. Wolf and I picked up a handful and challenged each other for the highest number. Deedee yelled at us to leave the dice alone. This wasn't rock-paper-scissors, he told us. Dungeons & Dragons was serious business. I told him he should be extra thankful to have us as friends. Especially since he'd forgotten the Pringles.

The doorbell rang. Deedee and I both looked at the clock. We had called for pizza only ten minutes ago.

"Maybe Bench managed to weasel out of dinner," I said.

"Yeah, maybe," Deedee said.

Wolf smiled as he stood up. From his seat, Deedee had the best angle on the front hall, and I watched his expression shift from curiosity to confusion. I spun around to see who was standing there, though I really should have guessed.

"Greetings, oh dungeony ones," Rose Holland called from the front door. "I come bearing gifts."

She held up a bag of Funyons and a two-liter of bargain-brand red cream soda and smiled. Deedee's mouth hung open. I kept mine shut. Wolf took the snacks and gave Rose a hug, the second in two days that I'd seen. "I wasn't sure you were going to make it," he said, escorting her into the kitchen.

"You kidding? Hang out with three world-class geekazoids like you on a Saturday night? How could a girl say no?"

I could think of approximately three *hundred* girls at Branton Middle School who would have. They actually wouldn't have said *no*. They would have said, *Are you kidding*, or, *Um*, or *Seriously?* In fact I couldn't think of a single other kid in the entire school who would have given the offer to sit around with the three of us and roll for saving throws a second's thought. But Rose was obviously an exception.

"Is that the pizza guy?" Wolf's mom called down the stairs.

There was a pause. Wolf looked at the two of us, as if he

expected us to answer, but we were speechless.

"No, Mom," he called up. "It's just a friend."

It's important to keep some things to yourself. If Jamie Juarez could have kept his superfluous nipple a secret, I'm sure he would have. It would have saved him a lot of grief. Same goes for Katherine McKinney's habit of chewing on her toenails or Daniel P.'s unfortunate long-standing history of bed-wetting that earned him the name P-Diddly. That's what happens when people find out.

Dungeons & Dragons was like that. Forget that half the kids in school probably went around slaying dragons and stashing loot on their PlayStations or iPads. It's different when you actually have to roll the dice. It's all about degrees. Mention you like to play board games and you're probably okay. Break out the Monster Manual and start talking about the difference between fifth-edition and fourth-edition rule sets, you might as well give up on ever getting a date to the eighth-grade dance.

That's why I was a little surprised to see Rose at the door.

Deedee pulled Wolf aside and the three of us had a quick huddle by the table.

"This isn't going to work," Deedee explained. "You're all at level seven. If she comes in now she'll throw everything off balance. She'll muck it all up."

It was a good excuse. Much better than saying that Wolf had crossed the line, inviting someone else into our game without permission, someone who probably knew nothing about constitution checks and critical hits. Someone we'd have to teach everything to. Lunch was one thing. This was different.

"I don't want to ruin your game," Rose said, eavesdropping. "If it's a problem, I can just sit and watch."

Sit and watch? Who in their right mind wants to sit and *watch* three guys play Dungeons & Dragons?

"It's not a problem," Wolf said, breaking the huddle prematurely. "We'll just bump up your stats a little. You'll be fine. Right, Deedee?"

Wolf and Deedee stared at each other. It was up to the dungeon master. It was Wolf's house, but it was Deedee's game. Wolf got to decide if she stayed. Deedee decided if she played. I was just glad neither of them was looking at me.

"She'll need to make a character," Deedee sighed.

Meaning that there were four of us playing, just like always. But not exactly.

We took our seats around Wolf's scarred kitchen table, Rose between Wolf and me but closer to him, and Deedee patiently explained the absolute least she had to know to get started while I poured myself a cup of the soda. "You'll need to choose an avatar," Deedee told her. He had a whole trove of little plastic figures. He picked out the tallest—an orc war chief, hulking and muscular, holding a giant ax. "Maybe this one?" he said.

Rose rifled through the box. "Who is this little guy?" she asked, holding up a short, pudgy-looking figure about half the size of the one Deedee held.

"That's a gnome," Deedee said. "They are good at making things."

"Like origami," Wolf added.

"I'll be him, then," Rose said. "What's his name?"

"You get to decide," I told her. "You get to make up everything. Name. Profession. Backstory. All of it. It's the best part about it, really." At least I thought so. Of course, maybe that was just the poet talking.

"So you're saying I can pretty much be anything I want?"

"Within reason," Wolf said.

"And within the roll of the dice," Deedee added.

"In that case," she said, setting the tiny plastic gnome in front of her, "my name is Moose."

We all looked at each other. You could hear the carbonation popping in our cups. I was no stranger to tense silences. I'd once witnessed my mother yelling at my father in the middle of a Walgreens loud enough for everyone waiting at the pharmacy to hear, including the guy waiting in the drive-thru. The quiet that followed that incident wasn't quite this awkward.

Rose shrugged off our stares. "What? You think I'm going to let some stupid little nickname get to me? Screw that. My name is Moose Wrathbringer and I'm a spell-casting ninja with a history of carrying out covert assassinations for top-secret guilds. Or something."

"You can't do that," Deedee said. "You can't be a spell-casting ninja. For starters you're a gnome, and the stat requirements, plus the rules for multiclassing, prohibit you to—"

He suddenly stopped talking, his mouth cinched tight, eyes bulging. Rose had reached out and taken his hand, just grabbed it from across the table. By the look on his face you'd know that no girl had ever held Deedee's hand before. I watched his Adam's apple jump like he'd swallowed a grasshopper.

"It's all right, Deedee," Rose said softly. "I *can* do it because *you* are the dungeon master, and *you* can do anything. Which means I can *be* anything, even a spell-casting ninja gnome named Moose, because that's what this is all about. We don't always have to play by the rules." She let go and Deedee seemed to relax, though he moved his hands to his lap and kept them there.

"Yeah. All right," he said, his voice catching. Wolf handed Rose some dice and we created her character, deciding how strong and wise and smart she would be. "Stronger, wiser, and smarter than the rest of you," she said with a grin. By the time

Moose Wrathbringer was born the pizza had arrived and Wolf paid with the money his mother left on the counter. Equipped with a slice of greasy pepperoni and a magic katana, Rose yelled for us to "get our adventure on."

Deedee talked us through the scenario, which started, predictably, with the three of us sitting around a table at a tavern. Eventually we ended up in a graveyard and then descended, with typical foolish courage, into a crypt, where we came across a horde of zombies. I tried to sneak around them so that I could find another escape route but I fell into a pit due to a failed perception check. Wolf tried to sing a song that would paralyze them, but it turned out they were immune. Normally this would be about the time that Bench would whip out his double-bladed Battle-Ax of Bleeding and go ballistic, but Garthrox the Barbarian was out to dinner with his parents celebrating "the catch."

Which left us with Moose.

"You guys are in trouble," Deedee said.

Rose licked her fingers and pointed to the cardboard chits that represented the undead horde shuffling toward us. "All right. I got this. I cast a spell of absolute zombie annihilation on the whole lot of them, sending them back to the foul abyss or zombie-making factory from whence they came."

"You don't have a spell of absolute zombie annihilation," Deedee informed her.

"How do I get one, then?"

"There is no such thing."

"Well there should be," Rose insisted. "What *do* I have?"

"You have a spell of scorching touch and your sword."

"Spell of scorching touch. What is that—is that like I light my finger on fire and go around pointing it at people?"

"Pretty much," Wolf said.

"That sounds lame. I'll just use the sword."

"It's called a katana," Deedee said.

"Its name is Charlene."

Six eyebrows shot up around the table. "*Charlene*?" I questioned.

"Yeah, why? Is that a bad name for a sword?" Rose asked.

"No. It's fine," I said. "I just thought, you know, you'd want it to be, like, something more . . . intense."

"Fine. Her full name is Charlene the Freakin' Crazy Sharp Sword That Will Cut Your Head Off If You Make Fun of Her." Rose gave me a challenging look.

"That's much better," I said.

"Okay," Deedee sighed. "But I'm telling you now, Charlene or no Charlene, you're all better off trying to run away."

Rose took a Funyon out of the bag and crunched it mercilessly. "You don't know me very well, do you? Just give me the dice."

Deedee consulted the tables, compared Moose's stats to those of the zombies. Turns out she needed a roll of fifteen on a twenty-sided die to be successful. Otherwise we were about to have our brains sucked out of our skulls. Rose blew on the die. Deedee asked her not to do that anymore. She rolled a twenty, scoring a critical hit and decapitating the first zombie in line.

"That's how *I* roll," she said with a smile, which would have been vomitously cheesy if all of us hadn't already said it ourselves at one point or another.

After that Moose Wrathbringer went into a rampage, improbably rolling one high number after another, slicing and dicing through imaginary undead, shouting "Make way for Charlene!" with every toss of the die. She even stuck her flaming finger into the rotting guts of the last zombie, incinerating him from the inside out, just for kicks.

When it was finished, Moose had a pile of actually-dead-this-time undead at her feet and the stares of three boys who couldn't believe what they'd just witnessed.

"Garthrox is a wuss," Deedee whispered in awe.

Rose sat back smugly and popped another Funyon. "Never mess with a ninja wizard princess."

"Wait. When did you become a princess?" I asked.

"I just saved your sorry butt. I can be a princess if I want."

I didn't argue. Instead I went to take a drink and found my

cup empty. Rose reached under the table for the bottle of soda and poured me what was left. Then she tapped her cup to mine. "To Charlene," she said.

"To being whatever you want to be," I said.

We all tapped cups. Then we descended farther into the crypt.

By the time the adventure was finished—the Queen of the Vampires thoroughly staked, all the loot split between us—Wolf and I had both gained a level and Rose had gained two. Moose was almost where we were. It was still only nine o'clock so we eradicated what was left of the pizza, opened a box of fudge brownies, and watched old *Dr. Who* episodes.

It was a pretty much perfect night.

No one said anything about Bench. Maybe I was the only one even thinking about him as we all squeezed in on Wolf's family room couch, me and Deedee on the ends, Wolf and Rose in the middle, a little tight but workable.

Or maybe we were all thinking about him. But the game was over.

And there was no room left on the sofa anyways.

That night, after Deedee's mom dropped me off at home, I tried to call Bench, just to see how his dinner went, but his cell went straight to voicemail. I wasn't sure if I was going to tell him about Rose or not. I couldn't make up my mind. And I couldn't quite figure out what it meant that I couldn't make up my mind. Would Bench even care? And if he didn't care, what would *that* mean? I figured if he asked how the game went I'd just say it was all right.

"Actually, funny thing," I'd say after a pause. "Rose came over and joined in. She didn't use your character, though, don't worry." And then he'd ask something, maybe who invited her, or was it strange with her there, and I would say that it was fine, but that it would have been nice if he were there. I wouldn't say *instead*. I wouldn't say *too*. I would just leave it at that.

I definitely wouldn't tell him how much we laughed. How Rose gave Deedee such a hard time, saying her grandmother would make a better dungeon master and urging him to just make stuff up rather than taking five-minute time-outs to page through his three-hundred-page manuals. I wouldn't tell him how she beat all three of us at an arm-wrestling contest afterward, nearly throwing Wolf out of his chair. Or how she told me that her favorite American poet was Emily Dickinson—even though I've never heard anyone else our age admit to *having* a favorite American poet.

And I wouldn't tell him how, when we all said good-bye at the end of the night, she gave out more hugs. Not just to Wolf. To all three of us. I wouldn't tell him that I hugged her back, and not a limp one either. I stretched to reach all the way around.

I would just say it was all right.

Because it was.

I dialed his home phone and his mom picked up. She sounded apologetic.

"J.J. isn't home yet, Eric. He went out to dinner with some of his football friends. He should be home real soon. Want me to tell him you called?"

"That's all right, Mrs. Jones," I said, and hung up without saying good-bye.

THE QUIET

MOST PEOPLE WILL TELL YOU THAT THE WAR STARTED IN EARNEST that next Monday.

It was over by the end of the week.

I call it a war, but it wasn't really. It was more like a barroom brawl, the kind you see in old Westerns, where the piano player hides under his bench and the chandelier always gets shot down. It wasn't just one side against another. I'm not even sure there were any objectives, or, at least, everybody's objective was different. Some people were probably just trying to be funny. Others had taken Mr. Sword's lesson to heart and thought they could really change the world one sticky note at a time. Others were out for blood.

It wasn't about anything new. The same stuff kids have

done since Julius Caesar was thirteen, probably, showing off his designer togas and thumbing his nose at the poorly dressed peasants beneath him. Fights over who was prettier or more popular, who had whose boyfriend first, who had more money, more followers, more favorites. Fights about who said what when and to whom and why and whether that meant they weren't friends anymore or not because-I-never-liked-you-anyway and so on.

What made it unique was the battleground. Every skirmish took place on three square inches. Sticky notes were the weapons and words were the ammunition.

Whatever it was, it became clear by Monday that the tone of Deedee's revolution had shifted. Some of the messages were still harmless, quotes from philosophers mixed with *yo mama* jokes. There were earnest entreaties to *Hug a Teacher!* or *Kick a Squirrel Today!* There was an abundance of smiley faces and frowny faces and other emoticons to express our feelings, many of which got hurt when the notes got personal.

There was the note on Sophia Bauer's locker that said *Just another pretty* ugly *face,* where the "ugly" had been scrawled in after the fact. There was the note I heard four guys arguing about, listing each of them in order of attractiveness. There was the note Maggie Manklin found on the back of her chair with a simple sketch of a pair of puckered lips inching toward a bare buttocks. Maggie *was* kind of a suck-up, true, but that didn't make it any less hurtful. It didn't stop her from raising her hand seven times in science either, though.

There were a lot of questions. *Why do you follow me around everywhere? Why don't you text me anymore? What's that smell every time you walk by?* Some of them got corresponding sticky-note answers. Some of them were probably responded to in other ways.

There were the usual slurs, slings, and arrows. A lot of name-calling, though nothing on the level that Ruby Sandels had heaped upon Mr. Jackson. It hadn't quite gotten to that point yet. Not out in the open, anyways.

I tried to stay out of it as much as possible. In war, even if you're not the one firing the shots, you still have to keep your head down. It didn't make a difference. I'm pretty sure everybody in the entire school took a note at some point. My first was stuck to my locker with nothing but a big *L* on it, etched in red marker. Deedee was with me.

"Maybe it stands for 'locker,'" he suggested.

"I'm pretty sure that's not what it stands for."

"Could be worse." Deedee showed me a note that he'd found on his locker that morning. At the top it said *One Dweeb to Rule Them All.* Underneath was a drawing of what I assumed was Deedee, though his facial features were exaggerated, too-big eyes, too-big ears. They got his hair right, though. And he was holding a lunch box.

"How do you know I didn't put it there?" I asked. It was easier if you tried to laugh it off.

"Because you don't know how to draw," Deedee said.

I took the note from his hand and crumpled it together with mine, tossing them both in the bottom of my locker. Just another nudge. Besides, being Lord of the Geeks could be something to be proud of. Just maybe not in Branton.

Not everybody was able to brush it off so easily, though. Two boys nearly got in a fistfight outside the gym, one shoving a Post-it in the other's face. Then there was the note I saw Rebecca Goldsmith holding, handed to her with some emphatic lower-lip biting from her supposed best friend. I didn't see what the note said, but it sent Rebecca bawling in the direction of the girls' bathroom. A teacher eventually had to go in after her.

The bathrooms were the worst.

There were hundreds of sticky notes being posted all around the school, out in the open for all to see. But the really nasty ones—the ones with fangs—were either tucked into the slats of lockers or left on the bathroom mirrors. Like the graffiti scribbled on the backs of stall doors, the messages you found in the bathroom used a different vocabulary, easily worthy of a parental advisory warning. Some were crude. Others just outright vicious, intended only to hurt.

Except you didn't know who was hurting you. Almost all the notes were anonymous. Nobody had the guts to sign their name. You didn't know unless you saw the person actually stick the note, and even then you couldn't be sure. Some were passed along from binder to binder, backpack to backpack, until they reached their destination.

Most of them didn't stay up for long. The person the note was intended for would laugh, or cry, or groan, or growl, or just stare at it dumbly for a minute before crumpling it and tossing it or stuffing it in a back pocket to be forgotten. There were a few conscientious objectors who saw where it all was headed and tried to put a stop to it, taking down any note they saw regardless of what it said. For the most part, the students got to the worst notes before any of the teachers did.

But not always.

Unsurprisingly, Ms. Sheers was the first to pounce, pausing her explanation of differential equations midsentence, her eyes narrowing on the third row.

"Can I see what you're writing, please?" she said, circling in typical bird-of-prey fashion around Casey Hillman's desk. Casey slapped her hand over the sticky note, but it was too late.

"Just copying down the homework assignment."

"I haven't assigned any homework yet."

Checkmate. For a moment I was certain Casey was going to stuff the paper in her mouth and try to choke it down secret agent style before Ms. Sheers could pry her lips apart, but instead she melted in her seat while Ms. Sheers took the note from her. "Did you write this?"

Casey nodded meekly. Ms. Sheers pointed to the door and told Casey to wait for her outside. Then she turned to address the rest of us, holding the note up—backward, so we couldn't see what it said. "I don't want to see any more of these in my class for any reason, do you understand? If I see them I will confiscate them and you will go straight to the office."

We all nodded. I noticed a few people tucking their yellow stacks back into their bags. Ms. Sheers had that enough-is-enough look in her eyes. And something else. Sadness maybe. Disappointment. She followed Casey out of the room, closing the door with a little more emphasis than usual, though even with it shut we could still hear Ms. Sheers's voice. *Disrespectful. Irresponsible. Call your parents. Take this note to Principal Wittingham immediately.*

I didn't see Casey for the rest of the day. That's how it is in war. One moment somebody is sitting right there next to you and the next moment they're gone.

I decided to keep my own pad of notes in my locker from

that point on. I had a few things I wouldn't mind saying to a few choice people, but it wasn't worth getting sent to the Big Ham for.

And besides, I wasn't sure it would do any good anyway.

Right after math I looked for Bench on the off chance that he wanted to at least *walk* to lunch with me. He hadn't been on the bus that morning. I hadn't seen him all day, in fact. We didn't have a class together until the afternoon, but you still ran into people—people whose routes and schedules you'd memorized. Maybe he was at home sick. Maybe his head exploded after reading about himself in the paper. I hadn't even had the chance to tell him what an awesome catch it was.

Or to ask him about dinner with his friends.

He wasn't waiting at the corner of the hall, so I walked to the cafeteria by myself. Wolf, Deedee, and Rose were already there. I didn't even bother to get in the lunch line, just went straight to the table.

"Have any of you guys seen Bench?"

There was a round of worried glances, Wolf to Rose to Deedee to me, full circle. Then, finally, Deedee looked sideways, almost guiltily.

I'm not sure how I missed him when I walked in. The table he sat at was easily the loudest in the room, seven kids packed around the circle, all members of the football team, all dressed in blue and white, in uniform even when not in uniform. Number 80 had his back to me, but his jersey made him impossible to miss. Part of me hoped he would turn around at that moment and catch me staring at him, just so I could read the expression on his face, to see if he would smile with embarrassment or offer an apologetic frown—something, anything. But he didn't look my way.

"He was there when I came in," Deedee said. "I figured if I came and sat down he might grab his tray and come sit with us." Deedee spooned up a glob of tapioca pudding, then plopped it back into the cup. Over in the corner Bench appeared to be telling a story to the other guys, who were all laughing. One of his football buddies slapped the table and the sound startled me. I felt something swell and catch in my throat and I forced it down, deep into a hole that had opened inside me.

"It's all right," Wolf said. "He's a big boy. He can sit wherever he wants. Besides. His stock has gone up."

I turned back to our table, but my eyes kept flitting back to Bench and the people he was with. They were his teammates. Friends by association, I guess. But they weren't his tribe. For two years he'd *never* sat with them. Not once. And yet, as much as I wanted to feel surprised, I guess I wasn't. I knew the difference between surprised and disappointed. As I watched him laughing, I couldn't help but think about what the bus ride home would be like that afternoon. There were a couple of student athletes on bus 152. They weren't on the football team, but I wasn't sure it would matter—there was nothing keeping him from sitting wherever he wanted. I nudged the empty chair next to me with my foot, maybe a little harder than I meant to. Rose's voice piped in.

"Did you see all the notes this morning?" she asked, looking at Deedee but mostly just trying to change the subject I think. "They're everywhere now. It's insane."

"Speaking of insane, you should show Frost *your* new picture," Wolf said.

For the first time since sitting down I noticed he had swollen gray circles under his eyes. I wondered if his parents had been arguing all night again. "What picture?" I asked, tearing my attention away from Bench.

With a groan Rose pulled a sticky note from her front pocket, smudged at one corner. "It's no big deal," she said, "really. It's even dumber than last time."

On it was another drawing in black ink, similar to the one before, though this one was much more elaborate. It showed a station wagon puttering down a road. Tied to its roof was a moose, its eyes just two big *X*s. The moose's tongue stuck out comically.

"That's terrible," I said.

"It's just a joke," she said. "He looks funny with his tongue hanging out like that, don't you think?"

"It's not a joke," Wolf said. "It's obviously a threat. You should tell somebody." He turned to me. "Tell her she should tell somebody."

"I did tell someone," Rose interjected before I could tell her anything. "I told you. Besides, you really think I'm afraid of whatever idiot drew this? I'm a ninja wizard princess, remember? This," she said, holding the note between them, "this is nothing."

"It's not nothing," Wolf muttered. "You can't just ignore it."

"Why not? You do," Rose fired back. "What about that note on *your* locker this morning?"

Wolf shot her a look. It seemed like a warning, but Rose didn't flinch.

"What note?" Deedee asked.

"It's no big deal," Wolf said. "Just the usual stupid crap. It wasn't anything like this." He plucked the dead moose drawing from Rose's fingers. She snatched it right back.

"What did you do with it? Can I see it? What did it say?" Deedee's questions were aimed directly at Wolf, but he ignored them, continuing to stare at Rose.

"He crumpled it up and threw it away. Just . . . like . . . so."

Rose squeezed her drawing into a wrinkled ball and stuffed it in her still-full carton, sloshing milk up over the side. "There. Gone. Now we don't have to talk about it anymore."

For a moment I thought Wolf was going to reach over to Rose's tray, grab the carton, and fish the crumpled note out. Instead he just said, "It's not that easy."

"I didn't say it was easy. I just said we didn't have to talk about it anymore."

For the first time since she'd sat with us, Rose and Wolf were not laughing with each other. They stared, arms crossed, a silent stalemate. Deedee looked down and stirred his pudding. Behind us, Bench's table erupted with laughter again.

I had to look. Fear of missing out. Bench was shaking his head, flashing his teeth through that double-wide grin of his. I felt the hole inside open even wider.

"I'm going to get some food," I said.

Deedee looked at me gloomily. Wolf and Rose continued to glare at each other. I stood up and pushed my chair in and headed for the line, not hungry, just needing to get far enough away that I couldn't hear Bench and his buddies over the usual cafeteria chaos. All the voices mixed together again, a hundred conversations that I wasn't a part of, blending to a steady incomprehensible roar. I stood in line and closed my eyes.

212

No words. Just noise. It wasn't the same as quiet, but I didn't want quiet.

I just didn't want to know what people were saying.

School is never quiet. Even in the library there's whispering, giggling, shushing. In class somebody's always making some comment or another.

But that doesn't mean quiet's always better.

In the last year before the Big Split, the quiet moved into our house for good, settling over everything like a blanket of heavy snow. My parents had stopped fighting. In fact, they'd stopped saying anything at all.

The silence felt so much a part of us, I imagined it sitting in the empty chair across from me at the dinner table, a ghostlike figure made of smoke or mist, one foggy finger perpetually at its lips. My parents wouldn't even ask for the other one to pass the butter. Instead they would reach across the table, sometimes knocking over other things along the way. My mother couldn't stand it for long, so she would use me as her excuse to make noise, asking me for the third time about my day or about homework or something random. Did I need new socks? How was the chicken? And once, did I notice that it was a new moon today?

You don't notice it's a new moon, I told her. The absence of something isn't remarkable. Unless it's the absence of conversation. Then it's painfully obvious.

After dinner my father would escape to his study to work and my mother would do the dishes and I would fight back against the silence. Turn on the television. Listen to music. Hum to myself. I would go out and shoot baskets only so I could hear the ball bricking off the backboard, the sound of it striking the pavement—*thump, thump, thump*. Silence was better than shouting, I told myself. But it wasn't. It was just another kind of bad.

The night before he moved out, there still wasn't even any shouting. Just a conversation—the briefest one in history, I think—carried out at the dinner table. After ten minutes of quiet my mother put down her fork slowly, setting it on the edge of her plate. Even that sound, the metal on porcelain, was startling, like the clang of a church bell. She folded the napkin in her lap and set it on the table. Then she looked across the bowl of mashed potatoes at my father and said, "I can't do this anymore."

"Do what?" he asked.

"Just sit here and do nothing," she said.

They stared at each other for a few seconds, then my father nodded and reached halfway across the table for the salt.

And that was it. In the silence that followed it was decided. They were done. And I could hear my heart in my chest. *Thump. Thump. Thump.*

There are times when I envy Wolf and his house full of shouting. There are times when I wish my parents had gritted their teeth and kept fighting, even if the end turned out the same. That way, at least, I would feel like they'd given it everything rather than simply given up. But that's not how it happened. It happened in quiet. The mashed potatoes congealing on our plates. The three of us chewing and chewing as if we were afraid to swallow.

There are some nights even a can of Prego can't save my mother's cooking. The pasta was undercooked—she called it *al dente,* which I assumed was Italian for "crunchy." I sat across the table from Mom, who was still wearing her name tag from work. Less than eight hours ago Casey Hillman had been kicked out of math and sent to the office for a nasty note that she'd apparently written to her BFF, who was now neither a BF or even an F. Six hours ago, I sat at the lunch table and listened to Bench cracking jokes with a bunch of other people who weren't part of his tribe while Rose and Wolf held a wordless blinking contest. Three hours ago I rode home on the bus alone—or at least with the seat to myself. It's not that Bench sat with someone else—he wasn't on the bus at all. Maybe he had practice. Maybe he got a ride. Maybe it was no big deal and I was worrying too much. But so many maybes didn't change the fact that I spent the ride home with my head pressed against the window, biting my lip and wishing I'd brought something other than *Julius Caesar* to bury myself in.

At least at home you didn't have to worry about who to sit with. I split open my fourth crescent roll and slathered it with butter while my mother told me all about her day. One advantage to the Post Sarasota Shuffle is that our dinners weren't quiet anymore. My mother did most of the talking. She also played music, and half the time the television was on in the background. She was afraid of silence.

That was all right. I'd much rather talk to her than to Dad. In fact, I'd rather talk to her than most anyone. So long as we avoided certain topics. But tonight there was something on my mind.

"Can I ask you a question?" I began.

Mom cocked one eyebrow, suspicious, her own buttered roll halfway to her mouth. She was usually the one to start our conversations. "Of course."

"Were you ever popular?"

She cocked the other eyebrow. Both barrels now. "Seriously?"

"It's just a question."

"I know, but you don't have to say it like *that*."

"Like what?"

"Like with the *ever*. 'Were you *ever* popular?' How do you know I'm not popular now?"

I shrugged. I hadn't really thought about it. Adults didn't have to worry about that stuff. "Okay. Are you popular?"

She grunted, setting her roll back on her plate. "Are you kidding? All the tottering old men who come to the dentist's office think I'm the greatest thing since color TV."

I pushed my still-stiff pasta around the plate some more, trying not to think of my forty-year-old-mother flirting with some sixty-year-old men. "But back when you were in school. When you were my age," I pressed.

"Oh. When I was *your* age. Sure. I was popular, I guess. At least I think so. I had friends."

"That's not the same," I said. *I* had friends. Even Winston Ferman had friends, though I was kind of just assuming that—in theory he would have to, wouldn't he? You find your people. It doesn't mean you're popular. When you're popular you don't have to find anyone; they find you.

"Well, I had a *fair number* of friends. A lot of people signed my yearbooks. And I wasn't really picked on. Does that count as being popular?"

I thought about the red letter *L* on my locker. The cartoon moose tied to the roof of the car. The notes and the nudges. All the kids like Jason and Cameron giving kids like Wolf and Deedee and me a hard time. Maybe Mom was popular. Or maybe it was just different when she was growing up. "What about Dad?"

Mom nearly choked on her water. "Your father? Oh god, no. He was *never* popular. Not that it mattered to him. In fact, that's one of the things that I liked about him at first—the fact that he was always in his own little world, that he didn't care a bit about what anybody thought of him. It made him sort of . . . mysterious."

I never thought of my father as mysterious. What was mysterious about a man who went to work in his boxer shorts and drank orange juice straight out of the carton? But I could easily picture him in his own world. "You mean he didn't have *any* friends?"

"There were people he hung out with sometimes. But no. I'm not sure he had any true friends until he met me. And when he did . . ." Mom paused, put down her fork, and leaned across the table. "Is there something going on at school? Something you want to talk about?"

I pictured my dad, working up the courage to come sit at Mom's table—if that's even how it happened. I wondered what her friends thought when they saw him standing there. If they let him have the empty seat or pushed him away. I wondered what they called him behind his back after he left. What kinds of notes they left in his locker. "No," I said, but I knew that wasn't going to be enough for her. My mother's looks could pull confessions out of hardened criminals. "It's just that, there's this new kid at school, and she's having kind of a hard time fitting in—" I figured I could always start with Rose and work my way up from there.

"*She?*" Mom narrowed her eyes and gave me a sly grin, like she'd just cracked the code.

I put down my fork. "You know what, it's not a big deal. Just forget I said anything."

"No. Tell me. I want to know. Because if this is about a girl, I can help you."

"Right," I muttered. "Because you're *such* an expert on relationships."

My eyes dropped immediately to my plate. It just slipped out. Words are like that sometimes. There was a really long pause. The old quiet creeping in. I looked up to see her frowning. "Sorry. I didn't mean—"

"No, you did," she said, clearly hurt. "But it's okay. What I meant is, I remember what it's like to be thirteen and wanting people to like you. It's not easy." She reached across the table and gently took hold of my wrist.

"But I'll tell you this, kiddo—being liked isn't even *close* to the same thing as being loved. Got it?"

I nodded and she took that as her cue that she could let go.

"I think next time I'll boil the noodles a little longer," she said, and pushed her plate away.

After the table was cleared I let Mom help me with homework—I didn't actually need it, but I could tell it made her happy getting involved, and I still felt like a jerk for what I'd said. We built an Inter-Continental Ballistic Missile out of a paper towel roll for my history presentation (Wolf was in charge of the poster—he had much neater handwriting), complete with the letters *USSR*, which, as it turned out, didn't have the word "Russia" in it at all.

When she finally said good night after asking me again if there was anything else I wanted to talk about, I waited for her door to shut, then snuck past it down the hall.

The office at the new house was nothing like the study at the old one, with its tall bookshelves and mahogany rolltop desk full of unpaid bills, where my father would sit for hours writing his articles and ignoring the rest of the world. The office at the new place was actually just the extra bedroom, complete with a day bed, a scratched-up student desk Mom had found at Goodwill, and a couple of IKEA shelves lined with whatever cheap paperbacks Mom and I picked up at library sales. We had a lot more books once, but Dad took most of them with him, minus the Frost, which was mine now.

Mom got to keep the photo albums, though. There weren't a ton of pictures. Mostly family vacations to Cancun and Canada. One album was filled with pictures of me running around the house in my diaper or smearing carrots in my hair. You're never more photogenic, apparently, than when you are half naked and covered in pureed vegetables. My toddler years were equally well documented. Probably because I was an only child. After that the pictures sort of trailed off. You take more pictures when people are having a good time.

Next to the albums sat what I'd come for. My mother's high school yearbooks, a layer of dust from the new house already settling on top of the layer of dust carried over from the old. There were four of them; I had seen them before. For a school project on family trees once I needed a picture of my parents as kids. Mom was easy; Grandma had thousands, most of them Polaroid instants with the glossy black back and white frame. But for Dad's we actually had to scan his freshman year picture in one of these yearbooks and blow it up.

I slid the first year of Midvale High's *Reflections* off the shelf and opened it to the inside cover, reading the messages scrawled there. She was right. It was full of signatures. My mother was *awesome*. And *the coolest*. She was *totally rad*. There were phone numbers from boys named Dan and Jacob, asking my mom to call sometime over the summer. Someone with the nickname of KK said she would always remember something called "the marshmallow surprise." Another girl named Sarah wrote, *I'm sick of not having the courage to be an absolute nobody.* I'm guessing it was from a book. I didn't know if it qualified as an aphorism or not. On the inside back cover it was more of the same. The whole thing was filled with signatures.

She really was popular.

I took the next year off the shelf. Looked for familiar names. KK was there again. And Sarah. And some others. The pages were still filled, but the handwriting was bigger. Some drawings took up a good amount of space. My mother was still *cool*. She would still *be missed*. But her junior year, there were fewer messages. Sarah wrote a long note that took up half of the back page, telling my mother what a good friend she was and that next year would be different. She didn't say how.

By her senior year the number of signatures in my mother's yearbook had dwindled to fewer than ten. The girl named Sarah signed it simply, *Good luck out there.* There was a note from someone named Mr. Feldman, presumably a teacher. On the cover page there was an angry tornado of blue ink, nearly clawing clean through the page. Something had been written there once, something I'm guessing my mother wasn't interested in seeing again.

On the back inside cover there was only one name. My father's. Following a short message, two sticky-note-worthy words.

Love always, it promised.

It mattered. Who signed your yearbooks mattered. I sat with

the last year in my lap until I heard a sound out in the hallway and silently slid all four of the books back into place. I waited for my mother to close the bathroom door before sneaking back to my bedroom and shutting off the light.

I lay there in the darkness, looking up at the ceiling, thinking about my mother's yearbooks, the fact that there were fewer and fewer signatures in each one, wondering how something like that happens. And how much, if anything, it had to do with Dad. I never heard her say anything about anyone from high school. Had never heard her mention a Sarah or a KK or anyone else whose names were inked on the inside cover. Most of the friends she had now either came from college or were colleagues from work. Where did they all go? Did they leave her or did she leave them? Where was her tribe?

Maybe that's how it worked. Maybe the people you know when you're a kid are destined to be just a bunch of signatures in your yearbook when you grow up. I didn't want to believe it though. I thought about Bench sitting on the bus next to me. And Deedee reaching into his front pocket for his die.

And Wolf bent over one of his models, putting all the pieces into place.

And Rose, standing at the edge of our table, eyeing the empty seat.

I thought about Dad, reaching for the salt, having run out of

223

things to say. How do you keep someone from leaving when it's clear they don't want to stay?

I bent over and grabbed my jeans from the floor, pulling out the note that I'd found in my locker that afternoon. Not the one that had been stuck to the outside with its lone capital letter. This one I'd found shoved through the slots, right before dismissal.

I knew who put it there. I recognized the handwriting.

SORRY ABOUT LUNCH, it said.

Bench always wrote in all caps.

Then, a little smaller underneath.

IT'S NOT ABOUT YOU.

It wasn't about me. Sure.

But I'm still the one who rode the bus home alone.

THE OFFER

THE DAY WOLF AND I NEARLY BLEW UP HIS HOUSE WAS THE SAME day my parents' divorce finally went through.

They had been split city for a while—I'd already visited Dad once in Tallahassee—but there were questions concerning my father's income and custody arrangements and who got the left-overs in the fridge or whatever. My mother refused to talk about the details and I didn't ask. If it happened to come up she simply said, "I'm working on it," and let it go at that, and I let her let it go. But finally the papers came through and Mom had to visit the lawyer to sign on the dotted line, so I went to Wolf's to hang out. Deedee was out of town and Bench had baseball practice for the entire afternoon, leaving just the two of us. There was nothing wrong with two sometimes. It wasn't four, of course, but spending the afternoon with Wolf was infinitely better than sitting at home eating Cap'n Crunch straight out of the box and watching SpongeBob reruns in my underwear.

It was too hot to be outside, so we holed ourselves up in his room, underneath the plastic jets and painted starships, listening to music and flipping through his impressive comics collection. It was big enough he had to keep them in giant plastic tubs under his bed. None of them were in sleeves—that was more like something Deedee would do. Wolf didn't see value in the books beyond what he got from reading them. He was also strictly a Marvel guy, but I didn't hold it against him.

We sat and read and ate and occasionally said something to each other. After an hour, we'd practically burned through an entire bag of Cheetos. Wolf held the last one up for inspection.

"Turds," he said.

"Huh?"

"Cheetos. They look like turds. Little cheese turds. Especially the stubby ones. I never noticed that before." He was sitting cross-legged on his bed with a copy of *X-Men #25* spread out in front of him. The one where Wolverine has his adamantium sucked out of his pores by Magneto. Brutal stuff. Good stuff. I looked at the Cheeto like it was some divine artifact worthy of a museum. He wasn't wrong. They did sort of look like that. I'd always imagined them more as tree roots.

"When I was little I thought they were supposed to look like toes. Cheese-toes," Wolf said.

"I'm pretty sure nobody's toes look like that," I said.

"I think my grandmother's toes probably look like this." He popped the crunchy cheese turd in his mouth and started chewing.

"And I'm pretty sure you have now ruined Cheetos for me for life."

Wolf gave me a giant grin with bright orange mush smeared across his teeth.

"Really? You're disgusting." I buried my face back in *The Incredible Hulk*. The ticked-off green behemoth had just ripped a helicopter out of the sky and was tying its propellors like shoelaces. There were days I wished I could do that. I'd tie a couple of kids' arms behind them and hang them from the flagpole so everyone could point and laugh as they walked by.

"So it's like, official," Wolf said, his teeth no longer orange. "Your parents." He made some kind of chopping motion with his hands.

"They aren't being beheaded. They're just getting divorced," I said. Wolf was just staring at me though. "What?"

"Nothing. It's just kind of a big deal, don't you think?"

He was serious. This wasn't the first time one of us had brought up parents or divorce or how nobody in their right mind should get married. You find people who share your interests. Wolf and I were both interested in complaining about the poor choices our parents had made, primarily in each other. "You think I should be pissed off or something?"

Wolf shrugged. "You're not? *I* would be."

I shrugged back. "Honestly, it's been so long coming, I just don't care anymore."

That wasn't completely true. I did care, but not as much as I thought I would. Or maybe thought I *should*. This wasn't like the day Dad left, or any of the days leading up to it, or even some of the days that came after. Those days were harder. This was just papers. I didn't need a lawyer to tell me that my parents couldn't stand each other anymore. I just needed one to tell me how many weeks I'd spend in Florida each year. It was different for Wolf. He was still knee-deep in the middle of it. "But you're still going to stay with your mom most of the time, right?" Wolf asked.

"I'm not leaving, if that's what you're worried about." Maybe it *was* something he was worried about, beause he seemed to relax a little.

Wolf sighed. "If my parents ever split, I don't know who I would want to live with. I think it would be hard, only seeing one of them on weekends or whatever. I'm not sure I could handle it."

"It gets easier after a while," I said. "You get used to it." Mostly you get used to it.

"Maybe. Still sucks though." He was giving me that look, like he was waiting for me to tell him where I hid the buried treasure or something. "I know that it's, like, against the rules. But if you ever feel like you've just got to get something off of your chest . . ."

His voice trailed off. It was one of those awkward moments where you're right on the verge of saying something all emotional and cheesy and stuff, something that might cause you to crack and get the waterworks going or at least feel itchy and uncomfortable.

"Thanks for the offer," I said. "Seriously, though, it's fine. I'm going to go home and everything's going to be the exact same as it was yesterday."

"Not the *exact* same. Your mother will be legally back on the market."

"Okay. Now you're just being creepy."

"What? She's kind of pretty . . . for a mom."

"You can totally just stop talking, like immediately."

Wolf made a production of zipping his lips. The moment had passed. I stood up and shuffled through the spread of comics on the bed until I found one with Spidey stuck to the side of the *Daily Bugle*, Mary Jane cradled in a nest of webbing below. He'd saved her yet again. Must be nice, having someone come to your rescue all the time.

"What do you think? Mary Jane or Gwen Stacey?" I asked. Real girls were hard to talk about, almost as hard as divorces. But comic book characters were fair game—and it was certainly better than talking about my mother. Wolf gave me a strange look. "I mean, I know how it ends up. But, like, if *you* had to choose. If you were Spider-Man and had to just pick one, who would it be?"

He put down his comic and leaned his head against the wall. "As Spider-Man or Peter Parker?" Wolf asked.

"Um . . . you do know how superheroes work, right?"

"Yeah, doofus. I'm just thinking maybe it could be both, you know? Like Peter could date Mary Jane and Spidey could go for Gwen. Why limit yourself?" It was an interesting question.

"Never work," I said. "Spider-Man spends half his time saving Mary Jane anyway. Gwen would get jealous." It reminded me of kids at school, fighting about who liked who more. "You have to decide. Dr. Octopus is standing there with both of them covered in dynamite or something—"

"Dynamite? Seriously?" Wolf asked. "What is this, like the 1940s?"

"Fine. They're strapped to missiles or whatever. And he's all, 'Take your pick, Spidey. MJ or Gwen.'"

Wolf shrugged. "I'd save them both."

"You can't save them both."

"Suck a Cheeto. I'm Spider-Man. I'll find a way."

"Just choose," I said.

"No."

"Redhead or blonde?"

"Forget it."

"Neighborhood love or classmate crush?"

"God, you're annoying. Has anyone ever told you just how annoying you are?"

"Just pick one."

"Maybe I don't *want* to pick one."

"You have to pick one," I insisted.

"I don't *have* to," he insisted right back. "Maybe they're not my type."

"Just do it already."

"Fine. Then I choose Betty Brant," Wolf said, clearly exasperated with me.

I blinked at him.

"Who the *heck* is *Betty Brant*?" She sounded like something out of an old Bugs Bunny cartoon.

"She was a secretary at the *Daily Bugle*. She was Peter's first love. Just nobody knows about it because it's not in the movies. So there." Wolf made a *nyah* face at me.

"Holy crap. I think you have officialy outnerded Deedee."

Wolf's face went serious. He pointed a finger at me. "You take that back."

I weighed Wolf's roomful of plastic models against Deedee's replica of Bilbo's sword. "Fine. I take it back," I said. "But you can't pick Betty freaking Brant. It's against the rules."

"You don't make the rules," Wolf said. "And I'll choose who I want." Then he threw his copy of *X-Men* at me. Magneto hit me in the face. Who in their right mind doesn't pick MJ?

Wolf looked forlornly at the empty bag of cheese turds. "You still hungry?" he asked.

"Yeah." My stomach gurgled. Power of suggestion.

"I could ask my mom to make us something," Wolf said. "Or if you want, we can just heat up a can of SpaghettiOs."

"Sounds good to me."

I assumed he knew what he was doing.

That's how it was between us. I just assumed everything was all right. That he had it under control. Until I saw the microwave catch on fire. Then I knew I'd have to keep an eye on him.

Because he'd do the same for me.

Ms. Sheers wasn't the only one with her hawk eyes peeled. That Monday afternoon the entire teaching staff of Branton Middle School had gone on high alert, stripping notes off doors, off windows, fishing them out of recycling bins. Gathering evidence. The Big Ham probably had a file full of the nastiest ones gathering in his office, ready to be dusted for fingerprints in order to discover who the culprits were. And to think that Deedee had started it by welcoming me to the Dark Ages. It kind of felt like the Dark Ages, assassins sneaking down the halls in between periods to plant little poisonous notes on lockers.

It wasn't a surprise, then, when the ax came down. On Tuesday morning in homeroom, right after the Pledge of Allegiance. The new commandment was delivered over the morning announcements in Mr. Wittingham's signature grunt.

"It has been brought to my attention by members of the faculty and several students that many of you have been using sticky notes to leave inappropriate and even insulting messages around the school. While I understand that, for most of you, this was intended to be fun, several faculty members have expressed concerns about messages they consider offensive. This kind of behavior undermines our mission here at Branton Middle School, which is to educate in a safe, nurturing, and inclusive environment. Therefore, until further notice, students are banned from posting such notes anywhere on school property. If any member of the faculty or staff sees a student doing so, the notes will be confiscated and a message will be sent home for that student's parents." He paused to let the weight of his pronouncement settle in. "Now here's Mrs. Kelly's sixth-grade English class with a message about our upcoming canned food drive."

I stopped listening and watched as more than one student tucked the sticky note they had been writing under their textbook or back into their backpack. This was probably the first time in Branton Middle School history that a principal had officially banned a school supply.

In English, Mr. Sword took some responsibility.

"Friends, Romans, countrymen. Lend me your ears," he began, one hand leaning on his desk. "You heard Principal Wittingham this morning. I've seen some of the messages you all have been writing to each other. Most of them are innocuous"—Mr. Sword liked to toss around words that most of us didn't even know how to spell, probably to help us expand our vocabulary, but also maybe to show that he was still the smartest one in the room—"but I've seen some that were very . . . disappointing."

Mr. Sword looked at me. At least he *seemed* to be looking at me. He was actually scanning the room, taking in everybody, but whenever a teacher gets to you, you sense a pause, whether there is one or not. I'm not sure *why* he'd fixate on me. The last note I'd even bothered to write was the one *he* told me to.

He was obviously thinking the same thing. "When I gave you guys that assignment last Friday I was trying to teach you something," Mr. Sword continued. "I thought if I forced you to share your words with the rest of the school you'd discover a greater appreciation for them. I guess I was wrong."

A snicker from behind me.

"Something funny, Mr. Kyle?" Mr. Sword focused his attention on Noah, sitting behind me, making it almost feel like he was staring at me again.

"No, Mr. Sword. It's just—I think *some* people are overreacting. We're just playing around. I don't think anybody meant anything by what they wrote."

Several students murmured their agreement. Then Wolf spoke up again without raising his hand, though his voice barely notched above a whisper.

"What was that, Morgan?" Mr. Sword prodded.

"I said, it means something whether *they* mean it or not."

"You're absolutely right," Mr. Sword said. "You can't know for certain what someone else is going to think or feel about what you've written. Some people are sensitive to things you might not be."

"You said it. Not me," Jason Baker responded under his breath.

"Maybe some people are just completely *in*sensitive jerks," Wolf murmured again.

This time Jason leaned in and kicked the back of Wolf's chair. "What did you say?"

Wolf turned around this time, face red, mouth working into a snarl. "I said maybe you should just shut your big fat mouth for once."

"All right, gentlemen," Mr. Sword said, one hand raised in a call for peace. Jason ignored it.

"You got a problem, *Morgan*? Because you know how I feel when you look at me like that." Both Noah and Cameron snorted. Wolf's face only got redder.

I put a hand on his arm. "Let it go," I whispered, but he jerked his arm away. He turned back to the front and stared straight ahead, slinking down in his seat. The class took a breath. Mr. Sword watched for two seconds, three. He looked like he was about to say something, but then he just turned to write on the board.

Behind us Jason mouthed something to Noah Kyle, who whispered, "Totally." I had a pretty good guess at what Jason had said.

Maybe Wolf did too. He reached into his backpack for a thin stack of notes—the same ones Principal Wittingham had just banned—and hurriedly scrawled something on the top one. Then he stood up, pushing the desk away from him with a nerve-grating screech. Mr. Sword turned, but he couldn't get to Wolf before Wolf slammed the note down on Jason's desk. We all arched up out of our seats.

It was a more colorful version of the word "butthole." And there was an arrow pointing directly to Jason.

Wolf stood beside Jason's desk, shaking. I knew I should do something, say something. I'd never seen Wolf like this. Those fingers that danced over his piano keys, that painstakingly held tiny plastic pieces of miniature ships in place, were balled into white-knuckled fists. Jason started to stand, to get in a nudge, maybe, or just to get in Wolf's face, but Mr. Sword was there finally, one hand on each boy's shoulder, holding Jason down in his seat and pushing Wolf back a step. He snatched the note from Jason's desk and balled it up, then turned to Wolf.

"Wait for me in the hallway."

Wolf didn't move. He stood his ground, jaw clenched tight, refusing to speak. Mr. Sword spoke in an even voice, bending down to put his face right in front of Wolf's, eclipsing Jason's smug grin.

"Hallway, Morgan. Please."

Wolf shook his head. Then he turned and grabbed his pack and bolted for the door. I tried to get his attention, but he wouldn't look at me. He didn't look at anybody, not even Rose.

Mr. Sword stood over Jason. "You and I will talk after class," he said sternly. "The rest of you, start reading act three, scene two of *Julius Caesar* silently to yourselves. I don't want to hear a *sound* when I come back in this room. Understood?"

Mr. Sword had never talked to us that way before, so we all just nodded. He raised a warning finger and then followed Wolf out into the hall.

We all followed directions. At least half of them, anyways. There was no sound to be heard, even after he closed the door.

We were all too busy trying to eavesdrop through the cinder-block walls.

I didn't see Wolf for the rest of the day. After the blowup in English, he went home, maybe because he had to, maybe because he wanted to, maybe both. Deedee told me that he saw Wolf's mom in the Big Ham's office before third period, hands flying, clearly upset. Principal Wittingham probably didn't know what he was getting into; Mrs. Thompson knew how to fight. In the end, she took Wolf home, and I made a mental note to call him as soon as I could and make sure everything was all right. I had never seen him go off like that.

As the day dragged on, I didn't see near as many notes either. But I still saw enough to know that the war wasn't over. At lunch, it was just the three of us. We talked over what had happened and agreed that Jason Baker was, indeed, exactly what Wolf had called him. Then Rose told us stories about some of the jerks at her old school who made Jason look like Mahatma Gandhi. She made Branton Middle School sound like an oasis of brotherly love.

"Wolf will be all right," she said as the lunch bell rang. But for the first time since I'd met her, Rose Holland didn't sound too sure.

That afternoon, I rode the bus by myself again, passing the empty seat next to Sean Forsett. During the ride home I watched two seventh graders make tiny spit wads the size of BBs and then drop them from behind in Sean's thick, curly hair, seeing how many they could get to stick before he noticed. I almost said something. They were up to eleven when the bus hit my stop.

My mother met me at the door wearing an apron and a smile. "They gave me the afternoon off because I had too much overtime," she explained, her voice unnaturally bouncy. The house smelled like cinnamon and burning. "I've been baking."

"That's great," I said. Then I grabbed the phone and went in my room to call Wolf. I sat for a minute, trying to figure out what I'd say, but before I could dial, the doorbell rang.

"Can you get that?" Mom yelled from the kitchen. "I'm elbow-deep in bananas."

I put down the phone and shuffled down the hall, thinking it might be Wolf. Maybe he'd biked over to see what he'd missed at school. Or maybe he'd come just to talk. I opened the door halfway and peeked.

"Surprise?"

Rose stood in front of my house in her olive green army

jacket, her hair in her face, hands tucked in her pockets. With her standing a step below, we were almost on even footing.

"Who is it?" Mom yelled over the radio.

I almost said, *a girl*, which would have been a huge mistake. So instead I said the same thing Wolf said to his mother. "Just a friend from school."

"Is it Bench?" Mom called back. Mom used our nicknames. She was the only parent who did. Except for mine; she never called me Frost. Probably because Dad was the one who introduced us in the first place.

Rose stepped up and leaned her head in the door. "It's Rose Holland, Mrs. Voss," she shouted carelessly. "I came to get your son's help with an assignment. We have English together."

I heard the radio snap off and felt my stomach shrivel into a hard little knot. No doubt the sound of a girl's voice—even one as husky as Rose's—would come as a surprise to my mother. I considered dragging Rose with me outside, shutting the door behind us, but it was too late. Mom appeared in the hallway holding a towel.

"Oh. Rose. Hi," she said. You could see her processors firing. She looked at Rose, at me, then back at Rose. She was ready to jump to all kinds of conclusions. I decided to stop her.

"We're writing an essay on Shakespeare," I said. "Rose asked if I'd look over hers." It seemed plausible enough.

240

"Your son's an excellent writer," Rose said, playing along. "Probably the best in the class."

The only thing Rose had ever read of my mine was the aphorism I stuck above the water fountain that day. And the one email I'd sent with its nonwinking smiley face.

My mother beamed, her forehead wrinkles smoothing. "Oh. Well. That's not a surprise. Did he tell you about the time he won the fifth-grade poetry contest?"

Rose rolled her eyes. "Are you *kidding*? It's all he ever talks about." I flashed her a what-Sharpie-have-you-been-sniffing look. She ignored it. "Your house is lovely, by the way."

"Well. Thank you, Rose. Maybe my son will be polite enough to show you around before you two get busy."

Everything stopped. Heartbeats. Pumping lungs. The earth's orbit around the sun. I let out an involuntary squeak, but Rose kept up her polite smile. My mother closed her eyes, face turning strawberry. "Sorry. Not that you're going to *get busy*. I meant before you have to get started on your work. . . ." She folded the dish towel in her hands over and over. "Right. Okay. Back to my banana bread." She looked at me apologetically, then hurried back into the kitchen.

I cleared my throat, scratched the back of my head. "Well okay, then . . ."

241

"Forget it. She seems cool," Rose said, no doubt seeing the crimson in my own cheeks. "How could you not like someone who knows how to make banana bread? Best food combo since chocolate met milk."

"Not necessarily when she makes it," I warned.

Rose tugged on her jacket, wrapping it tight around her. It was cold enough outside that the grass crunched underfoot in the mornings when I walked to the bus. I looked over her shoulder, down the street. Deserted. No one to see Rose Holland inexplicably standing at my door. "Can we talk?" she asked.

"Yeah. Sure."

"Like in*side* the house?"

Oh. Right.

I nodded, then stepped out of her way. I pointed down the hall. "We can work in here," I shouted loud enough for my mother to hear. I followed a few steps behind and shut my bedroom door, pressing my back up against it.

Rose Holland stood in the center of the room, *my* room, taking it in. She was the first girl ever to do so. And I was sure she was regretting it almost as much as I was.

The room was a landfill. My mother let me keep it that way because she had a hard enough time keeping up with the rest of the house. Now I regretted not at least stuffing the dirty laundry into the always-empty hamper. Only members of the tribe ever came in here, and I never cared what it looked like to them—but with Rose, I felt exposed. The World of Warcraft posters. The empty Coke cans. The bedspread with the Tardis on it. Hadn't she said she liked *Dr. Who*? She sat and watched two episodes with us. Except people say things sometimes just to fit in.

I spotted a pair of dirty underwear on the floor and tried to stealthily kick them underneath the bed, hoping she hadn't seen them when she walked in. They ended up getting caught around my big toe and I had to do a little dance to shake them off. Luckily Rose's back was turned. I took a deep breath and realized that the whole room exuded a mustiness, sort of mildew meets armpit. I wondered if I should open a window. Or go get some Febreze.

Rose didn't seem to notice though. "It's almost exactly as I pictured it," she said, nodding.

I'm not sure what gave me more pause: that Rose Holland could accurately guess what my room looked like after only knowing me for a week, or that she spent time even trying. She explored for a second longer, then sat on my bed. I must have had an odd look on my face, though, because she smiled.

"Let me guess. You've never had a girl sit on your bed before."

"My mom used to read me stories as I fell asleep," I said. "Does that count?"

"Not really. But it's kind of awesome. My parents didn't read to me much. Though they never said anything about me ducking under my sheets with a book and a flashlight and staying up for hours."

She stood back up and walked over to my desk, spotting the sticky note hanging from my computer monitor, the thank-you with the snowman sketch. I was afraid she might ask me why I kept it. I wasn't sure what I would tell her. Or maybe she would notice the half-formed origami lizard sitting in my trash can. But she didn't say anything about it either, just moved over to my window, which looked out over the algae-crusted pond that sat between two rows of nearly identical houses. "It's pretty."

"I wouldn't swim in it," I said. "I know some boys who've peed in that pond."

"*Some* boys," Rose repeated slyly, then shrugged. "It's still pretty. Your house is nice, too."

I realized just then I had no idea where Rose lived. She always just seemed to materialize everywhere, apparating like Harry Potter. "How did you find it?" I asked.

"It doesn't take an FBI investigation, Frost." She put her lips close to the window and exhaled, then drew a thick round smiley face in the breathy smudge filling the pane. "Actually, Wolf told me."

I didn't move from my spot by the door. I figured if things got too awkward between us I could make a break for it. Run away from my own house, leaving my mom to deal with the girl I left in my room.

Girl. In. My. Room. I glanced nervously at my bed, thinking of the spiral-bound notebook tucked underneath.

"He said you wouldn't really mind."

"I don't," I said quickly, scratching the back of my neck. It felt like I was breaking out in hives. I tucked my hands under my armpits to keep from fidgeting. "So you guys must talk a lot." I meant to phrase it as a question, but it came out more like an accusation. She didn't seem to notice, though. She pulled out my desk chair and plopped down in it backward, chin settling on the top.

"We've known each other for a week," she said. "I guess I've only known all of you for a week, but with Wolf it feels like longer." A lot had happened since Rose Holland showed up, it seemed. The phones. The notes. The catch. It felt like longer to me too. "I guess we do talk a lot," she continued. "He's easy to talk to, don't you think?"

I nodded. He was. So long as you followed the rules.

"We don't talk about you, though, if that's what you're worried about."

"Who said I was worried?" I untucked my hands from underneath my armpits and ended up shoving them in my pockets. From down the hall my mother started belting out some old song to the radio.

"*And* she sings?"

245

"Better than she cooks," I said. I moved toward the now empty bed, away from the door. "So what *do* you two talk about?"

"Me and Wolf? You know. Stuff," Rose said. "Life. Anything. Everything. We talk about his parents a lot. And my parents. And school. Books. Movies. You guys."

"Us guys?" I prodded.

"Yeah. You. Deedee . . . Bench." She left his name just sort of hanging there. Like some kind of bait. I didn't take it, though. I was still stuck at the "you."

"You just said you didn't talk about me."

Rose tugged on a strand of tawny hair hanging in front of her face, twisting it around and around. "Okay. We don't talk about you *that* much. But we do sometimes. He worries about you."

Why was Wolf worried about me? The last I checked I wasn't the one who got sent home for scribbling an inappropriate note. I wasn't the one leaping out of my seat trying to start a fight. I wasn't the one anyone should be worrying about.

"He worries about what you think," Rose continued. "He worries about your guys' friendship." She kicked off with her feet and took a spin in the swivel chair, as if gathering momentum for what came next. When she stopped she was looking at the floor, and in that moment I remembered the Rose from that first day, coming down the hall, afraid to look up. Ignoring the

246

gawking of all the kids around her. Feeling nervous and awkward, no doubt. Like a boy with a girl in his room for the first time and a pair of underwear wrapped around his toe.

"That's why I came, actually. I know what's going on. I know I'm the reason Bench doesn't sit with you anymore."

I sat down on my bed and made some pathetic sound, like *pfft*. Rose saw right through it.

"*Pfft* me all you want," she said. "I'm not an idiot. I could tell he didn't like me from the beginning. I probably should have just left you guys alone after that first day. I would have, except I ran into Wolf after school and we started talking. The next day he asked me if I wanted to keep sitting with you guys."

Of course he did. Wolf asked. I didn't ask. Bench certainly didn't ask. *Rose Holland's going to do what Rose Holland wants to do.* I made a production out of straightening a corner of my bedspread, the closest I'd come to making it in several months, trying to think of something to say.

"I almost said no," Rose continued. "But that first day most of the kids at the other tables just gave me these dagger looks when I walked by, like *don't you dare.* You guys were different. I honestly didn't know Bench was going to eat somewhere else."

I thought about the note I found folded in the bottom of my locker. *IT'S NOT ABOUT YOU.* "That's all because of the

247

game." I said. "He's kind of a big deal now. Sitting with his football friends."

Rose shook her head. She knew right away I was lying. Bench had stopped sitting with us before the catch. He just hadn't started sitting somewhere else yet. "It's okay, Frost. I'm tough. I can take it. You can't be friends with everybody. It was worse at my old school. Kids there didn't even bother with notes, they just told you right to your face. I had a nickname there, too, you know."

I knew enough of Rose's names already. I didn't need another one, but she told me anyways.

"Dozer."

"Dozer?"

"As in bulldozer, minus the bull. Though maybe that was implied." Rose laughed. I figured that gave me permission to at least smile, but I didn't.

Instead I said, "That sucks."

Rose shrugged. Then she reached into the wastebasket under the desk and rescued my misshapen komodo dragon, turning it over and over in her hands. She started to unfold it, carefully, wrinkle by wrinkle, crease by crease, flattening and smoothing. She didn't even bother to read the riddle Bench had left me.

"I had a really hard time at my old school. It wasn't just the names. Girls would play pranks. Put stuff in my backpack. Drop things in my lunch. Boys would make these . . . jokes. I told my

dad that moving schools wouldn't help. I wasn't going to suddenly look different. Kids weren't suddenly going to change. But
he said it didn't matter. What mattered was my attitude. I could
start over, be myself, and I'd make new friends."

"You find your people," I whispered.

Rose looked up from her folding. "What?"

"Nothing. Just something my mom says all the time. You
find your people and you protect each other from the wolves."
Except, I guess, Wolf was her people. Funny. I'd never put those
two together before.

From the kitchen Mom started to really croon. I covered my
face with my hands. "Wow," I said through an embarrassed half
smile. "I really *am* sorry."

"Don't be. It's awesome. She has a great voice. And she sings
like there's nobody listening."

"Except *we're* listening," I protested.

"And yet, I don't think she cares," Rose said, and I remembered her laugh, loud and unafraid and unapologetic. She took
another spin in my chair. "A mom who sings old pop songs and
makes banana bread and says completely inappropriate things to
total strangers. You're lucky."

She didn't say anything about a dad. I wondered if Wolf
had told her about my parents. Maybe she noticed the pictures
in the hallway—all of them of just me or of just me and Mom.

Mom didn't cut out my father's face or anything—she just got rid of anything with him in it. There were no pictures of her on the walls of his apartment down in Florida either. "Your mom doesn't say completely inappropriate things to total strangers?" I asked.

"My mother has difficulty coping with reality. I mean, she actually gets medicated for it. Except the pills she's on make her tired all the time, so she has to rest a lot. And Dad . . ." Rose took a deep breath. "My dad's great, but he works all the time. It gets lonely after a while. It helps to have someone to talk to."

The chorus came floating in again from the kitchen. "Wolf's a good guy," I said. "He really likes you."

Rose laughed. "I'm pretty sure I'm not his type," she said.

She looked at me knowingly, as if waiting for me to say something, to take it back, but I had no idea what to say. A poet at a loss for words. She shook her head and added, "You're right. He is a good guy. And I know he's a good friend." She paused, her eyes cast up at the ceiling, hands pressed together in her lap. "Which is why if you want me to leave you alone, not sit with you anymore or crash your games, just let everything go back the way it was . . ."

Her voice trailed off.

Before she came along. Just me and Bench and Deedee and Wolf. The perfect square. I glanced at the window, where her smiley face had disappeared, out over the backyard and the porch where my father once handed me a book and told me to read out loud, and a line from that same poem struck me. *Yet knowing how way leads on to way, I doubted if I should ever come back.*

Rose looked at me uncertainly. The offer was on the table and she was waiting for my answer. The thing was, I knew no matter what I said, things would never go back to the way they were before. Not exactly. Even if I wanted them to.

"No," I said.

Rose flinched. "No?"

I shook my head, backpedaling. "Oh . . . no . . . Not *no*, like, *no, don't sit with us. No*, like it's all right. I don't care."

"You don't *care*?" she asked, confused.

"No, not like, I don't *care* care. Obviously I *care*. I just don't care. I mean . . . you know . . . it's cool. Whatever you want to do." Then before my brain could step in and edit, I blurted out, "You're cool."

I swallowed hard and stared at my carpet—one of the few spots not covered in dirty laundry. Five seconds passed, then Rose stood up and crossed the room so that she was standing next to me and I felt so small all of a sudden. She opened up her right hand and handed me back my folded scrap of paper, the one she'd rescued from my wastebasket. Somehow, while I wasn't looking, she had transformed it.

"What is it?" I asked, staring at the fish in her hand.

"It's a phoenix, derr," she said.

"Phoenix?" I whispered.

"You know? Mystical bird? Bursts into flames, then rises from its own ashes? What kind of nerd are you?"

I took it from her and made a production out of turning it this way and that till I held it at an odd angle toward the light. "Oh. Yeah. I see it now. Totally." I set it on the one straightened corner of my bed. "Thanks."

Mom's jam was over. A commercial for air freshener came on. Rose walked to the door. "I really do like your room," she said again. Then she left.

Or at least she tried to. But my mother caught her trying to sneak out the front door. "Oh no you don't. You're taking a loaf of this home with you." Mom held out a brick of banana bread, wrapped in foil.

"Oh, no, really, Mrs. Voss. I shouldn't," Rose said, declining the offer, but I came up beside her and told her that it was non-negotiable. Some things you can't say no to.

"Saves me from eating it," I whispered. "And besides, I'm almost positive it will stick to the roof of your mouth."

She took the loaf of bread with a thank-you. "Maybe I'll bring it to lunch tomorrow," she threatened.

Then Rose Holland winked at me. Right in front of my mother.

That night I wrote my one hundred and fourteenth poem. I number them, like Rose's favorite American poet, Emily Dickinson. Not because I particularly like Emily Dickinson. It's just easier than coming up with titles all the time.

Poem 114 was about a girl made of paper. She flies on the currents of the wind, going wherever they take her, aimless and free, not caring at all what the people down below even think of her, if they can see her or if they even believe she exists. Until, one day, she gets lonely and looks at the bright orange circle in the sky and imagines it's the eye of a giant. And she imagines that the giant is just as lonely as she is, so she flies toward him.

But it's a mistake. The heat of the sun's rays scorch her, like Icarus and his wax wings, and she catches fire. The paper girl turns to ash, a thousand tiny pieces scattered. And all of her is suddenly blown in different directions, sent to all ends of the earth, so that she can never be whole again.

Because she's not a phoenix. She's just a girl who got too close.

When I finished I tucked it away with the rest of my poems. Shoved underneath my bed with one pair of dirty underwear.

THE
BET

THE SWOLLEN PURPLE PIMPLE OF THE SCHOOL'S ONGOING WAR OF words came to a pus-filled and potentially explosive head the day Deedee almost got dunked. Before that it had stayed mostly on the page—or in our case, the yellow square. But there was always the possibility that words wouldn't be enough. That somebody would push it one step further.

Deedee-Day. Which isn't really funny, I know, but looking back, all of it—Rose, the catch, the game, the notes—they all seemed to be building to that moment in the boys' restroom and the downhill slide that followed.

There was no way of knowing it at the time. No portents of doom. No crows circling overhead. It wasn't raining frogs. It wasn't raining at all that Wednesday, just overcast and cold like it had been all week, everyone coming to school with pink ears because we are too cool to wear hats. The only thing strange that day was that Wolf didn't show up. He wasn't feeling well and convinced his mom to let him stay home—at least that's what Rose said when she met me by my noteless locker that morning. "He texted me this morning to let me know."

"He didn't let me know," I said.

"I'm letting you know," she said.

I shut my locker. They were almost all noteless now, thanks to Principal Wittingham's proclamation and the darting eyes of the sweater-clad authorities prowling the halls. The open-field warfare had vanished. The number of notes decorating the halls dwindled from hundreds to dozens. Like the cell phones packed away in clear plastic tubs in the front office, the stacks of notes were tucked in the bottoms of our backpacks.

But the war was far from over.

The sticky notes were still a perfect weapon—secret and succinct—but you could tell the rules were changing. The volleys and retorts, once restricted to three square inches, spilled back over into conversations. Shouting matches could be heard down the hall. You'd go to watch and see two kids yelling at each other about who said or didn't say what until a teacher's voice hollered at them to get to class. The notes had brought out the worst in us.

And some of us weren't all that great to begin with.

I do wonder if it would have gone differently if Wolf had been with us that day. I know it would have gone different if Bench had been, but I'd barely even seen him since "the catch." He had stopped taking the bus in the mornings, and I'd heard he was hitching a ride with David Sandlin, the team's tight end, whose father dropped them off on the way to work. It made sense—they lived only two blocks apart. But he only lived a few blocks from me too.

When I did see Bench, in class or in the halls, his reaction depended on who he was with. If he was by himself, he'd stop and we'd talk for two minutes about nothing in particular, which is to say, not Wolf or Rose or where he sat at lunch nowadays or why he lied about going out to dinner with his family, because these weren't two-minute conversations. If he was walking with someone else, though, he would just nod, which was my cue to just nod back.

We were still friends, the nod said. But things were different now.

Which is a shame, because had Bench been with us, I'm pretty sure Cameron Cole and his buddies wouldn't have done what they did.

At least I hope not.

✦ ✦ ✦

With Wolf out for the day, the seat between Deedee and me sat empty in English, and for a moment I expected Rose to come fill it, but she stayed in her usual spot by the door, as if she was worried about taking Wolf's place. I passed Deedee a note while Mr. Sword was scrawling a timeline of ancient Rome on the board.

Did Rose come to visit you yesterday?

He mouthed the word *Huh?* The perplexed look on his face elaborated: *Why would you even ask me that?*

I shrugged. *Just curious.* Deedee flipped the note over and started to scrawl something on the back, but Mr. Sword turned around and Deedee was forced to tuck it into his lap. The Big Ham had already suspended four kids for using sticky notes, but some of the teachers were slower to enforce the rule than others. The reason Wolf wasn't suspended for his dig at Jason was because Mr. Sword crumpled the evidence and threw it away. Mr. Sword, who just last week had encouraged us to share our most profound thoughts with each other on these same yellow squares. When he got hold of a note now he didn't even bother to read it, just balled it and tossed it in the wastebasket. It was his way of protecting us from a trip to the office, he said, though I suspect he was trying to protect us from more than that.

Mr. Sword finished his timeline of the events in Caesar's life and turned to the class. "Why do you think Brutus kills himself at the end of the play?" he asked.

"Um, spoiler alert?" Samantha said.

"It would be, Ms. Bowles, if I hadn't asked you to finish it last night."

I flipped through the pages like everyone else, hoping by looking busy I wouldn't get called on.

"Well, let's start here. Why do you think Antony calls Brutus the 'noblest Roman of them all' at the end?"

"Maybe they were into each other." It was Noah Kyle this time, though I could hear a chorus of snickering from behind.

"What was that, Mr. Kyle?"

"Nothing. I just said that maybe they were besties or something."

Mr. Sword looked irritated, eyes narrowing, homing in. "Have you even bothered to read the play, Noah? Or any book this year for that matter?" Noah coughed and shrank down in his seat, but I could see the corners of his smug little mouth twitch.

Mr. Sword shook his head. He called on Amanda, who'd managed to finish the play while redyeing her hair, apparently—it was green today. "The other conspirators did what they did because they were jealous of Caesar's power," she said. "But Brutus thought he was really doing what was best for Rome."

"Excellent. But does that make it *right*?"

Again nobody raised their hands.

"Seriously, people. Is it all right to murder one person in cold blood if it will improve the life of thousands of others. Is that justifiable? Yes, Simone."

"Who cares? I mean, it's not like any of *us* is going to go out and kill anyone." For some reason, half the class found this amusing. Mr. Sword did not.

"We are speaking hypothetically, Simone," he said, weaving between our desks. "And it doesn't have to be murder. I'm sure there's been some time in your life when you've used that same logic, some point where you decided the reward was worth doing something you *knew* was wrong. Maybe you stole something. Or maybe you cheated on a test. Or maybe you teased somebody, knowing it would help you to fit in better with your friends." He stopped between Jason and Noah. "Would you pick on one kid if it meant a dozen more would like you?"

"Everybody already likes me," Jason said.

From across the room Rose groaned. Jason shot her a dirty look. Mr. Sword bent down and spoke softly in Jason's ear, but it was loud enough that I could hear. "That's probably what Caesar thought, too."

At least that shut them all up for the rest of class, though once I looked back to find them passing a sticky note between them, Noah to Cameron.

And I didn't like the look on either of their faces.

Deedee, Rose, and I walked to lunch together, stopping by Deedee's locker so he could grab his lunch box and check for notes. More people had taken to folding the Post-its in half and stuffing them into the slatted vents at the top of the locker—that way the teachers couldn't come by and peel them off. Nobody had left Deedee any messages. Not today at least.

We walked toward the cafeteria and Deedee and I stopped by the restroom, Rose joking that we were a couple of girls and saying she'd wait for us in the hall.

Deedee took a stall—he always did his business behind closed doors, regardless of number. I stood and waited for him by the sink and read the two notes that were stuck to the side of the trash can. One showed a crude drawing of Principal Wittingham—you could tell by the glasses and the tie—except he was sporting a snout that took up half his face and the words "Pig on Patrol" were written underneath. The other note informed anyone who cared that Tracy F. was a word I'd rather not repeat. I didn't know who Tracy F. was, but I took the note down regardless and threw it in the trash. I left the one about Wittingham up though. It made me smile.

Deedee emerged and took the sink next to me. He looked at the principal's piggish face and frowned. "Kinda rude," he said.

"Kinda funny," I countered.

"I guess," Deedee said in that way that lets you know he doesn't agree in the slightest. "I almost regret starting it now. The whole note thing." He spoke with the resigned sigh of a superhero lamenting the fact that he has to go save the world yet again.

"I think you're giving yourself too much credit," I said. "Besides, if it wasn't this, it'd be something else." I looked at the old markings on the stall doors, typical middle school graffiti, curse words and crude drawings done in Sharpie and thick pencil scratches. At least the sticky notes were easier to clean up.

As if reading my mind, Deedee reached across me and crumpled up the note about Principal Wittingham. He tossed it toward the can, but it bounced off the rim onto the floor.

He was bending down to pick it up as the bathroom door opened and Cameron walked in, followed by Noah and some kid a year younger than us that everyone just called T. I didn't know what the T stood for. I didn't know much about the kid at all except that he was taller than me and hung out with Jason and Cameron and them. He probably attended the same summer camp for how to most effectively be a jerk.

Cameron's eyes fell on Deedee standing by the sink. Noah and T stood by the door. They made no move toward the bank of urinals or the stalls, and I could feel that spreading, hair-tickling tingle that's your body's way of telling you to pack up and go.

I looked at Deedee—a warning shot to suggest that he hurry up and finish drying his hands—then I walked past Cameron, squeezing between him and the wall.

Just make it to the door. That was the key. Just make it to the door and the hallway and the rush of other kids headed to lunch and the occasional wandering glance of a teacher and the chance to blend back into the crowd. But as soon as I took another step, Noah Kyle stepped in front of me, blocking my way. He actually crossed his arms, pulling a page right out of the Hollywood thug handbook.

"Excuse me," I said, hoping to strike a tone that was polite but also a little threatening, but Noah acted like he couldn't even hear me. I tried to sidestep him, but he matched my movement, continuing to block the door. I looked back over my shoulder. Behind me Deedee stood his ground, the used paper towel bunched in his hands, his *Lord of the Rings* lunch box still sitting on the edge of the sink. Cameron stood in front of him, between us, blocking Deedee's way. He held out his hand.

"All right, Aardvark. Let's have it."

It was a name they'd used before. Close enough to Advik to supposedly be funny, though I never heard anyone but them laugh at it, ever. They also called him Apu sometimes, because it was the only other Indian name they knew—sometimes that would get a giggle. There'd already been one sticky note telling

Deedee to get back to the Kwik-E-Mart this week. Probably left by one of these guys.

Cameron snapped his fingers, then opened his hand again, right in Deedee's face.

Deedee handed over the used paper towel. Cameron swatted it to the floor.

"Not that, dumbass. Your good-luck charm. Your little geek cube. Hand it over. I want to see it."

He meant the die. Deedee's special die.

Deedee flashed me a look. The meaning was obvious. *Oh crap*. That was a given. But also *How does he know?* Everyone knew that Wolf was a piano prodigy and that I wrote that one poem, but we had always kept that die to ourselves. Deedee's lips moved, his mouth working, but no sound came out.

"Just back off, Cameron, all right?" I took a step toward him, but as soon as I did, the kid named T came up behind me and put a hand on my shoulder. I shrugged it off, but it popped right back, squeezing this time. Everything seemed to be escalating much too quickly, veering out of control. At least out of *our* control.

"I just want to see it," Cameron said again. "You keep it in your pocket, don't you? I'm sure not going in after it."

The boys behind me laughed. "He'd probably like it," Noah said.

263

"Probably," Cameron said, keeping his eyes on Deedee. "Just like his friend. *Et tu*, Patel?" T still had his claws dug into my arm. I could get free, if I wrenched hard enough, but I hadn't figured out the step after that. If Wolf were here, it might be different. We'd at least be even. But as it stood it was three against two. If Deedee and I even counted as two. "C'mon. I just want to see if it's true. Then I'll let you go."

Deedee looked at me and I nodded. Sometimes it was just easier to give them what they wanted. Usually it was just a laugh at your expense. That's probably all this was too. Deedee dipped two trembling fingers into his front pocket and fished out his ebony die with the gold-emblazoned dragon on it. He held it up.

"There," he mumbled. "Happy?"

He went to stuff it back in, but Cameron snatched it from Deedee's hands and took it between his thumb and forefinger, holding it up to the dull halogen lights, catching its reflection in the dingy mirror. He shook his head.

"Can you believe this?" He turned and showed the die to his friends, the ones I could hear breathing behind me. Deedee made a move to snatch it back, quicker than I would have thought him capable of, but Cameron cupped it in his fist and pulled it away.

"You've seen it, all right. Now give it back." Deedee's face burned. I looked at the reflection of the door in the mirror, thinking somebody was bound to come in and break this up any second now. More likely they would see what was happening and then turn the other way, but even that might be enough. Times like this, a kind of spell seems to take hold and you feel like time has stopped for everyone but you. Unfortunately the door stayed closed.

"Seriously, Cameron. Just give him the die back," I said, trying to keep my voice steady. Cameron exchanged looks with his two buddies, some predetermined signal. He took a step toward one of the closed stalls.

"Is it true that you actually roll this thing to make decisions?" he asked.

"Who told you that?" Deedee said through a shuddering breath. I could tell he was doing his best to hold it together. Begging or crying would just encourage them. He could run. That was an option. T wasn't holding on to his shoulder. Deedee could bolt for the door and maybe slip past Noah Kyle, go find a teacher or something, but he just stood there watching Cameron's hand.

Cameron ignored Deedee's question. "So, what?" he said. "I pick a number and if it comes up, then that's what I do?" He kicked the stall door open. "All right. Let's try it. I'll roll. If it comes up evens, I'll flush this thing down the toilet, doing you a favor. Giving you the freedom to grow up and start making your own decisions for a change. But if it's odds . . ." He turned and grinned at his friends. "If it's odds, we'll have to try something else."

The boy behind me laughed again. Noah said, "He's probably small enough to fit." Deedee held his stomach with both hands and bit hard into his upper lip. He looked at me, desperate. I'd had enough.

I wrenched my arm free with a painful jerk and took a step toward the stall where Cameron was standing. "All right. Freaking hilarious, like always. Now just give him his stupid die back."

I didn't get more than two steps before Noah and the boy named T teamed up, each of them taking an arm now, trapping me between them. Deedee still stood by the sink, paralyzed. "Please don't," he croaked, but Cameron ignored him.

"So how about it? Evens or odds?" And without waiting for Deedee to answer, Cameron tossed the ten-sided die against the wall. Deedee suddenly came back to life, collapsing to all fours and scrabbling across the filthy bathroom tiles, but Cameron crouched down and grabbed his shirt, pulling him backward. The die rebounded and spun for a moment before settling down, dragon side up.

"That's a one, isn't it?"

Deedee didn't say anything. Just stayed there on his hands and knees.

"Not your lucky day, I guess."

Cameron lifted Deedee up the by armpits, locking his arms and dragging him toward the bathroom stall. I couldn't see Deedee's face, but I could hear him pleading, breathless. "Please don't, Cameron. Please don't. Please, please, please . . ."

"Not my call," Cameron laughed. "The die has spoken."

I couldn't help but think of how many times one of us had used that exact phrase.

There was the sound of scuffling feet, of Deedee kicking the walls of the bathroom stall. I tried to wrench my arms free, grunting with the effort, but the other two held tight. Deedee screamed just as the bathroom door swung open, then squeaked closed. The grips on my arms slackened as the two kids holding me twisted around, twisting me with them.

Rose stood in the doorway, leaning against the frame, periwinkle eyes taking everything in. She let out a low whistle. The other two boys let go of me and I took a cautious step toward her.

Cameron stood halfway in the stall, arms still wrapped around Deedee. "This is the men's room. You're not supposed to be in here," he said.

"If it's really a men's room then neither are you." Rose smiled, almost daring him to laugh. Or maybe daring him not to. I'd seen that look before. "Let go of him," she demanded.

I had said the same thing less than a minute before, of

course, but I wasn't Rose Holland. She was taller than all of them, her face taut, lower lip tucked under her top teeth, and I realized this was the first time I'd ever seen her really, truly angry.

Cameron unwound his arms and pushed Deedee away, nearly running him into the bay of sinks on the other side of the room.

"We were just playing a game," he said. "We made a little bet. He owes me."

Rose glanced at me. I shook my head. "He was about to dunk him," I said. "He stole Deedee's die." She turned back to Cameron, glaring.

Cameron shrugged and gave Deedee's ten-sider a kick, causing it to skitter into a corner. "Whatever. The dweeb can keep it. We're leaving anyway." He took a step toward the door.

Rose didn't budge. "Not yet you're not."

Cameron froze, only a few feet away from her. Obviously he hadn't factored Rose Holland into the equation when he followed Deedee and me into the bathroom, but he wasn't going to back down either. "You're going to stop us from walking out that door? You're a girl . . . loosely speaking," he added. Noah snickered.

"A girl who's strong enough to knock your teeth out. . . . Loosely speaking."

Noah stopped laughing. Cameron thought about it for a

second, swallowed hard and thick, it seemed, then blew her off with a wave of his arm. "I'm not going to fight you, if that's what you're thinking. I wouldn't hit a girl. Even one like you."

Rose shrugged. "Fine. Then since you are in the mood to make bets, how about you and I make one. If you win, I'll let you dunk all three of us. But if I win, you have to walk around school with a note stuck to your shirt the whole day that says whatever I want it to."

Deedee looked at me and sniffed. Cameron and his friends exchanged glances. I tried to catch Rose's eye and ask her *what the heck do you think you're doing* with a carefully constructed facial expression, but she wouldn't take her eyes off of Cameron.

He shook his head. "You're kidding, right? That's the stupidest thing I ever heard."

Rose's voice was like steel. "Take the bet or take a swing. I'm good either way."

Deedee and I stood next to each other, looking from Rose to Cameron and back again. Possible she was bluffing, but I didn't think so.

"She's nuts, man. Let's just go," T said, but he didn't move. He couldn't. Rose was blocking the door. There was absolutely no chance of squeezing by. Not without her permission.

"I'm serious. You want to walk out of here, you take the bet. Otherwise we just end it right now." She looked down at her black boots, the toes scuffed gray. I wondered if she'd ever kicked anyone with those boots before.

Cameron clearly didn't think she was bluffing either.

"All right. Fine. Whatever," he said, mustering the necessary bravado to save face with his friends. "You want to roll the geek's stupid little die again?"

Rose shook her head. "No dice. This is Branton," she said smugly. "There's only one way to settle a bet around here, right?"

"The Gauntlet? Are you crazy?"

The three of us were sitting on a bench outside the cafeteria. Deedee was still shaking, the snot crusting over on his shirt sleeve. After Cameron and his friends left—only after Rose stepped aside and agreed to *let* them go—Deedee collapsed to the bathroom floor by the trash can and started sobbing. Rose knelt down and wrapped an arm around him, whispering, "It's all right," over and over. I picked up his die and put it in his hand, but he just grunted and threw it across the room, where it ricocheted off one of the urinals. It took a few minutes for him to calm down enough to stand up and leave the restroom, enough time for two other boys to come in, one of them at least having the kindness to ask if we wanted him to get help. Rose thanked him and told him everything was fine, she had it under control. Then she got a wet paper towel and helped Deedee wipe his face.

We found the bench in the hall and put Deedee between us, propping him up on both sides. We were already ten minutes late to lunch, but it didn't matter. Wolf wasn't here and Bench was sitting somewhere else. There was nobody else who cared if we showed up or not.

"We should just go tell Wittingham," I said. "Forget this stupid bet thing. I mean, have you even *seen* the Gauntlet? There's no way. It's nuts. Totally nuts. This is insane."

I was talking quickly, I realized. I wasn't as shaken up as Deedee, but then I wasn't the one who'd been dragged into the stall either.

Rose, on the other hand, seemed unfazed. "It can't be any worse than having your head stuck in a toilet."

"But if you lose, then we are all going to have our heads stuck in the toilet," I said.

"I'm not going to lose."

"You don't know that," I said.

"Neither do you," she countered. "Besides, telling the principal won't work. Trust me. This kind of thing happened at my old school all the time. You report it and it becomes your word against theirs. Maybe they get suspended, but probably not. Maybe you get blamed too. Doesn't matter. Either way, it'll probably end up the same as before. Or worse."

"It's not like that here," I insisted.

271

"It's like that everywhere," Rose said. "This isn't my first rodeo."

I shut up, remembering what she'd said before, about what it had been like for her in Chicago. Dozer—the bull was implied. I wondered how many times she'd been where Deedee was now, sitting on a bench, blurry eyed and trembling. Wondered if she ever had people on either side of her, holding her up, or if she had always had to sit up by herself.

"What if he doesn't even show?" I asked. Half of me suspected that Cameron only agreed to the bet to get out of the restroom before things got messy, before he found himself on his knees, looking for a missing tooth beneath the sink.

"Then he loses. But don't worry, he'll show," Rose insisted. "Word will get around. He knows what people will say if he doesn't. You said yourself, the Gauntlet is the place where scores are settled."

"It's the place where bones are broken," I amended. "And there's no way you're going to make it all the way down. It's impossible."

"I don't have to make it all the way down," Rose said. "I just have to make it farther than he does."

Sitting between us Deedee sucked up a noseful of snot. He looked hopefully up at Rose. "If you do win, what are you going to write on the note?"

"First things first. I have to win," she said. "Which means there's one thing we've got to take care of."

My stomach lurched. "Oh God. Please tell me you know how to ride a bike."

"Of course I know how to ride a bike," Rose scoffed. "I just don't happen to *own* one."

THE RUN

NOTES WEREN'T EXACTLY NEW. DESPITE WHAT DEEDEE MIGHT THINK, he didn't invent them as a form of communication. I bet Ancient Egyptian schoolchildren shuffled little bits of papyrus back and forth, scratched up with hieroglyphics poking fun at the pharaoh. The Founding Fathers probably passed around bits of parchment with a poll on them: *On a scale of one to five, how cool are you with the current tax on tea?* I could see Shakespeare passing a note to some girl—or boy—with checkboxes that asked, "Art thou besmitten with me" or "Art thou *besmitten with me*-besmitten with me."

My parents used to pass each other notes back in high school. Afterward they wrote letters. They went to the same college right after graduation, but about halfway through my mother transferred to a community college closer to home so she could help take care of her father, Grandpa Steve, who had a stroke. During those two years my parents saw each other every other weekend, but they filled the spaces in between with writing. There was no Skype, no texts or Instagram, only email. And yet my father insisted on pen and paper, on the minty-bitter taste of envelope glue. Mom once told me that she thought Dad was an excellent writer—the thing he was best at, really—and if it weren't for those letters she probably wouldn't have hung around. Dad's words wheedled their way into her heart and got stuck there.

When they got married there was no need to write to each other anymore. And when my father finally did go far enough away, they had nothing left to say, except *How's Eric?* And *Have you mailed the check yet?*

I sometimes wonder where those letters got to—the ones from college. Maybe Dad took them with him and they are stashed in some dilapidated shoe box in the corner of his closet. Maybe my mother recycled them along with credit card offers and coupons for takeout Chinese.

It makes you wonder where they *all* go, all the letters and notes, the thank-you cards and the birthday invitations, the little missives scrawled along the edges of grocery lists, the doodles on the cardboard backs of spiral-bound notebooks. All those messages, so important, so pressing, so necessary.

Maybe Wolf's right and they never really disappear. Even after they're crumpled and thrown away, they linger and become ghosts. Not the kind that hide up in the attic rattling your shutters, but the kind that follow you wherever you go, coming back to you like an echo, like when something leaves a bad taste in your mouth. I don't know if that's guilt or regret. My father would probably be able to tell me. My mom too.

I *do* know that in the heat of the moment, people will say things that they haven't thought through, things they don't really mean. The words come from somewhere deep in the chest and take the first turnoff, bypassing the brain and heading directly for the mouth, and only afterward do you realize what a gonzo mistake you've made.

Like . . . I don't know . . . making a stupid bet that is probably going to get you killed.

It was decided—through the passing of stealth sticky notes, of course—that Rose Holland and Cameron Cole would run the Gauntlet at five that same afternoon, only a week after Evan Smalls bruised his shoulder, sprained his ankle, and busted up his bike. It seemed too soon, too little time to prepare, but there was a threat of rain at the end of the week, which would only make the Gauntlet more treacherous. Besides, as Cameron was heard mentioning to his friends in the hall, this time of year was prime moose-hunting season.

It was also decided—after some debate—that Rose would borrow my bike. Wolf's had been broken since the summer, busted chain, and Deedee's was too small even for him, a twenty-incher that his parents hadn't realized he'd grown out of yet. If Rose tried to ride that little Schwinn, she'd look like one of those tricycle-riding clowns at the circus. My bike was old, but at least it was almost the right size.

I only knew one person who owned a new bike. A black-and-gold Diamondback, twenty-four speed. It was Bench's Christmas present last year. But as soon as I mentioned it, Deedee's face turned green.

"No," he said. "We're not asking Bench."

I opened my mouth to ask why, but then I realized. Because Cameron Cole knew about Deedee's die. Which meant somebody had to have told him. Maybe that someone wasn't Bench. Maybe it trickled down from somebody else. Like a game of telephone, whispered from ear to ear, jumping from text to text. It didn't matter. Deedee was convinced that Bench had blabbed.

"You don't know for sure that he said anything," I said, but Deedee shook his head again and looked at Rose.

"Your bike will be fine," she told me.

"In fact," Deedee added, "I hope he doesn't even come."

That seemed too much to ask. The moment Cameron agreed to the bet, word spread like pinkeye, working its way through the underground channels. The first showdown of the year: Cameron Cole versus Rose Holland. There had been a couple of solo runs, like Evan's, but no head-to-heads. Add to that that this was the first run between a girl and a guy in the history of the hill, and only the fourth time a girl had tried to run the Gauntlet ever, and it became plain as white toast that anyone who could sneak out of the house and make it to Hirohito Hill would be there to watch.

Everyone but Wolf. He hadn't been at school and Rose asked me not to call him. "I already know what he's going to say. It's best if he doesn't even know."

It wasn't my call. It was my bike, sure, and Deedee's honor, but it was Rose's bet and Rose's body—her bruises and potentially broken bones. She didn't want Wolf there for whatever reason, so I didn't call. That didn't mean he wouldn't find out, of course. But maybe he wouldn't find out in time to try to stop her.

We met outside my house after school and I brought out Rose's ride, a ten-year-old Huffy, once painted red, now looking more like rust. My mother snagged it for twenty bucks at a garage sale.

Deedee had a can of barbecue Pringles in hand, munching nervously. "Oh. *Now* you bring them," I said.

Rose ran her hand along the frame of my bike. "We'll have to raise the handlebars," she said. "I'll need to steer. And raise the seat too."

"You won't need to raise the seat," I told her. "You won't even need to pedal. It's got eighteen speeds, but you won't need any of them." The Gauntlet only had two speeds: way too fast and abrupt stop. "Steering is all that matters. And balance." I thought about Bench's formula for making it down the Gauntlet. "And not letting go."

"And faith," Deedee added.

"You need to relax," Rose said, looking at Deedee and pointing to the can of chips. "What's the worst that could happen?"

I didn't want to say, but as Captain Dramatic handed over the Pringles, he immediately launched into a lecture on the history of the Gauntlet and its storied atrocities. "The *worst* that can happen? Let's see. In oh-four, Jimmy 'Breaker' Beeker earned his nickname on the hill. Compound fracture. The bone sticking out, blood-black gore and everything. And in oh-eight some kid named Carlos from another school nearly lost an eye to a tree branch. He had to have surgery and wore a patch for three months. Everyone calls him Cap'n now. And supposedly thirty years ago, a kid who lived in the neighborhood near the bottom actually *died*."

Rose stopped, hand stuck in the can of chips. "Are you serious?" She looked at me. "Is he serious?"

"He didn't die going down the hill," I corrected. "He had leukemia. He passed away in the hospital. Kids just tell that story to scare other kids."

"I'm telling you what I heard," Deedee insisted. I took a moment to appreciate the irony. This is how we got in this mess to begin with. People telling other people what they heard.

"First to die while biking down a hill. Not a record I want." Rose straddled my bike. It still looked too small for her. She was a real-life Goldilocks. Nothing quite fit, but she didn't let it deter her. She steered the bike down the driveway and Deedee and I watched her pedal up and down the street a few times, looking not-too-wobbly. Then she asked us to stand out in the middle of the road and pretend to be trees so she could practice weaving in between us.

"No," Deedee said. "I don't want to be a tree."

"Do you want your head stuck in a toilet?" Rose fired back.

The toilets in the boys' bathrooms were cleaned once at the end of the day and by then the smell was beyond atrocious. There was a reason somebody put a sticky note on one stall that read *Now Entering Chernobyl, Population 0.* It was not the kind of bath you ever wanted to take.

We took our places in the street and I closed my eyes as Rose whipped past. Her green jacket brushed against me, but that was as close as she got to knocking me over. She maneuvered around us half a dozen times, only riding over Deedee's foot once. He was almost positive she broke it, but that was just Deedee being Deedee.

Afterward the three of us sat in my garage and finished off the chips. I felt a little better. Rose had shown that she was capable of consistently maneuvering between two trees. Or at least two humans posing as trees. On a straight, level, paved road. Going five miles an hour.

There was a chance she would survive. I sucked the red barbecue powder from my fingertips.

"You know what this is like?" Deedee said as Rose funneled the crumbs from the can into her mouth. "*Game of Thrones*. Like when you have a trial by combat and you get to choose your champion. That's exactly what this is."

"Your parents let you watch *Game of Thrones*?" Rose asked. I couldn't tell if she was impressed or appalled. Maybe she was just jealous.

"Of course not," Deedee said. "But I got the books from a used bookstore and I read them late at night while my parents are asleep."

I smiled. This kind of deviousness surprised me coming from him. "And how is this anything like *Game of Thrones*?" I asked.

"Well, in the books if you're accused of something, like poisoning a king or stabbing your cousin, you can call for a trial by combat to defend your honor. But you don't have to do it yourself. You can choose the person who will fight for you."

"And you chose me," Rose said, smiling. She reached over to punch Deedee playfully, leaning over me. Her hair smelled like coconuts.

"Technically you volunteered," I corrected.

"And how does it usually turn out? This trial by combat?" Rose asked.

Deedee scratched his head. "Honestly? Somebody gets their head smashed in."

We all let that thought sink in. Deedee forced a smile. "It's pretty good stuff, though," he added. "Really bloody."

I asked if I could borrow the books when he was done.

At 4:35 we started our quiet walk to the hill. I volunteered to push the bike, saying Rose should save her strength, get focused, or whatever it was people did before they plummeted to their death. We passed a gas station and Deedee insisted on stopping and getting a pint of milk. "For when you win," he said. "Like in the Indy 500." Rose said okay, as long as it was chocolate. In the end she ended up drinking it on the way to wash down the barbecue chips.

Up ahead you could see the outline of Hirohito Hill peaking above the houses like a green sunrise. A couple of kids from BMS passed us riding their own bikes. I saw one of them point and say, "There she is. *That's* Rose Holland."

"You're famous," I said.

"I'm infamous. There's a difference."

We cut through the last neighborhood and across the field, past the fence through the gate that was never locked. You could already see the crowd forming at the top, half the school, it seemed, an even bigger crowd than turned out for Evan's run, everyone bundled in jackets, huddled in groups. I didn't see Bench, but that didn't mean he wasn't in the crowd somewhere.

Looking at the tree-studded slope, I felt a heaviness. Part of it was just dread, recognizable from my first day of school or the moment in the bathroom leading up to this, but there was something else. A sense of significance. It felt like the kind of thing that you might even tell your children about when they asked you what it was like growing up. I'd never had a friend run the Gauntlet before.

A friend.

Rose Holland was about to risk everything for us. For Deedee and me. Suddenly, overlapping the dread and the weightiness, came stomach-worm-squirming guilt for not telling someone. The principal. My mother. Deedee's parents. I'd convinced myself that Rose was right. This was how you handled things. You didn't go to the adults. You sucked it up and made outlandish bets about who could make it down a hill on a bike without killing themselves.

She said this was the only way to settle it.

Maybe. Maybe, if she won, it would mean more than just saving us from a dunking. Maybe Cameron and his friends would learn something. The embarrassment. Just the thought of it, of all the kids he'd picked on—that they'd all picked on—laughing at whatever it was that Rose forced him to wear around school the next day.

Trouble with that was, I wasn't sure she was going to win. Nobody had ever died running the Gauntlet, but the rest of the stories Deedee told about it were true. Some of the trees held the carved initials of the riders they had taken out, chiseled reminders of how dangerous it was. I was on the verge of telling her not to go through with it. We would find another way to deal with Cameron Cole.

But I didn't have to.

Standing there, at the bottom of the hill between us and the summit, hands stuffed in the pockets of his brother's hand-me-down leather jacket, Wolf squinted and frowned at us. He'd been waiting. Somehow or another he'd found out. He walked right up to me and grabbed the handlebars of the bike—my bike—and wheeled it around, heading back the other way without a word.

"Wolf. Wait," Deedee called. "What are you doing? We *need* that."

"No you don't," Wolf said over his shoulder.

I thought about all the kids up on top of the hill, wondered if they were watching us, and if so, what they were thinking. That Rose Holland had taken one long look at the Gauntlet and wussed out, probably. That she was chicken.

"Hold up," Deedee pleaded, Rose and I following behind. "Don't you know what's happening?"

Wolf stopped and spun. "Don't *you* know what's happening?" he said, looking at all of us. "What were you even thinking?" He was mad again. Just like he'd been in English the day before. It seemed, by his stare, that his last question was leveled directly at Rose. It took her a moment to say anything. She draped an arm around Deedee's shoulders.

"I'm his champion," she said. "I'm defending his honor." She said it half jokingly, but Wolf didn't even crack a smile.

"I heard about what happened in the bathroom," Wolf said, looking first at Deedee, then at Rose. "I know what this is about. But I'm telling you it's not worth it."

"And I say it is," Rose countered, grabbing hold of the seat of the bike so Wolf couldn't drag it any farther. "I'm sick of what those pricks do to Deedee and Frost and you and everyone else and I want to see Cameron Cole eat dirt, all right?"

Wolf let go of the handlebars and Rose let the bike fall to the ground. We stood in a circle around it, all four of us, but it was obvious this conversation was just between the two of them now.

"You can't stop me," Rose said.

"I could call your dad."

She shook her head. "By the time he gets free from work and gets out here I'll be down that stupid hill already. And it would take my mother half an hour just to get dressed and find her car keys. Face it, Wolf, in five minutes I'm going to ride down that hill. Now you can either stay and support me and be there when I screw up and crack my head open, or you can turn around and go home and pretend like this has nothing to do with you. But decide now, because I'm taking that bike and I'm riding down that stupid freaking hill."

Wolf stood over the bike, trembling. He looked up at all the people waiting at the top. "It won't solve anything," he said. "You know that."

"Maybe," Rose said. "But it will mean something to me. And it will mean something to Deedee." She looked over at Deedee, who nodded. "And maybe, if we're lucky, it will send a message."

"If we're *lucky*," Wolf said, "we won't have to call for an ambulance."

"That too." Rose leaned in close to Wolf, so close that their chapped cheeks almost touched. "I need to do this. I know you understand."

Wolf bent down and picked my bike up. For a moment I was certain he was going to keep walking away, but then he aimed it back toward the top of the hill. "I don't *even* believe you."

"Just so long as you believe *in* me."

Had either of us said it, Deedee or me, it would have been gag-worthy, but coming from Rose it was different. We didn't laugh or make fake vomit sounds. We just stood there for a moment, the four of us, looking at each other. "All right," Wolf said.

Slowly, silently, we trudged up the less-steep side of Hirohito Hill, Wolf and Rose leading the way, Deedee and me walking behind, the crowd parting for us the same way they'd parted for Rose her first day at school. At the front of the pack of kids clustered at the top, Cameron stood next to his bike, staring at the slope, looking uneasy. Noah Kyle stood on one side. Jason Baker stood on the other. Jason and Wolf exchanged loaded glances, then Wolf quickly looked away. The crowd was library quiet, nothing but indistinct murmurs, all of them huddled in one large mass to break the wind that had picked up, threatening to topple the bikes where they stood. Rose walked over to Cameron, and for a moment I hoped she would just deck him and get it over with, just knock him to the cement-hard ground. Instead she extended her hand.

"We have a deal. Whoever makes it the farthest," she said.

"Yeah, whatever," Cameron said. He waved off her handshake and spit on the ground by her boots. Rose didn't budge.

"Say it," she pressed.

"Fine. We have a deal," Cameron said. "I can't wait to see if your fat head even fits in the toilet." Cameron's friends laughed, but you could tell they were nervous. Maybe just as nervous as I was. I doubted it though.

Rose walked back and stood between Wolf and me. "So what do you think? Good day for a ride?" She looked at the rustling leaves. The wind would be at her back so she'd go even faster. Lucky her.

I looked down Hirohito's worst side. It had only been a week since I'd last stood there, but it looked different this time. The trees had started shedding in earnest, making for a few skeleton limbs that threatened to reach down and snatch an unwitting rider from her bike or snag the back of her ratty old army coat and yank her backward. It looked steeper too, almost straight down. I tried to carve out a path with my eyes, but there was no clear line of sight to the bottom of the hill. Everywhere you looked were branches and bark. I noticed a broken beer bottle that had been smashed against one tree, its dark brown glass glinting in the indifferent October sun. A red glove stuck out of the leaves about a quarter of the way down. I wondered who it once belonged to.

"Yeah . . . you really don't have to go through with this," I said as Rose threw one leg over my bike. The hill beckoned with rows of forty-foot teeth.

"You're not worried about me, are you, Frosty?" Rose shot me a sneaky kind of smile. "You're too cool to worry, I thought."

"I'm not worried," I said. "I just agree with Wolf. It's not really going to prove anything."

"Sure it is," she said. "It's going to prove that a moose can ride a bike. Besides, sometimes you just have to shut up and *do* something, you know?" She turned and looked at Deedee. "Wish me luck." Deedee nodded. He looked like he was about to lose his Pringles in the grass by his feet.

Rose turned to Wolf and reached out with one hand. He took it and squeezed.

"All right," she said. "Let's show these kids what a ninja sorcerer princess from Chicago can do."

Cameron pulled his bike in beside Rose's, close enough that he could reach out and push her over if he wanted. The crowd closed in behind. I thought I saw crumpled dollar bills being passed around. Not unusual, but it made me wonder what the odds were. No doubt Rose was the underdog. This was the first time she'd ever even *seen* the hill.

"She's never going to make it," Deedee whispered beside me.

"She's going to make it," I said.

She wasn't going to make it. It was a matter of physics. Too much speed. Too many trees. She was a rookie. It wasn't even her bike. Of course I didn't think Cameron would make it either. So then it would simply come down to who crashed first.

Noah Kyle stepped up between the two of them and raised both of his arms into the air, holding them there for several seconds, just to build suspense, then brought them down like twin ax blades.

Both bikes tilted forward, each taking only one push before the Gauntlet swallowed them whole.

There wasn't a crowd when my father made his run. The one that would take him all the way to Florida. Nobody came to wish him good luck. He'd already said good-bye to the people at the magazine he wrote for, and most of the neighbors were so clearly on my mother's side that there was no real point in saying good-bye.

In fact, my mother tried to argue for the two of us not being around when he left either, saying it would be too hard, that it would complicate matters. If it were up to her, Dad would have snuck away in the middle of the night, maybe standing in the doorway of my bedroom while I slept, watching the rise and fall of my chest like a tide sweeping in and out, maybe whispering something to me, a line from a poem (Frost, of course), or just an *I love you*, hoping to say it just loud enough to wake me but not. Then he would vanish.

But my mother didn't get her way, and I got to be there when he left, packing up the last of his portion of the loot. My father insisted he didn't need much. It all fit in the back of the SUV. Mostly books and clothes. The laptop computer and the smaller television. His baseball mitt that he used when he taught me how to catch. The box that I painted him for Father's Day when I was five. His collection of ball caps. The SUV was stuffed to the tinted windows, spilling over into the passenger seat, but it didn't matter. He wasn't taking any passengers.

There were no tears either. There had been enough of those. There had been a dozen conversations and explanations—none of which I remember because I didn't believe any of them. Probably he said something about two people realizing they simply weren't right for each other. Undoubtedly he said something about loving me no matter what. More than twenty times I was told that it was absolutely not my fault that he was leaving. Which meant it was all their fault. Which meant I could just be mad at them instead.

And I was. Angry enough that I told myself I wasn't going to hug him or say good-bye or even open my mouth. I was going to clench my teeth and jut my chin and narrow my eyes and just stare so that he would know it. That was my plan, anyway. The plan of a ten-year-old who knows he can't get what he wants.

Dad said good-bye to my mother, actually giving her a kiss on the cheek. She told him to drive safe and to text her when he got down there. Then he sat down next to me on the porch.

"It's twenty-five hours by car, but only three by plane," he said. "And it's just a couple months until summer break and then your mother will let you fly down. There's a place where you can actually swim with stingrays. Touch them and everything."

Teeth clenched. Chin jutted. Eyes narrowed.

Dad ruffled my hair, then took the Tigers cap off his head—the one that he'd had since college—and put it on mine. It was way too big and covered the tips of my ears. I didn't move. I didn't take it off. I was a statue.

But when he wrapped his arms around me, something inside collapsed, crumbled like a tower made of wet sand. My hands shot around him and clenched fistfuls of his shirt, hot face buried in his chest, pressing close and tight so I could barely breathe, wanting to burrow as far in as I could go. And we sat there like that on the porch for what seemed like an hour. Long enough for my mother to go back inside. Long enough for me to remember how it felt to have him breathing next to me.

He waited for me to let go. I had to be the one. But as soon as I loosened my grip just a little, he pulled away. Then he stood up and looked one last time at the house we'd lived in for most of my life. He told me good-bye and I love you and we'll talk soon, all the things you're supposed to say. And I went back to clenching my teeth as the truck drove off, absolutely positive that, at that very moment, I was the most miserable kid in the universe.

I sat and watched him go, even long after there was nothing more to look at. Then I went inside, slamming the door behind me, loud enough, I hoped, for everyone in the world to hear.

I could barely watch her, pulling down the brim of my cap to half cover my eyes. The crowd erupted the moment they took off, both bikes instantly diverging, choosing different paths. You could see Rose struggling to maintain her balance, the front wheel wobbling over the uneven terrain, my old bike listing one way and then the other. And she hadn't even gotten to the middle of the hill yet, where the trees clumped even closer together. Most of the kids were hooting and hollering, incomprehensible grunts and shouts, but a few were calling out Cameron's name. Deedee had his hands in front of his eyes, splayed open like he was watching a horror movie. Wolf just had his fists clenched, but he was watching all the way.

A third of the way down, Rose brushed against the trunk of one tree, catching the right handlebar and wrenching her wheel around, sending her off course, or at least onto a new one. I felt sure she was going to wipe out right there, but she somehow recovered, adjusting to the new trajectory, instantly rebuilding her speed. Cameron was ahead of her. He seemed to have found a fairly well-worn path—maybe he had planned the route ahead of time—and it made all the difference. If Rose bit it now, she'd lose for sure. I tried not to think about what the boys' toilets smelled like, the ring of brown and yellow crust along the rims. Tried not to imagine the cold water on my lips, up my nose, in my hair.

The crowd around me started calling Cameron's name louder. I don't know that they were friends of his, particularly. Friends' friends. Or maybe it was just that he was in the lead. In middle school, all other things being equal, you side with the kid who has the best chance of winning. In front of me Deedee had given up on his finger slats and buried his face completely in his hands. "I can't watch," he murmured.

I couldn't not.

Beside me, Wolf was unshakable, pumping his fists, his cheeks pink from the wind. "C'mon, Rose! You can do it!" he shouted at the top of his lungs. Some of the kids standing next to us gave him looks. I didn't say anything. She probably couldn't even hear her name above the din of the other kids. Maybe she couldn't hear anything over the wind in her ears. I put my hands on top of my father's cap, holding it in place. Every muscle in my body tightened. "She's going to make it," Wolf said to no one in particular.

They were two-thirds of the way down the hill, both of them weaving, ducking beneath branches that threatened to clothesline them. Rose hit a bump and actually went airborne for an instant and I held my breath, hanging on to it, even after she landed. It was difficult to make out either bike through the colonnade of trees.

"Holy crap," Deedee whispered beside me, and I knew he was watching again. "I don't believe this."

I nodded. I'd never actually seen anyone make it this far before. Heard stories, but never actually *seen* it. They were almost to the bottom now. Both of them. This wasn't just a bet. It was an actual *race*. For the first time in Branton history two people could conquer the Gauntlet at the same time.

Then I saw the back of Cameron's black-and-red jacket suddenly rise into the air, for just a second, before it disappeared, swallowed by the green. The Gauntlet struck quickly, biting once, and dragging him into the dirt.

He was down.

Less than a second later, Wolf pointed.

"There she is!"

My blue Huffy shot through the wall of trees at the bottom of the hill at breakneck speed, its rider a mostly green splotch from this far away, jacket flapping behind her like a cape. The bike skidded sideways, sliding to a stop. The rider hopped off and thrust both fists into the air.

The crowd instantly shut up. Every mouth dropping open in disbelief.

Rose Holland—the Moose, the Dozer, the girl who took the empty seat at the table and made phoenixes shaped like fish and once told me that my mom was cool and that she liked my room—Rose Holland had conquered the Gauntlet.

I couldn't hear anything over the sound of my own cheering.

THE MESSAGE

IT TOOK THE REST OF US THREE TIMES AS LONG TO MAKE IT DOWN the hill. As we skidded and slid, grabbing hold of each other's jackets to keep our balance, Deedee wrapping both arms around me at one point, we passed a cluster of kids already huddled around Cameron, Noah and Jason among them.

I stopped to appreciate the damage. It wasn't the worst I'd seen, though he was clearly in pain—grimacing through skid marks of dirt on his face, a crown of leaves in his hair. Rose had given him a bloody nose just like she'd threatened, she'd just let a tree branch do it for her. A few gawkers took pictures with their phones. If I'd owned a phone I probably would have taken one too. Jason yelled at everyone to go away as he tried to help Cameron to stand. Most of the kids were passing right by him, though, heading down to the bottom. To Rose.

She stood in the center as a crowd circled around her, huddled up with Deedee and Wolf. Kids were taking pictures of her, too. Rose Holland. The conqueror. Deedee was bubbling over, blabbing away like a little kid who's just been to the movies, going on and on about how that was *the greatest thing he'd ever seen*, though he had only kept his eyes open for half of it. Wolf was speechless; he just held on to the bike like he was afraid it might take off without us.

"Thanks for the ride," Rose said as I pushed my way through the crowd.

"Thanks for not wrecking it," I said back. "And for, you know, making it to the bottom in one piece. That was . . ."

I didn't have the words to describe what it was. I usually had plenty of them, even if I seldom said them out loud, but this time I was at a loss.

"It was freaking *epic*!" Deedee said.

Wolf leaned up against her. "I still don't believe you," he said. "But it *was* pretty awesome."

We all basked for a moment in Rose's glow, in the admiring looks of the other students, some of whom had probably been chanting Cameron's name only minutes before. I couldn't help but think of Bench and the catch, and how he must have felt being lifted up and carried out of the end zone by his teammates. To be surrounded by people who suddenly see something spectacular in you—something they might have overlooked before. Deedee wrapped both arms around Rose and squeezed until his face turned purple.

I wasn't sure what had just happened, but I knew it was big.

The crowd around us slowly broke up, though Rose got an appreciative nod from Evan Smalls—for beating the Gauntlet, for beating Cameron, maybe for both. We walked around the base of the hill, Deedee pushing the bike now, as if he was her noble squire leading her steed, Wolf and Rose pressed so close together you could barely slip a sticky note between them. I walked a pace behind, glancing at everyone we passed, trying to read their expressions, figure out what they saw when they looked at us. Most of them were on their phones, probably texting about what had happened: *Rose Holland runs the Gauntlet, crushes Cameron Cole.* In five minutes the rest of the student body would know.

I looked back once to see Cameron limping in the opposite direction with his friends. The crest of Hirohito Hill was nearly empty now, but I caught one familiar face looking down at us, standing all by himself.

I put up a hand, more out of instinct than anything, and was happy to see Bench wave back.

By the time we got to my house, my mother was already there.

Even worse, she invited everyone for dinner.

This was after she asked us where'd we been, assuming that four kids walking home long after school let out were probably up to something. The other three looked at me. It was my mom, so whatever I coughed up, they would go with it.

"Study group," I told her. "For science. We have a quiz coming up on the laws of motion."

I don't know what possessed me to add the last part. Deedee sniggered, almost losing it completely. Rose just made it worse. "Newton's third law: For every action there is a reaction of equal or greater force," she added.

Like, you try to stick my friend's head in the toilet, I make you eat a tree and show you up in front of the whole school.

Mom seemed to buy it, at least. "You should all stay and eat," she said. "I can throw something together real quick." She kept her eyes on Rose as she spoke, as if she still couldn't believe there was an actual girl hanging out with us. For a second Rose looked like she was about to say yes, but both Wolf and Deedee had experienced my mother's cooking before.

"No, really, Mrs. Voss. I appreciate the offer," Wolf said. "But I should be getting home."

"Me too," Deedee seconded. Rose nodded along, looking disappointed.

"At least let me give you all a ride, then."

We piled into the Civic, Rose, Deedee, and Wolf squeezing into the back, giving the smallest member of our posse the wedgie seat. I watched them pressed tight, thinking of those cans of snakes that pop out when you pull off the lid, imagining them bursting through the windows. "Aren't we missing one?" Mom asked as she started the car. "Where's Bench?"

I couldn't give her a good answer if I'd wanted to. I imagined him still standing at the top of Hirohito Hill looking down on us. I wondered who he'd been rooting for. I didn't see him standing with Cameron and his friends. He hadn't been standing by us either, though. Had it been me running the Gauntlet, I know he would have been there, front and center, cheering me on. At least I wanted to believe it. "He's not in the same science class," Deedee said, which wasn't even the half of it.

I heard Rose whispering to Wolf in the backseat. It made me antsy, sitting in front, wanting so badly to twist around and keep talking about what had happened and instead biting my tongue with my mother right next to me. But she knew more about what was happening at BMS than she let on.

"So what's this I hear about sticky notes at school?" she

asked, taking her eyes off the road and putting them squarely on me. Those eyes were killer. The Eye of Sauron had nothing on my mother.

"What about the what now?" I mumbled, trying to sound only vaguely interested.

"Principal Wittingham sent out a recorded message this afternoon about a ban on sticky notes due to . . . how did he put it . . . a rash in hurtful and derogatory messages being spread around school. You all aren't involved in any of that, I hope."

I shook my head, playing innocent. *Involved? Us? Pfff.* The backseat was quiet.

My mother sighed with relief. "Good, because I work with Elizabeth Browner, and she said her daughter Caroline—you know Caroline?—apparently she came home yesterday absolutely beside herself, bawling over something somebody posted about her in the girls' locker room."

Caroline Browner. I knew her. She was a seventh grader. Popular, pretty. In other words, Deedee probably had her locker number memorized. I'd always assumed she was untouchable, the kind of girl who was above teasing. "What did it say?"

"Liz wouldn't tell me, but she said it was terrible. I swear, sometimes kids can be so cruel."

"Can't argue with you there, Mrs. Voss," Rose said from

between the seats. "But we can be sweet *some*times." Out of the corner of my eye I saw Wolf lean his head against the window, watching the world pass by, a twitch of a smile on his face.

"I just want to make sure you're okay," Mom said, glancing at me again. "That you're all okay," she added, looking in the rearview mirror.

"We're just fine," Wolf said. He sounded like he meant it, too.

We dropped him off first since he lived closest, and he and Rose whispered to each other again. I could see his parents through the bay window having a discussion—you could almost hear them through the glass. Wolf thanked my mother for the ride and said he'd see us all tomorrow, then he stood on his sidewalk for a moment, staring at the house, as if he didn't quite recognize it. My mother frowned, and for a second I thought she was going to roll down the window and tell Wolf to get back in the car and just come home with us, but Wolf adjusted the straps of his backpack and trudged up the driveway. I wondered if he'd go straight to the piano and try to drown his parents out or maybe hide away in the garage and finish his battleship. My mother shook her head and backed out, saying something about Wolf being such a good kid.

"Can't argue that either," Rose said.

We dropped Deedee off next and I watched him give Rose

another thank-you-for-saving-me-from-the-toilet hug. Mom turned to the backseat.

"You'll have to tell me how to get to your house, dear."

I still had no clue where Rose lived. I imagined an apartment complex, or one of those older, one-story houses across from the old bottling plant, judging by the secondhand clothes, the almost-empty lunch trays, and the things I'd heard people whisper about her in the halls about her parents, mostly how her mom didn't work and how they moved here because they couldn't afford Chicago anymore. Except as we turned down streets, following her directions, the houses only grew larger and the fences taller, till Rose told us we could stop and let her out. We sat at the end of a driveway leading up to a big wood-trimmed house with a white-columned porch and perfectly square-shaped hedges. You could just make out the cement lining of an in-ground pool in the backyard. Rose Holland's house was enormous.

"You sure you don't want me to pull all the way up?" Mom asked, probably wanting a better look.

"No, really. This is fine," Rose said. "Thanks for the ride, Mrs. Voss. See you in school tomorrow, Snowman," she said. The brightness of her voice had dimmed, the thrill of running the Gauntlet already starting to fade, I guess.

Or maybe, like Wolf, she simply wasn't all that happy to be home.

I rolled down my window to wave. "Hey. If you need help, you know, thinking of something for that writing assignment tomorrow, just let me know." I winked at her to make sure she got the message. She rolled her eyes.

"Don't worry," she said. "I'll think of something. Bye, Mrs. Voss. And thanks again for the bread the other day. It was delicious."

"I like that girl," Mom told me, still plenty loud enough for Rose to hear.

We waited until she'd disappeared up the winding driveway, then my mother seemed to inch her way along, marveling at the size of the houses we passed. "What do Rose's parents do again?"

"Her father works long hours," I said. "That's all I know."

But I knew a lot more than that. I also knew now that Rose Holland could afford brand-name clothes if she wanted. She could wear something besides tattered combat boots and that same old ratty jacket. She could probably carry a purse studded with *real* sapphires, and host parties on the weekend for people who actually went to parties. She could be a lot more popular, probably, if she wanted to. Could get people to pretend to like her, at least.

305

Instead she spent last Saturday saving us from a horde of zombies.

My mother sighed as she wound her way through Rose's neighborhood. "We used to have a house like this," she said.

That night, after a late dinner of leftover spaghetti that could stick to the roof of anything, I went to my room and prowled the feeds and walls and chat rooms, looking for a picture from the afternoon, hoping to catch one last glimpse of Cameron's bloody nose posted on some other kid's timeline, but I couldn't find anything. This was the Gauntlet, after all. You had to be careful about what you put online in case parents watched over your shoulder.

It was all right, though. Cameron Cole's punishment was far from over. He'd made the bet and he'd lost. I lay in bed wondering what Rose had in mind. Something horrible, I hoped. Something that would make him melt from embarrassment, wicked-witch-in-the-rain style. Something that would make him feel the way Deedee felt, watching his die roll across the filthy bathroom floor, scrabbling on his hands and knees after it.

Wolf was wrong when he said it wouldn't change anything. It *had* to change things. I could feel it already. Tomorrow the whole school would see what total losers Cameron and his friends were, and I, for one, couldn't wait.

Eventually I managed to fall asleep, dreaming of the possibilities, a paper phoenix under my pillow. No doubt a lean and hungry look on my face.

I woke up the next morning with a Christmasy feeling in my gut, eager to get to school.

Post-it notes were officially banned at BMS, of course, but a deal was a deal. If Rose had lost we'd all be sporting swirly wet mops of hair, our shirt collars damp with toilet water. But she didn't. Cameron smacked wood three-quarters of the way down Hirohito Hill and it was payback time.

He promised to wear it the whole day—Rose's note saying absolutely *anything* she wanted. So many delicious possibilities. On the bus ride in—sitting by myself—I wrote down some ideas, just in case she'd had a case of writer's block.

Beaten by a ninja sorcerer princess

Teachers, please don't make me sit, I just got my butt kicked

I'm docking punny becaud a twee bwoke my node

Or a big fat capital *L*. Just like the one that someone— maybe even Cameron—had left on my own locker a few days ago. I had a dozen suggestions by the time the bus pulled into school, ranging from clever pun to demoralizing put-down. I was a poet, after all. I had a way with words.

Turns out, she didn't need my help.

That's when I realized the true brilliance of Rose Holland.

The butter-yellow note was already stuck to Cameron's chest as he moped through the hall before first period, attached with a safety pin to make sure that it wouldn't "accidentally" fall off. I read what she'd written and shook my head in admiration.

It was perfect. Had it been anything else, it wouldn't have worked. Maybe Cameron would have refused to wear it. Or he would have worn it proudly, knowing the first teacher or administrator he saw would tell him to throw it away. Anything derogatory or insulting would have drawn too much attention, or the wrong kind of attention. But this was different—masterful in its simplicity. Maybe it wasn't an aphorism, but it spoke to a basic truth. And it was awesome.

Cameron walked through the school with his head down most of the day, sitting quietly in his classes in the corner. To my surprise, and probably everyone else's, including Rose, he kept his word. Literally. He never once took the note off. He didn't touch it, as if he were afraid the paper itself might burn him or something.

The teachers didn't say anything either, despite the fact they had a mandate to confiscate any note they found. But this one, they let slide. Maybe they had heard what had happened, or, if not, they made an educated guess. They couldn't see the bruises on Cameron's legs, but there was no mistaking the purple hue of his nose, like a squashed eggplant set between two bloodshot eyes. Maybe, they thought, the message was worth sharing, no matter who it was pinned to, after everything that had happened, after all the things they'd read. Whatever the reason, they let him wear it. And I relished every moment I passed him in the halls.

Until I saw him heading straight for Deedee's locker after the final bell. I tensed and looked for Rose but couldn't find her. Wolf was gone, too. Probably they were somewhere together. It was just Deedee and me all over again. I crossed the hall quickly, standing by his side. "Cameron," I whispered in Deedee's ear, nodding. Deedee's eyes exploded from his skull. Desperate, I even looked around for Bench. Instead all I found was Mr. Parker, one of the science teachers. At the very least I knew he would intervene if things got physical again—if Cameron tried to push us into the boys' restroom for the swirlies he felt he owed us.

The boy with the note on his chest stopped less than two feet from us and Deedee stepped even closer to me, his backpack held in front of him like a shield. The purple nose and painful-looking raspberries on his arms made Cameron look even more dangerous than usual. The day was over. All bets were off. Rose's note had humiliated him and now he was going to take it out on us.

He brought his hand up and Deedee flinched, expecting a

shove at least, but Cameron was just reaching for the note. He ripped it free of its pin and stuck it to Deedee's locker.

He didn't say a word. His face was wooden, no smiles, no grimaces, no leers. He just turned and walked away, leaving Rose's half-torn note hanging lopsided by one sticky corner for everyone in the hall to see.

I'm Sorry

Deedee peeled the note off and held it between us. His whole body shook with relief. "Looks like we won," he said.

I took Rose's note from him, rubbing my thumb over the words. "Yeah," I said. "Looks like it."

The war was over. I was sure of it. Deedee was sure of it.

But we were both wrong.

There was still one last message to be posted.

Whoever left it broke the rules, scrapping sticky notes for something stronger. There was no paper to peel off. Nothing that could be easily erased. This message was written in permanent marker, thick black lines that couldn't be missed.

There had been thousands of notes over the last week, so many you kind of grew numb to them. So many snide remarks. So many loaded looks. But this one was different—and it wasn't just the fact that it was scrawled in marker, filling half of the locker door. It was what was written underneath. It was a kind of code, but the meaning was absolutely clear.

I turned the corner the morning after the apology, and saw Wolf standing in front of his locker, an invisible barrier between him and the cluster of students surrounding him, watched him reach out and trace the black letters with one finger. He set his backpack slowly on the ground and took two steps back, his body rigid. He looked down the hall, cheeks flushed, eyes flashing as he spotted something. Or someone. I reached out to stop him, to say *something*, but he brushed past me, storming down the hall until he was face-to-face with the person he'd locked onto.

He grabbed Bench by his jacket and shoved him against the row of noteless lockers.

Bench hit with a hollow metalic thud. He didn't push back. If he'd wanted to, he could have put Wolf on the ground, arms pinned behind him. He was always the strongest of the four of us, but he didn't even try to pull Wolf's hands off.

"It wasn't me, Morgan. I swear," he said.

Morgan.

The sound of his own name—his real name—coming from Bench seemed to take Wolf by surprise.

"I don't even believe you," he said.

Bench looked over Wolf's shoulder to me. He was looking for help, I knew, but before I could do anything, Wolf let go and took off, bolting down the hall and out the back door of the school, leaving his backpack beside his locker, with its parting shot written in all caps for everyone to see.

THE CONFESSION

THE WAR DIDN'T END WITH AN APOLOGY. IT ENDED WITH SOMETHING else. A phrase that somebody had cooked up and started passing around. An inside joke that didn't stay inside for long. Even if you didn't know what it meant, you could probably ask the person next to you and they would tell you. Or you could figure it out from the way Wolf dropped his bag and pushed Bench up against the wall, escaping through the back door before anyone could stop him.

One last message on locker B78, in permanent marker that couldn't be scrubbed off, that would have to be painted over in order to cover it completely.

TOTAL ROMAN

Nothing. Almost nothing. Nonsense. Except it wasn't.

Because words don't always mean the same thing to everyone. Because their meanings can change. And because word gets around.

And because this wasn't the first time.

I told you I knew how the war began and how it ended. I told you it began with Ruby Sandels, but that wasn't true either. It started long before that.

It starts the moment people see you for the very first time. Standing on the corner. Waiting in line. Walking down the hall. They get an idea in their heads. Maybe it's because of your shoes or your haircut or the kind of phone you have. Maybe it has to do with the neighborhood you're from, what team you're on, whose side you take. Whether you look at the other person the right way or even look at them at all. Whether you are too small or too big or too just-right. Maybe you like the wrong kinds of movies. Maybe you're in the wrong kinds of clubs. Maybe you're just the easiest target.

It starts on a day in early September, a little over a year ago. The beginning of seventh grade. Still warm enough to dash out and check the mailbox in bare feet but cool enough that you tucked your hands into your sleeves while waiting for the bus. Me and Wolf, sitting in the locker room before gym, getting changed. A couple of kids we hardly know look over and see us looking back at them without their shirts on. One of them says to Wolf, "What're you lookin' at, homo?" The other laughs.

That's it. A word. A nudge. I don't think much of it. I'd been called the same for even less. I can't even remember who said it that day, whether it was Jason or Cameron. It could have been either of them. It could have been anybody. Wolf looks down at the tiled floor, then over at me as if to say, *Can you believe those guys?* And I shrug, as if to say, *Just forget it.*

And I did. But Wolf didn't. Because sometimes words are like shadows. They follow you around.

It doesn't take much. A poem. A catch. A glance. A roll of the dice. And it doesn't matter what's true and what isn't. Doesn't matter what you think you know about yourself. The things you have the guts to tell people and the things you don't. You get your label, and then you get ignored, or sometimes you get teased, but mostly you go about your business, thinking things that you would never say out loud, not to someone's face.

Because there are some words you know you can't say. Not out loud. Not without getting into serious trouble. You might whisper them to your friends, but you would never write them down. Instead you find some other way. A secret code. An inside joke. Something you've been whispering to your buddies for the past two weeks. Something *they* start to whisper, till it catches on. *He's so Roman.* It spreads. And everyone knows what it means, but nobody says anything.

Until it's written on your locker for all the world to see.

Wolf didn't show up at all for first period. I squirmed in my seat all through English, kept glancing at his empty desk. Twice I twisted around to look at Cameron and them, but they just stared straight ahead, completely enthralled, it seemed, with a lecture on the dangers of hubris, Mr. Sword asking us, again, if we thought the characters in *J. C.* deserved what was coming to them. If justice had been served. I had my doubts.

After class I pulled Deedee and Rose aside and told them what happened. Deedee let out a grunt like I'd just punched him in the gut. Rose looked stone-faced.

"Any idea who put it there?" she asked.

I had ideas. She probably had the same ideas. But neither of us knew for sure. Like most of the messages that came before it, the message on Wolf's locker didn't come with a signature.

"Do you think he went back home?"

I shrugged. I didn't know where else he might have gone. Outside of his parents and his older brother, the people who cared most about him were standing right here.

The bell for second period clanged above us. Rose chewed on her lip, clearly working something out in her head. Then she said she'd catch up with us later. I walked with Deedee to math.

"It was probably Cameron, that prick," Deedee spit. "Trying to get us back. I knew something like this would happen."

I didn't bother to remind him that he was the one who said it was over. That we'd won. It could have been any of them. Cameron. Jason. Noah. Or somebody else they knew. Somebody they put up to it. "It might not be that hard to find out," I said. Maybe it was just a matter of asking the right person.

Rose intercepted us by Deedee's locker right before lunch. "Grab all your stuff," she said. "We're leaving."

"Now?" I asked.

Rose glanced around, keeping her voice low. "We can't very well call him, can we? So we're leaving. He needs us."

"But we'll get in trouble," Deedee said.

"*Wolf's* in trouble," Rose said. "Do you want to roll for it or can we just go?" Deedee shook his head. She looked at me for backup.

"Right behind you," I said. Deedee groaned as he nodded.

We let Rose take point.

We used the door by the gym. There was a moment of hesitation, crossing the threshold, that sense that what you are doing is wrong on some level. But it was a really *low* level by comparison, so I quickly got over it. And it was easier with Rose in the lead, striding purposefully through the door like she owned the place. *Rose Holland is going to do whatever Rose Holland wants to do.* Bench had called that one. For a second I thought he should be here with us. That he should be the one marching us out the door instead.

No. Not instead. Too. He should be here too.

We skulked across the school parking lot and crossed the street, walking for a long ways in silence until Deedee couldn't stand it any longer. "What happens when we don't show up next period?"

Rose shrugged. "The teacher makes a note of it. Probably somebody calls our parents and tells them we weren't in class." She didn't sound at all concerned. I was pretty sure she'd done this kind of thing before.

"And what am I supposed to tell my parents?"

"You tell them a member of the tribe was in trouble," I said. Rose turned to smile at me. I gave her one right back. Deedee wasn't finished panicking, though.

"What do we do if he's not at home?"

"We go looking for him," Rose answered.

"Looking where?"

"Everywhere," she said.

I suddenly had this image of Wolf on his brother's moped, taking the highway out of town. Except he wouldn't do that. He wouldn't run away from home. He wouldn't leave us. Not over this.

"And what do we even say when we find him?"

Rose turned and put her hands on Deedee's shoulders. It reminded me of the night we played Dungeons & Dragons and she grabbed his hand and told him anything was possible. This time he didn't even flinch. "We'll figure it out," she said. "The important thing is that we are there for him. All of us."

We didn't have to hunt Wolf down, though. We didn't even have to knock on his door. I heard a sound, like the pop of a firework, as soon as we turned down his block. Then I spotted him, standing in his backyard, holding a baseball bat. He saw us coming—he looked right at us for a moment—but then he went back to what he was doing without so much as a nod.

He stood on his cement patio with that aluminum bat—probably left over from his brother Simon's days in Little League. At his feet sat a parade of to-scale painted tanks and airplanes and sports cars, all lined up single file. It had to be his entire collection, brought down from his bedroom. Wolf had taken one of the bar stools from his kitchen and set it in the grass at the edge of the cement. An aircraft carrier—the one from his dresser—sat on top, sticking out over the edges.

The three of us came up to the gray picket fence that lined Wolf's backyard, tall enough to reach Deedee's chin. Rose called out his name.

"Go away," he said, just loud enough for us to hear. He adjusted the grip on his bat. I'd seen almost all of these models. I'd heard their names, their histories, how long it had taken to build each one. I'd even helped him glue a piece on here and there. I knew the aircraft carrier was one of his favorites—it had taken him six weeks to put together. Which is why I dreaded what was about to happen.

Wolf spread his feet and swung the bat, driving it hard into the hulking ship.

Crack.

The U.S.S. *Enterprise* exploded, a dozen miniature fighter jets shooting into the sky before landing in the grass, nose first, the deck of the ship splintering and flying off into a bush. The majority of the hull soared ten feet before sinking into the lawn, an unsightly gash in its side. Beside me Deedee jumped involuntarily.

I surveyed the yard and my stomach felt like it was suddenly full of squirming maggots. This wasn't the first casualty. There were already pieces everywhere, half hulls and busted chasis. Wolf's backyard had been turned into a plastic scrap heap, turrets and wings and wheels and engines, scattered and broken, littering the ground. It looked like a war zone. I thought of my uncle Mike. What were the render safe procedures here? Probably he'd say that it was too late. That the bomb had gone off already.

Probably he'd say to take cover and keep your head down.

Something pinched my arm and I looked to see Rose holding on to me. Wolf bent over and took a model car—a red Corvette—and set it on the stool. He wasn't crying, though it looked like maybe he had been. If anything, he looked distant now. Determined. His lip curled as he took his stance again, bringing the bat over his shoulder.

"Wolf, man. Hang on," I said, but he swung anyways, the Corvette taking it in the trunk and sailing out over the yard, fifteen feet or more. Wolf, apparently not satisfied, walked casually over to the model and proceeded to smash it to pieces. Swing after swing. You could hear the plastic splintering, see the red shards popping up out of the grass.

"Wolf, stop," Rose shouted. She started to circle around the fence toward the gate, but a look from Wolf made her pause. *Don't get too close,* the look said. *I don't want you to get hurt.* He walked back to the porch and selected another model—a B-29 Superfortress—setting it gently on the stool, positioning it just right. He glanced back at us and I could see the humiliation in his eyes.

"Leave me alone," he said, hefting the bat to his shoulder again. "Go home."

"Wolf, seriously," Rose said. "Put the bat down. It's going to be all right. Tomorrow we can go talk to Principal Wittingham.

We can find out who wrote it. We'll get it taken off your locker. Just let us come in."

Wolf dropped the bat to his side. "What difference does it make? So they clean my locker or give me a new one? They're just going to write something else on it. It's not going to *end*. Your stupid ride. That stupid apology. None of it made any difference, just like I said." He turned back to the stool. "Besides. I'm not going back to that school again."

The bat went up. Swung forward. *Crack.* I winced as the bomber snapped in two, its tail end twisting, propellers spinning skyward.

Wolf reached for another.

I looked to Rose. She stood there with her hands gripping the curved points of the fence, like a row of spears. *Good fences make good neighbors.* That's what the poem said. But there was Wolf, destroying something he'd worked so hard to build, piece by piece, and us on the other side, only feet away though it seemed like so much farther. I thought about all the times I'd been to this house. Standing in this same backyard chucking water balloons. In his driveway lighting bottle rockets. Sitting on his couch watching TV. Standing outside his living room, listening to him play, note after perfect note, afraid that if I got any closer, he'd stop.

Now I was afraid that he wouldn't. There were still a dozen

models by his feet, but at the rate he was going, there would soon be nothing left.

"Wolf, let's just talk about it," I said.

He turned and glared at me. At us. "Forget it!" he snapped. "Just leave me alone."

Rose looked at Deedee and me. I'd never seen her panicked before, not even staring down the mouth of the Gauntlet, but at that moment she looked lost. "What should we do?" she asked. "You know him better than I do."

I wasn't sure that was true anymore. Back when it was just the four of us, it was easy. We all knew our place. We counted on Deedee for the drama. We counted on Wolf to be reasonable. We counted on Bench to stick up for us. But here was Wolf, no longer reasonable, slugging away at his models, and Bench nowhere to be seen.

And me? What did we count on me for?

Standing on the other side of the fence, watching Wolf destroy the things he loved, I realized I hadn't done anything. This whole time, I'd simply stood there and watched, a part of the chorus, afraid to speak up, afraid I'd somehow make it worse.

I was tired of feeling helpless. But before I could do anything, I needed to know who was responsible. I put a hand on Rose's shoulder. I think it surprised her. It surprised me a little too. "I've gotta go."

Deedee looked at me like I was crazy. "What? Go where?"

"I'm sorry," I said. "There's something I really need to do. You got this?"

It was a stupid question, I knew. The three of us on one side. Wolf on the other holding a baseball bat and yelling at us to go home. Deedee shook his head emphatically, but Rose nodded. She understood.

"Yeah, we've got this," she said, putting her hand on top of mine.

I gave Wolf one last look, but he ignored me. He took another swing, and more pieces went flying as another busted battleship was buried in the grass.

I could still make out the explosions of cracked plastic, even once I was a block away.

The Joneses lived on the other side of the district from Wolf, in a two-story house with a brick front and a big enough backyard that you could play Wiffle ball and never have to worry about hitting it over into the neighbor's. I'd ridden or walked the stretch between Bench's house and mine with its goose-poop-bombed sidewalks a hundred times, so many I could do it backward without tripping over the cracks in the cement. Bench and I were the two members of the tribe who were closest to each other, his house on the way to school so I was always picked up first. Why I was always the one who saved the seat.

I walked slow, planning out what I was going to say. I wasn't even sure he would be home yet. School had barely ended by the time I reached his neighborhood, but I decided that if he wasn't there I would wait. I would sit on the curb until he showed. I wasn't going to leave without an answer.

Like with Wolf, I heard him before I saw him—*thunk, thunk, thunk*—turning the corner to find him in his driveway, basketball in hand. I followed the rhythm of its bounce as he drove to the hoop then pulled up to nail a jumper, all whisper, no clang. He was always a better shot.

Bench spotted me at the end of the drive and immediately looked up and down the street. I remembered doing the same when Rose showed up at my door. I'd been doing it for weeks now.

"Just you?" he asked, bouncing the ball twice before tucking it under his arm. I came farther up the driveway so we could talk without yelling. I'd never yelled at any of my friends. Not really. Not yet anyway.

"Just me," I said. He had to know why I was here, but I said it anyway. "We need to talk. About Wolf."

Bench looked at me, shielding his eyes from the sun. Even in the chill air he'd already worked up a sweat. "What's there to talk about? It wasn't me. You know that. *He* knows that. At least he should." He started bouncing the ball again, except he didn't dribble this time so much as pound, as if he were trying to bust up the blacktop with each bounce. He turned and took another shot, bricking it off the backboard this time. He hissed a word that Ruby Sandels had already gotten in trouble for.

He seemed mad, which just made me angrier. What did *he* have to be mad about? I got to the ball before he could, snatching the rebound, holding it at my side.

Bench put his hands on his hips. "Give me the ball, Frost."

I shook my head. "You still owe me one, remember?" I shifted it to my chest. I was determined to get his attention. Determined for him to look me in the eyes and tell me the truth.

Bench smirked. "Right," he said. "I owe *you* one. Whatever, man. Just give it here."

He lunged for the ball and I twisted, starting an absurd game of keep-away. He reached out with one hand, attempting to knock it out of my grasp, and I moved the other way. He swiped and I dodged, the two of us choreographing some ludicrous dance in his driveway. Finally he got both hands on the ball and wrenched it from my arms with a grunt, the rough rubber scraping the underside of my chin.

"Grow up," he said.

Bench dribbled twice then took another shot, bricking it again. It rebounded right toward me and I kicked it on the first bounce. The ball sailed into his front yard, missing his head by inches.

"What the hell is wrong with you, man?" He was shouting now.

"What's wrong with *me*? What the hell's wrong with *you*?" I yelled back. First time for everything. I couldn't help it. "Right now our friend—your friend—is standing in his backyard smashing up all his freaking models with a baseball bat because of something some jerk wrote on his locker, and here you are acting like it's no big deal!"

"I never said it was no big deal. And I already told you, I had nothing to do with it!"

Bench tromped into the grass after his ball so that I had to keep shouting at his back.

"But I bet you know who did. Was it Cameron? Was it Noah? Jason? Or somebody else. Another one of your friends."

Bench froze, bent over the ball at his feet. "They aren't my friends." He came back to the blacktop with it cradled tight. "I don't hang out with Cameron and those guys. I don't even talk to them. You know that."

"But people say stuff," I reminded him.

"Not me." He lined up another shot.

"Yeah, right."

The ball clanged off the rim. We both let it roll past us

down the driveway and into the street. "What's that supposed to mean?" He turned toward me, taking a step closer. For a moment I thought he was going to push me and I braced myself.

"You're telling me you've never said anything about any of us. Not me, not Wolf, not Rose—"

"Don't bring her into this," Bench said, holding up a finger. "Everybody says stuff about her. *You've* said stuff about her." He stuck that same finger in my chest.

That stopped me. I couldn't remember what all I'd said about Rose in those first few days. I'd thought plenty of things. And I'd heard so many more and said or done nothing. "What about Deedee?" I asked. "You're telling me you've never said anything about him to the guys you hang out with?"

Bench frowned, shaking his head. Dead giveaway.

"I didn't tell Cameron about Deedee's stupid dice," he muttered.

"But you told somebody." I stared at him. People always told me I had my mother's eyes.

Frustrated, Bench threw his hands in the air. "Fine. I told somebody. Big deal. I was with some of the guys on my team— we were getting something to eat that night after the game." He paused, realizing what else he'd just let slip. The night after the game, after "the catch." The night Rose showed up at Wolf's door and saved us all from the undead horde. All of us but Bench.

"There were six of us. And one of 'em couldn't decide what to order so somebody else said 'flip a coin,' and I started laughing."

"You told them."

"I said I knew somebody who did that all the time. I was just kidding around," Bench protested. "Just a bunch of guys talking smack. They rolled their eyes, called Deedee a freak. That was it. I didn't know Cameron would find out or that he'd do what he did. I mean, who cares what Deedee keeps in his pocket?"

"Deedee, for one," I snapped. "And me. And you too. At least you used to."

Bench rolled his eyes, still trying to blow it off. "I told you. Cameron's not my friend. I can't control what he says or does. What any of them do."

Any of them. He knew. I knew he knew.

"You still shouldn't have said anything."

"Well, maybe Deedee shouldn't carry his toys around with him everywhere he goes. Maybe he needs to grow up too." Bench glared at me.

I glared right back. "Funny. That's what Cameron said before he tried to stuff Deedee's head in the toilet."

And where were you? I wanted to add. But I'm pretty sure he got the message. He took a step back, putting more space between us.

"What do you want me to say?" he shouted. "You want me

to apologize? Fine. I'm sorry you and Deedee got jumped in the bathroom, all right? I'm sorry I ever said anything about Deedee's stupid dice. I'm sorry I'm not there to babysit you guys every time you walk down the halls or sit and play your stupid little games at lunch. I'm sorry not everybody likes you or the people you hang out with. I'm sorry people call you names behind your back. Did I miss anything?"

"How about 'I'm sorry for acting like a total jackwad and completely dissing all my friends'?"

"I didn't diss you," Bench insisted.

"You left us."

Bench groaned, both hands on his head. "God, Frost, do you even *hear* yourself? You make it sound like we're some kind of secret superhero society. That's not how it is."

"You're wrong. You find your people," I said, repeating the mantra that carried me through those first two weeks in the sixth grade, my mother's promise that held up when a boy named J.J. came and sat next to me on the bus. "You find your people and you make your tribe."

"That's exactly what I'm *talking* about, man," Bench said. "There is no *tribe*. And even if there was, *I'm* not the one who changed things. You come here and blame me for screwing things up, but I'm not the one who invited that girl to come sit with us in the first place."

That girl. Maybe he didn't know what to call her. There were too many names to choose from. "So you're just going to blame it all on Rose, then?"

"*I'm* not the one looking for someone to blame," Bench yelled, jamming a thumb to his chest, stepping up, closing the gap between us again.

"You don't like her, so to heck with the rest of us?"

"I never said that."

"Or maybe it's Wolf you have a problem with."

"Man, don't *even* go there," Bench snarled.

"Because you know. You heard all the stuff people were saying."

"Just stop right now, Frost."

"Because it's easier to just go with the crowd than to stand up for your friends."

"That's not what I'm saying."

"Then what *are* you saying?"

"I'm saying that it's not even *about* you!" Bench shouted.

He was so close now that I could count his heartbeats through the throbbing veins in his neck. I didn't back away, though, even as he kept on yelling right in my face.

"Did it ever dawn on you that maybe I didn't feel like *I* belonged sometimes? That I might want to hang out with somebody else? That maybe, just *maybe* I might not want to be with you guys *all* the time? I mean . . . ," he sputtered, "I don't even *like* Dungeons and Dragons!"

Silence.

We stood right next to each other, bodies stiff, locked in an epic eyeball-burning staring contest, the kind that you expect to devolve into grunts and shoves as two kids wrestle each other to the ground. My lower lip started to tremble.

And then I laughed. I laughed right in his face.

I couldn't help it. It came out first as a snort, then a building giggle, high-pitched and uncontrollable and ridiculous, laughing so hard that my chest hurt.

Bench looked at me like I'd lost my mind, but then it hit him too, and he chuckled softly to himself.

"Which part don't you like?" I asked breathlessly. "The dungeons or the dragons?"

Bench shook his head. "None of it, man. Honestly. I was faking it the whole time."

For some reason that just made me laugh harder. I thought about so many Saturday nights at Deedee's house, rolling the dice, Garthrox the Barbarian shouting and swinging. Bench cutting up and carrying on. He had me fooled. He had us all fooled. "Seriously? I mean you *never* liked it?"

"I only played because I wanted to hang out with you guys."

I stopped suddenly, wiping hot tears from my eyes. *Wanted*

to. Past tense. "But not anymore," I said softly, sniffling.

Bench shrugged. I wasn't sure if it was an I-don't-know shrug or a that's-just-how-it-is shrug. I wasn't sure what to say. I felt drained. All used up. I flashed back to the night my father left, how I'd been the first to let go, just a little. I thought about the blank spaces in my mother's senior yearbook. About the empty seat next to me on the bus. I'd been here before.

I waited for him to talk first. When he did, his voice was softer.

"After that game last week, things were just . . . different. I can't explain it. I caught that ball and they all swooped in and lifted me up and carried me out and it was almost like I was this other person, you know? I mean, it was incredible."

"I was there," I said. "I saw." *I cheered you on,* I thought. *Even though you couldn't hear me. Even though things had already started to change between us, I was there. You just didn't realize it.*

"I didn't mean for what happened with you and Deedee. And I didn't have anything to do with Wolf. I swear. I'd heard people say it. I knew what it meant. But I didn't get involved. And I didn't write that on his locker. I swear."

"But you know who did," I pressed.

Bench looked back down the street again. I don't think he was looking to see if anyone was there. I think he just didn't want to look at me.

"This isn't about you either," I told him. It wasn't about him or me or Deedee or even Rose. This was about Wolf.

Bench took a deep breath and nodded. "Yeah," he said. "I know who wrote it. But if I tell you, you gotta promise me you won't go and do anything stupid."

I promised. I had no idea what I was going to do, but I promised anyways.

"All right," he said.

And even though there wasn't another soul around, Bench still leaned over to whisper in my ear.

THE RESPONSE

I KNEW. I KNEW WHO LEFT THAT MESSAGE ON WOLF'S LOCKER, AND I spent the whole weekend thinking of ways to break my promise to Bench, the promise to not do anything stupid.

I spent the whole weekend dreaming of breaking Jason Baker's jaw.

People say things. And when you are part of certain circles you hear them. Jason had been the one to come up with the phrase, then he bragged to one too many someones that it was his idea and Bench was close enough to hear. It wasn't a revelation. Jason had been nudging Wolf for as long as I could remember. All off-the-cuff, in-the-moment stuff to get a laugh out of his friends. But the locker felt different somehow. Premeditated and purposeful and permanent in a way his other comments hadn't been.

Which had me premeditating how to go about punching him in the face.

It was either that or rat him out to Principal Wittingham, though I wasn't sure what that would accomplish. No more notes, though. There was nothing I could write on Jason's locker that would hurt him as bad as he'd hurt Wolf. But maybe if I could dislocate his jaw, he wouldn't be able to talk for a while. That would be something.

Forget the fact that I'd never punched anyone before. Not like Rose. I Googled how to do it, just in case (strike with your knuckles, don't tuck your thumb inside, put your hips into it). I practiced on my pillow (the wall seemed too hard). At least he wouldn't see it coming. No way Jason Baker would expect the poet laureate of Branton to take a swing at him. It probably wouldn't fix anything—not in the long term—but I was pretty sure it would make me feel better.

And hopefully not just me. It had been a miserable couple of days. When I wasn't dreaming of fattening Jason's lip, I was leaving phone messages for Wolf that he didn't respond to. Sending him emails that he didn't reply to. Seeing him, again and again, his face salt streaked with dried tears, standing on his backyard, destroying a fleet of planes and ships, telling me to go away. It was the Big Split all over again, and I couldn't help but feel like I was on the verge of losing two friends at once, which only made me want to hit somebody even more. I wanted to just go knock on Wolf's door, but I was afraid he wouldn't let me in. And I wasn't sure what I would say.

"He's not talking to me either," Rose said when I gave in and emailed her my number, asking her to call. It made me feel better at first, knowing he was ignoring all of us and not just me, but then I felt worse, knowing he was shutting everyone out. "We just need to give him some space, I think."

And in the meantime, I thought, we need to protect each other from the wolves.

I sat on the bus that Monday morning, making and unmaking fists and grimacing back at the gray sky that had been threatening rain for days and was finally fulfilling its promise, weighing the pros and cons, knowing I'd probably get suspended if I started a fight, wondering if I even had the guts to go through with it. I blocked out the people around me. I didn't even realize the bus had stopped for a train and was running ten minutes later than normal. I played the whole scene out in slow motion, picturing the exact moment of impact, Jason's skin rippling out along his cheek, counting the individual droplets of spit spraying from his soon-to-be-split lips. I couldn't stop imagining it, because when I did, I just came back to Wolf standing in his backyard, baseball bat in hand, telling me that nothing would ever change.

Too many things had changed already.

The bus pulled up and I fought down the urge to vomit as I stepped into the rain, walking into school with my head down, hoping to avoid anyone I knew—Deedee, Rose, even Bench. I was afraid they would try to stop me. As soon as I entered, though, I sensed it. The hum. I saw the crowd of students spilling out into the main foyer from B Hall, even though the first bell had rung and everybody should already be heading to class. Instead they were all funneling to the same place, whispering, tugging on each other to hurry.

Whatever it was, it had to be serious.

I followed the buzzing crowd and found myself swallowed by a hive of students, all crammed together, all staring at the same something. I suddenly felt light-headed and put a hand against the wall to steady myself.

It was Wolf's locker. Newly painted. A brighter blue than all the rest.

What you could still see of it, anyways.

I caught sight of Rose near the front of the horde, towering over the students beside her, Deedee at her shoulder. She saw me on my tiptoes and beckoned me over. I pushed my way through until I was standing beside them both, right in front of locker B78. Except you couldn't actually see the locker number anymore.

Because of the notes.

The whole upper half was covered in them. At least a hundred. Maybe more. Different sizes and colors. Overlapping like links of chain-mail armor.

I just stood there and stared.

"Go on," Rose whispered to me. "Read them."

I started reading the closest ones silently to myself. One said, *You're Awesome!* Another, *You're hilarious!* Several notes simply said, *Morgan Thompson Rocks.* One note said, *You're So Talented You Make Me Want to Puke,* which I assumed was a compliment. There were several *Stay Strong*s and *Be Proud*s. There was at least one *I THINK YOU'RE HOT.*

There were so many.

Some of the messages had drawings: hearts and smiley faces and peace signs. There was a rainbow done in marker and another done in colored pencil. The latter was shaped like a flag.

There were quotes, too. Or maybe they were aphorisms. Some of them at least had a name attached. Henry David Thoreau and Martin Luther King. Taylor Swift. A pink note with fancy cursive said, *Be who you are and say what you feel, because those who mind don't matter and those who matter don't mind.* Whoever wrote it attributed it to Dr. Seuss, though I had my doubts, because it didn't rhyme. *Love thy neighbor as thyself,* said another. That one was signed by Jesus.

More than one square said, *You are not alone.*

And there were still more coming. I looked to see students with pads of sticky notes, slapping them into waiting hands. Kids leaned against the wall to scrawl something before making their way through the crowd to add their message to the locker. The collection of notes fanned out from the center, growing like a virus. Sprouting. Spreading.

Proliferating.

"They've been coming for the last twenty minutes," Rose said beside me, her voice hushed. "Not just students. Teachers too. Nobody even knows who started it." The second bell rang above us. We were all officially tardy now. But only a few students bothered to head off to class, and no teachers came to shoo us away. I spotted Mr. Sword off to the right. He was handing out blank notes too. "I wish Wolf was here," Rose added.

I looked over at her, then bent down and dug into my backpack, down to the very bottom, with its broken eraser tops and random bits of paper. I pulled out the crumpled sticky note—the one I'd meant to give back, the one that had been so easily dismissed the first time around. I smoothed it out as best as I could, then found the closest empty space, about halfway down. I was afraid it wouldn't stay, so I pressed hard. It stuck.

Wolf's aphorism on his own locker. *Words are ghosts that can haunt us forever.*

Behind me I heard a familiar snort of laughter and twisted to see first the breakable jaw and then the rest of Jason Baker's slug-worthy face at the edge of the crowd, whispering something to Noah Kyle. Noah smiled and shook his head.

I had absolutely no idea what they'd said.

I didn't care anymore.

I turned around and started pushing my way back through the crowd, heard both Deedee and Rose calling after me. "Frost. Hang on. Where are you going?"

I ignored them. I couldn't get Jason's arrogant smile out of my head. Sometimes you have to shut up and do something. Rose could appreciate that.

I got free of the mob and turned the corner.

And walked straight to Principal Wittingham's office. I didn't even bother to ask the secretary or wait for him to see me. I just barged in.

"I know who put those words on Morgan's locker," I blurted out. I'd almost said *Wolf's*, but then I remembered, he probably wouldn't know who Wolf was.

Principal Wittingham folded his hands in front of him with a sigh that suggested his patience had dried up weeks ago. "Thanks, Eric. But I already know who did it," he said. He nodded to the chairs across from him. The one closest to me was empty.

Bench looked up at me from the other one and nodded.

"I saved you a seat," he said.

Words accumulate. And once they're free there's no taking them back.

You can do an awful lot of damage with a handful of words. Destroy a friendship. End a marriage. Start a war. Some words can break you to pieces.

But that's not all. Words can be beautiful. They can make you feel things you've never felt before. Gather enough of them and they can stick those same pieces back together, provided they're the right words, said at the right time. But that takes more courage than you'd think.

I went to Wolf's house that night, after I'd told Mr. Wittingham everything I knew, after Jason was called down to the office and not seen for the rest of the day. Wolf's mother met me at the door. She looked exhausted, eyes swollen, shoulders slumped. I wondered out loud if it was a bad time, but she and Mr. Thompson both welcomed me inside. "He's upstairs in his room," Mrs. Thompson said. "And I'm sure he'd like to see you."

I had my doubts.

I tiptoed upstairs and stood for a moment outside Wolf's room with its colorful musical notes painted on the door. Any other time I probably would have just barged right in. This time

I fished a Post-it note out of my pocket that I'd brought for just this purpose and slipped it underneath.

It said, *Knock. Knock.*

After a few seconds I heard him laugh. It was the first time I'd heard Wolf laugh in days, and it made me smile. He opened the door.

"Hey, Frost," he said, motioning me inside, but I stopped in the doorway. His room looked strange without the planes dangling from their strings, the cars lined up at an angle on his shelves. It wasn't just empty. It felt *hollow*. It was as if a part of Wolf had been carved out of him and scattered all over the backyard.

"Didn't see you at school today," I said. By the looks of him, I guessed that he probably hadn't even left his room all weekend long. He sat on his bed with his back pressed to the wall, knees together, arms wrapped around them, as if he was determined to take up as little space as possible. "Wish you would have been there."

"I already know about the notes, if that's what you mean," he said. "It's not as if I don't hear things." He didn't sound angry, not exactly, but I still couldn't help but feel like there was accusation hidden in there somewhere.

"Rose?" I guessed.

Wolf nodded. "She also told me that you went to Mr.

Wittingham's office." He paused, then added, "Thanks for that."

I shrugged. "To be honest, Bench kind of beat me to it."

Wolf seemed surprised. Obviously Rose hadn't told him everything. "That's Bench for you. Always has to be first at everything," he said.

I wanted to tell Wolf the rest. About our shouting match and the things Bench had said, how it had nothing, really, to do with Wolf and everything to do with him. *It isn't about you.* But it was. It was about all of us. Maybe Wolf could sympathize with Bench feeling out of place, not quite knowing where he belonged. "He wants you to know he's sorry," I said.

"Bench told you that?"

"Well. Not in so many words."

"It doesn't take that many," Wolf remarked. And for a second I saw that flash of anger, that same one I saw when he slammed the note on Jason's desk, when he drove his brother's bat into his model bomber. Wolf shook his head. "He doesn't need to apologize. He didn't write that on my locker. I knew who it was all along. I mean, it's not like this was the first time."

Wolf sat on his bed with me still leaning against the doorway and told me about all the other things Jason Baker had been saying to him all year long. Most of them were names not worth repeating, whipered among his friends just loud enough for Wolf to hear. The Roman thing was the latest in a long string, but apparently Jason thought it was clever and kept at it, needling Wolf whenever he got the chance. Calling him Gayus Thompson. Coughing out the word *Romosexual*. Giving him that same legionnaire salute that he'd given the three of us at the football game whenever they passed each other in the hall.

And he wasn't the only one. Wolf had heard others whispering the same thing behind his back, a few kids who thought it was just as funny as Jason did. It caught on. Just like the notes.

"Jason Baker's a total class-A butt-munch," I concluded. I may not have gotten the chance to fatten his lip, but he sure deserved whatever Mr. Wittingham was going to dish out. I sort of hoped he'd be expelled. And maybe the Big Ham could dunk his head in the toilet a few times on the way out. But writing "Total Roman" on somebody's locker probably didn't warrant physical torture, whether you knew what it meant or not.

"That doesn't really help," Wolf said, "calling him names."

I flinched, suddenly feeling worse for thinking that would make him feel better. There'd been enough of that sort of thing the past two weeks. I was about to take it back—even though I didn't want to—when Wolf smiled.

"But you're right. He is. Class A for sure." He scrunched up my *Knock. Knock.* sticky note and threw it at me, hitting me square in the chest.

You got me, I thought, suddenly hearing Rose's voice in my head, wheedling herself into the conversation even when she wasn't around. I stood in the doorway and watched the last two weeks flash by in reverse, from the notes on Wolf's locker all the way back to that first moment when Rose Holland sat at our table. Jason and Wolf. Deedee. Bench. The Gauntlet. All the nasty messages. The ones that stuck and the ones that didn't. It seemed like somewhere along the line we could have stopped it. Kept it from coming to this, to me standing in Wolf's bedroom, feeling like I let him down.

"You still thinking you might not come back?" I asked.

Wolf nodded.

"Because of Jason Baker?"

"Screw Jason," Wolf said, scowling. "It's none of his business who I like and don't like. Though I sure as heck don't like *him*."

"Then why leave?" I asked. After all, he hadn't seen the notes yet. The new ones. His locker was covered in them. Maybe when he saw them, he'd change his mind. He'd realize we weren't all like Jason Baker. Most of us weren't anywhere close. But even as I thought it, I realized that wasn't true either. We were all guilty of saying something we probably shouldn't have. Rose's voice echoed in my head again. *I could start over, be myself, and there would be somebody who would appreciate it. I just had to find them.* But Wolf still had us. He had me and Deedee and Rose. And I told him that. Maybe not in so many words. Or any words, for that matter.

But I gave him a look that I hoped meant that the tribe was still here. That this was no reason to quit. Or not enough reason.

"Sometimes you need a change of venue," Wolf said. "I'm not leaving *you* guys behind. It's just this whole year so far . . ." He stopped, tapping his fingers on his knees for a moment, maybe playing a familiar tune or maybe just making one up in his head. "I just need to get away from the noise. Maybe a new school is the best thing for me."

I nodded. I understood. Maybe. A little. I didn't know how it felt to be Wolf, of course, but I knew about needing space. It was hard enough trying to figure out who you were, who you liked, what you believed in, what you were good at. Even harder with everyone else telling you what you should or shouldn't be. And even if you did figure it out, you still had to summon the courage to actually *be* that person, regardless of what other people thought. Maybe a new school *would* be different. It couldn't be too much worse.

Except it wouldn't have us.

"I'm sorry," I said. "Sorry if I let you down. If I wasn't there all the time."

"You're here now," Wolf said matter-of-factly. Ever the voice of reason. We counted on him for that. Maybe this was what he counted on me for—for just being there. I could do that. At least I could try.

We stared across the room at each other for an eternity while I worked up the guts to say something emotional and blubbery and totally against the rules. Something cheese-ball like *I'm with you every step of the way,* or one of the fortune-cookie nuggets pulled directly from the Post-its still hanging from his locker. But Wolf saved me by standing up all of a sudden with a sly grin on his face, a look that I'm pretty certain he picked up from Rose.

"I haven't had dinner yet," he said. "My parents have been so worried about my emotional well-being that they kind of forgot to feed me. You hungry?"

My stomach rumbled. Power of suggestion. "If you're asking if I want you to try heating something in the microwave again, I'm going to have to go with no." Burning the house down seemed like it might just push the whole Thompson family right over the edge.

"I was thinking ice cream, actually. Give Rose and Deedee a call. Make my mom take us out. Mr. Twisty's?"

I grinned and nodded.

I couldn't have said it better myself.

The next day Wolf came to empty out his locker, well after dismissal so as not to attract too much attention. We were with him—me, Deedee, and Rose. His mother was in the principal's office filling out the necessary paperwork required for his withdrawal from BMS.

It was official. He really wasn't coming back.

I'm sure the Big Ham was serving her apologies and promises on a platter, anything to get Wolf to stay and not to turn this into an even bigger deal than it already was, but for once Wolf's parents agreed on something. Branton Middle School wasn't the best place for their son.

When Wolf saw his locker he froze. It was completely covered now, every inch, the messages climbing up onto the wall above it. The day it happened, kids kept coming, adding to the ever-growing pile, making a mountain of notes, some stacked on top of each other so that by the last bell it looked like a paper blanket skirting the ground, a waterfall of words. So many notes. More, it seemed, than there were even students in the school. Even now, the locker still smelled vaguely of new paint, though that was probably just my imagination.

Rose and I stood on either side of Wolf, propping him up. We were getting good at that.

"It's pretty incredible," Deedee said. "Don't you think?"

Wolf didn't respond. Maybe he couldn't find the words. Didn't matter. He had plenty to choose from. He quietly ran his fingers over the notes, tapping them gently, as if he found some kind of melody there, a secret song that only he could hear. I wasn't sure he was even reading them, but then I saw him smile. He must have gotten to *I THINK YOU'RE HOT.*

"You can take them," I said. "Pretty sure they were all meant for you."

Wolf shook his head. "Nah. I think the longer they stay up, the better." He dropped his hands and stepped back. His voice cracked a little. "It's crazy. I don't even *know* this many people. I bet half of them barely even knew I existed." He leaned over and settled his head on Rose's shoulder, and we stood like that for a minute or two. I realized this was the last time I would ever meet Wolf at his locker and my heart started to ache.

"C'mon," Rose said. "Let's get your stuff, get out of this place, and go do something fun."

Wolf nodded solemnly and carefully opened his locker so as not to knock any of the notes free. It was practically empty inside already. His math textbook. A magneted mirror. An empty bottle of Coke and a BMS sweatshirt that he might never wear again.

And at the bottom, one last note that had been folded into an origami fish and shoved through the slats.

"I wonder who *that* could be from," I said.

Rose smiled knowingly. "I didn't write it, if that's what you're implying," she said. "I actually found it stuck to my locker the day of the Gauntlet. I don't know who wrote it, actually, but it seemed like good advice, so I stuffed it in here for you."

Wolf crouched down and unfolded the note. He held it out for us to see. It was written in black marker, all caps.

KEEP YOUR HEAD UP. KEEP YOUR EYES FORWARD. AND DON'T LET GO.

"I thought maybe you could use it more than I could," Rose said. "Besides. Everyone knows origami wombats are good luck."

"Wombat, huh?" I said.

Rose nodded. "Derr," she said to me. "What else would it be?" As usual I didn't have an answer. But I didn't mind being derred by Rose anymore. Some things just take time to get used to. I caught a glimpse of Wolf in the mirror stuck to his locker, maybe a little misty-eyed, the three of us standing behind him.

"You don't have to go," Deedee said, saying out loud what we'd all been thinking.

"No. I don't *have* to," Wolf answered. Then he stuffed the wombat in his pocket and softly closed the door.

THE INVITATION

WARS SHOULD TEACH YOU THINGS. THOUGH JUDGING BY HOW many humans have had, we must be terrible students.

Not me, though. I learned more in the two weeks following that first posted note than I did in the two years of middle school leading up to it.

Like you should maybe put your dirty laundry in a basket, because you never know when a girl's going to come along and see your underwear lying in the middle of your floor. And that there are better ways to let your emperor know he's being a jerk than stabbing him twenty-three times. And that people who get embarrassed by other people who laugh or sing too loud just don't have the guts to laugh and sing out loud themselves.

And you can't have it both ways. The road forks sometimes

and you have to choose. Just pick the path that looks the least perilous and watch out for the trees on your way down.

And you can't be friends with everyone, and even the friends you do make won't always last forever, which royally sucks, but as my mom would say, that's life.

And finally, if you can't say *anything* nice, like, not a single freaking thing, then maybe you should keep your big trap shut.

But if you do have something nice to say, and you feel a little awkward saying it, you can always write a note.

There were a lot of changes after Wolf left.

For starters there was the new policy on phones. Too many complaints flooding in from parents and students both, so the administration decided it was a fight that just wasn't worth winning anymore. The new policy stated that students could bring their phones into school but had to keep them in their lockers—they still weren't allowed in class. That didn't always work, of course, but for the most part the students followed along, happy for a compromise, and the teachers looked the other way, provided you weren't sucked into the screen when you were supposed to be turned on to linear equations.

I still didn't have a phone, so it didn't make a bit of difference to me one way or another.

The phone policy wasn't the only schoolwide change,

though. As soon as Wolf transferred, the Big Ham promised to start a new program to help combat bullying and discrimination in school. I figured that just meant adding more brochures to the rack in the counselor's office, but Mr. Sword volunteered to be the program adviser, so maybe not. I told him I'd help however I could. He told me that twenty other students had already said the same thing.

Post-it notes remained banned on school grounds. You could still find them sometimes, attached to someone's binder or stuck to the side of the toilet in the boys' room. I'm sure a few were still traded under the table, passed in secret exchanges in the halls, but for the most part you could tell they were done, especially since students could go back to texting each other between classes. The Sticky Note War, as it came to be called, ended the day we all used them to cover Wolf's locker.

It's not covered anymore. Now it's just the newest-looking locker in the school, sticking out from all the rest.

Don't get me wrong; the *fighting* wasn't over. The nudging and needling, the dirty looks and side-slung insults and behind-the-back tittering, that still happened, though I'd like to think there was less of it than before. You couldn't go a day without hearing someone say, "Not cool, man," in response to an idiotic remark. Jason Baker got an especially cold shoulder from most of the student body—that is, once he returned from his three-day suspension. He and Cameron Cole started skipping school a lot. I didn't miss them.

Ask most of the students about it and they'll tell you that the whole Post-it note thing was just a fad. They won't remember half the things they wrote, though they probably remember everything that was written about them. They certainly couldn't tell you who started it. Ashley R. probably. Or somebody on the basketball team.

Just don't ask Deedee.

He'll tell you he personally instigated World War Three.

We were a triangle now. At least at lunch.

The week after he emptied his locker, Wolf transferred to St. Simon's, the private K–12 school that was probably more than his parents could afford but was "worth it in the long run." It was Wolf's call—his parents ultimately left the decision up to him, and he didn't ask to borrow Deedee's dice to make it. I think he'd been wanting to go for a while. He just needed a nudge.

On paper, at least, it looked like an easy decision. St. Simon's had a 97 percent college admittance rate, but that wasn't why he wanted to go. They also had an excellent music program, with a jazz band and orchestra and everything. They were just as eager to have Wolf join them as he was to go there, apparently.

Probably more so. After all, there were a few good things Wolf was leaving behind.

I started sitting with Sean Forsett on the bus, the kid with the crazy curly hair. His stop was before mine in the mornings, so he saved me a seat. In all honesty it was more like a third of a seat, but that was all right. Turns out Sean was a writer too, short stories, mostly in the fantasy genre. He let me read a few and I had to admit they were pretty good. I mean, Sean was no George R. R. Martin, but I could see the potential. (Deedee had lent me *Game of Thrones*. I kept it hidden under my bed next to my poems. He was right. It was thoroughly educational.) After I read his first story I asked Sean if he ever played Dungeons & Dragons. He looked at me like I was nuts.

"To each their own," I told him.

We still played. Wolf, Deedee, Rose, and me. Just about every weekend. And even after everything that happened, Deedee still kept his ten-sided die in his pocket and used it to calculate the odds that somebody would trip in the cafeteria and bury their face into their spaghetti. But he also insisted I go with him to the restroom every time. And that Rose guard the door. We always went right before lunch, which was still the best period of the day, even though there were only three of us now. Bench still sat with his football buddies. Occasionally he'd look over at our table and wave. If I noticed I made sure to wave back.

The third day without Wolf I got my food and sat between Deedee and Rose. We had plenty of room to stretch out, but we tended to scrunch together anyway, taking up only half the table.

"Did you talk to Wolf last night?" I asked. "Find out how his first day at Saint Stuffy's went?"

Rose nodded, taking a bite of her peanut-butter-and-banana sandwich, prime mouth-roof-spackling material. "Yeah," she said through a mash of PBB, "he said it was all right. They have uniforms, apparently. And three times as much homework. And everyone knows everyone else, so it's pretty obvious when you come in right in the middle of things."

Rose would know. She was no stranger to starting over. "Did he make any new friends?"

"It's only been one day, Frost," Rose said. "But yeah. He said he met some nice people."

"That's good," I said. And I meant it, though I felt an ache. It wasn't jealousy, exactly, though that was part of it, having to share. I guess I wasn't sure I wanted Wolf to have a whole new set of friends yet. I didn't want him to forget about us. But I understood. You find your people. I wondered what they would call him. Maybe he'd try to pull off Amadeus this time. Or maybe he would just be Morgan. With us he would always be Wolf.

Rose punched my shoulder. Apparently I'd been staring off into space.

"Earth to Snowman. Come in, Snowman. Look, I made you something."

She handed over a fish folded from an old math quiz that she'd aced. She was incredibly smart, Rose Holland. A total nerd. Pure tapioca. And she ate deadly, tree-studded kamikaze hills for breakfast. She was frankly kind of awesome. And I was a little surprised she still bothered to hang out with us.

"What is it this time?" I asked, taking the paper fish from her. Knowing Rose, it could be anything.

She shrugged.

"That's the best part," she said, smiling.

"Hey, we're still on for this weekend, right?" Deedee asked. "I mean, I've got all new maps and everything."

"Absolutely," Rose said. Then she pointed to his tray and asked if she could have the rest of his pudding.

There'd been a rebellion.

At least that's how Deedee put it. Of course he was prone to exaggeration, but in this case we cut him some slack. He was the master, after all. He'd done all the prep work. We were just along for the ride.

"The goblins are revolting," he said in a comically deep voice that wasn't supposed to be funny at all. "They have risen up against their masters and are now planning a takeover of the entire kingdom, the world of men"—he looked across the table—"and women included."

"*¡Viva la revolución!*" I said, refusing to pass up a chance to tease the dungeon master about his limited Spanish.

"Charlene doesn't do goblins," Rose protested, twisting her little cardboard gnome around and around. We were all sitting at my scratched-up dining room table. Rose looked a little scrunched in one corner but it didn't seem to bother her. "She considers them beneath her."

"Swords don't discriminate," Deedee told her.

"Mine does," she said.

"I find that hard to believe," Wolf said.

Rose looked at Wolf and smiled. She reached for the bowl of chips—sour cream and onion—but he snatched it away from her. "Not until you promise to play fair," he said. "No making up random powers that you don't have, and no bullying Deedee into letting you reroll your dice just because you feel like it."

"You're such a downer," Rose teased. "Since when does Wolf

Thompson play by the rules?"

"It's the school uniform," I said. "Wearing khaki all day makes you tame."

"Lay off the khaki," Wolf warned. "I happen to look very good in slacks and polos. Besides. On Fridays we get to wear jeans."

"You rebel!" Rose snarked. We joked about Wolf's new, posh private school, but truthfully he seemed happy there and the rest of us were just jealous that it had an open campus and we still had to eat lunch in our obnoxious and odiferous cafeteria.

"Are we going to get started or what?" Deedee was getting impatient.

I nodded and poured us all a round of red cream soda, which had become the only beverage served in taverns across the five realms. Our little table was crowded with all of Deedee's maps and guides and his towers of dice and the chips and our cups. We'd started switching houses every week and it was my turn to host. Kind of a shame, because Rose had a gigantic basement with an expensive-looking poker table that was perfect for dragon slaying, plus a gargantuan TV and a fridge full of soda in the garage. I lobbied to move D&D night to her house permanently, but she said her parents would never go for it. Her mom wasn't much of a people person and didn't like loud noises, and even from all the way in the basement she could hear Deedee's groans whenever we set one of his minions on fire.

Noise wasn't an issue with my mother. That's another thing that made her cool. There were a lot of things, actually. She was in the kitchen only one room away, watching the oven, determined not to burn the homemade chocolate-chip cookies, and singing Janis Joplin so loud I almost didn't hear the doorbell ring.

"Did you order pizza?" Deedee asked, hopeful.

I shook my head and got out of my seat, the three of them following me to the door, probably because they thought I was lying. Outside the living room window you could see the first Branton snow starting to fall, a crystalline blanket the color and consistency of soft wool. I saw the car parked in our driveway, headlights on, still running. I recognized it instantly and my stomach lurched as I opened the door.

"Hey, Frost." Bench stood there in his BMS jacket, a cap pulled down to his eyebrows. He had his hands tucked in his pockets. "Hey, guys."

Deedee said "hi" back. Wolf and Rose waved. I glanced nervously behind me toward the dining room, to see if you could spot the table from the doorway with all the dice and figures spread across it. I wondered who told him we were getting together at my place tonight, but then I saw the look on Deedee's face and it was obvious. "What's up?" I asked.

"I know you guys are busy." Bench scratched his head

underneath the rim of his cap; he did that when he was nervous. "I actually just came by to tell you the last football game of the season is next week," he continued. "We're only four and six, and I know you're not really all into it, but Coach says I'll probably get to start this time. . . ." His voice trailed off.

"Oh," I said. "That's great."

I meant it. It really was great. Bench wasn't going to be "Bench" anymore. I'd have to find something else to call him. At least during football season.

"Yeah. So, you know. It'd be kinda cool if you could come."

He was looking at all of us. Not just me.

"Sure," I said, though I wasn't sure at all.

Bench focused on Wolf standing in the doorway behind me. "How's the new school? Good?"

"Yeah. It's good," Wolf said. "Things are all right."

Bench nodded. I couldn't be sure, but I thought he looked relieved, like that was really the reason he stopped by. To ask that question and get that answer. The rest was just an excuse. He glanced back at his car, where his dad was waiting for him. "Okay then. I guess I'll see you all around."

He was halfway down the sidewalk when Rose called out to him. "Bench, hold up."

She stepped outside, ignoring the snow that slushed beneath

her feet, seeping into her purple socks. You could see her cloudy breath and Bench's meeting in the cold as they faced each other. "I don't know what you've got going on," she said, "but we haven't started playing yet. And judging by the number of manuals Deedee brought, it's going to be epic. . . . That is, if it's all right with everyone else." She turned and looked in the doorway.

Deedee and I both looked at Wolf. It was my house. Rose's offer. Deedee's game. But we let Wolf make the call. After everything that had happened, it only seemed right.

Wolf shoved his own hands in his pockets, the cold air already pinking up his freckled cheeks.

"I think we can make room," he said.

And for a moment I pictured it, all five of us, crammed around the table somehow. Laughing and teasing and carrying on, snorting red pop and begging my mother for more cookies.

But I'm a sucker for a good image. I knew Bench's answer already, even before Rose asked.

"Thanks. Maybe next time."

Bench smiled, then walked to the edge of the driveway, put his hand on the car door, and stopped. In the amber glow of our porch light he looked older to me. A high school kid already even though high school was still half a year and forever away.

"No matter what happens," he said, "keep your head up. Keep your eyes forward. . . ."

"And don't let go," Rose finished.

Bench nodded and got into his car. His father waved as he pulled away.

The four of us stood in the doorway with Rose at the front of our pack and watched, and I realized that, from here on out, it would always be *maybe next time*. Maybe we'd all go see him in his last middle school football game. Maybe only some of us would. Maybe just one. Maybe there'd be summer days where we'd happen to meet up at Freedom Park and kick the ball around (his ball this time), or just sit in the grass and talk about nothing in particular—favorite bands, lame movies, the usual. But it would never be just like it was before. Two roads and so on. I couldn't predict the future any more than Deedee's dice could.

All I knew for sure was that it was cold outside. And the goblins were coming. And the villagers were counting on a backstabbing thief, a passionate bard, and a ninja warrior princess named Moose to come and save them, which we were going to do whether Charlene the Freakin' Crazy Sharp Sword That Will Cut Your Head Off If You Make Fun of Her wanted to or not.

And we would easily polish off both bottles of soda and all

the chocolate-chip cookies. Then we would squeeze onto the couch afterward with a bag of cheese turds and settle in for a couple more episodes of *Dr. Who*. Just enough room for the four of us, shoulder to shoulder, packed tighter than the trees on Hirohito Hill, telling each other that everything was going to be all right.

Without even saying a word.

ACKNOWLEDGMENTS

THIS BOOK WOULD HAVE BEEN IMPOSSIBLE TO WRITE IF NOT FOR THE dedication and support of so many people. Much praise goes to Jordan Brown, editor extraordinaire, for his wisdom, sensitivity, and artistic hand-holding. His patience and insight guided me through all seven hundred and forty-two drafts. To Deb Kovacs at Walden for continuing to believe I've got the chops to do this, and to Danielle Smith for helping to convince the rest of the world of the same. To everyone at HarperCollins: Katie Fitch and Amy Ryan, who designed the darned thing; Renée Cafiero and Christina MacDonald, who are continuously cleaning up my frustrating prose; Viana Siniscalchi, who frankly deserves more candy; and Alana Whitman and Caroline Sun, who somehow find a way to market my nutso ideas. To Rafael Mayoni, whose cover illustration looks exactly as I imagined it when I first started writing this book. Thanks also to Kate Jackson and Donna Bray for keeping me on the shelves. And to Zoey Peresman, whose insights and (good) nudges were immensely helpful during the revision process.

To my agent, Adams Literary, who does all the boring work so I can just frolic on the playground of my imagination every day.

To my parents, Wes and Shiela, and my wife, Alithea, for their unending support. And to my own kids, Nick and Isabella: thank you for being kind, for standing up for what's right, and for reminding me that everything I say matters.

One last thing.

Growing up, I was short for my age. Short and smart (but not *that* smart) and scrawny and often alone. This was the eighties. The Dark Ages. Back when "nerd" was still an insult, but that wasn't the worst thing I was called. The verbal bullying was steady, but I also remember being tripped, slammed into lockers, having things flicked at me. Once some kid put me in a choke hold until I passed out in the middle school parking lot. And yet I know I had it easier than many kids today.

Every day tens of thousands of kids stay home from school for fear of being bullied, but even that's no escape. The teasing follows them on social media, in texts and in emails, in whispers that get back to them, because words are ghosts. You don't have to go far to hear the kind of rhetoric that makes you wonder if the lessons we learn as kids ever stick with us as adults. Lessons about compassion and empathy, acceptance, and awareness. They aren't that difficult to teach—provided we grown-ups make an effort to model them and think about what we say before we say it.

And to any young readers out there who might see a part of themselves somewhere in this book, who feel like sometimes the Gauntlet can't be beat, just remember:

Keep your head up. Keep your eyes forward. And don't let go.

JOHN DAVID ANDERSON is the author of *Ms. Bixby's Last Day, Sidekicked, Minion,* and *The Dungeoneers.* A dedicated root beer connoisseur and chocolate fiend, he lives with his wife, two kids, and perpetually whiny cat in Indianapolis, Indiana. You can visit him online at www.johndavidanderson.org.